MISS PORTLAND

MISS PORTLAND

a novel

by
David Ebenbach

ORISON
BOOKS

ISBN 978-0-9964397-1-8

Orison Books
PO Box 8385
Asheville, NC 28814
www.orisonbooks.com

Distributed to the trade by Itasca Books
1-800-901-3480 / orders@itascabooks.com
www.itascabooks.com

Cover photograph by Emily Chambers. Used by permission
of her family.

Manufactured in the U.S.A.

ORISON
BOOKS

for Mom and Naomi,
who have come to rest

One

Zoe knew what other people didn't: she knew that life was perfectible. She knew that, when you were born, life was just handed to you like a pile of mismatched shoes and books and unwashed laundry, and most people thought that you had to carry that stuff around everywhere you went forever. But no. If you were lucky, at some point you realized you could set all the junk down and walk away from it. You could walk away and find something else that you actually wanted to hold on to. No— something that carried *you*. Something perfect that carried *you*.

And she knew these things because of Maine.

Maine because, when she was a girl, probably ten years old, Zoe's family took this one summer vacation there. It was just a little coastal town, nothing dramatic, but a town that, unlike Philadelphia, was slow-talking and had a pebbly beach right near the A-frame house they were renting and went all the way dark and quiet at night. That was the crucial part, the part she would always remember—that calm. That brand-new, totally unfamiliar calm. During the day there was the beach and the ocean, and every once in a while a tiny maritime museum in some other town or a no-nonsense seafood restaurant somewhere, no netting or life-preservers or other seafaring kitschy stuff on the plain walls, and one time they went to a state fair a half-hour away just to give her bored younger brother something to do—but that stuff, especially with her jangly family around, wasn't the calmest part. No—sitting on the back porch of the rental house as things went over to evening and beyond—that was it. After dinner she would settle into a chair, would stare out at the ocean and the beachscape in front of it, all the detail of the remaining beachgoers and the driftwood and patches of dune grass and so on. And then everything would begin to dim. The people would pack up to go home, to bring their noise and color away with them. And after even more dimming the landscape would start to get fuzzy, until she couldn't make out the dunes or the driftwood and instead everything was just soft. And even the ocean would seem to hush.

The thing was that Zoe had had no idea. She was ten years old and she hadn't ever known that the world could come to rest like that. Could become so still, so settled. Satisfied. Already by that time she had come to know the world as a loud and in-your-face kind of place, a bang and crash kind of place. Sometimes at school she would look out over the playground and all the other kids ricocheting off everything, and she'd get shaky watching all the movement, hearing all the sounds clanging into each other. It was so much, and it was all the time. But in Maine—in Maine, the day, every day, came to rest. Right there in her lap, like a warm cat.

Zoe hadn't forgotten that feeling, hadn't forgotten it at all in the two-and-almost-a-half decades since, even though she'd spent those years in uncalm places and uncalm ways. Maybe *because* she had spent them that way. If you looked at it like that, all the chaos in between then and now had just been preparing her.

Zoe stepped off the bus. She stepped off the bus, as a matter of fact, into her new life. She made a point of saying that to herself as her foot touched the ground—she said, in her mind, *I am stepping into my new life*.

Gordy was right there to meet her, in the lot in front of the Greyhound station. Gordy! Zoe could feel her heart bound across the concrete to where he was. And she followed along, right into the long arms that he put all the way around her.

Gordy came out of the hug and held her at arm's length. He was a lean man—you could call him wiry, but it was a good kind of wiry—with a long braid, a goatee, and such thoughtful eyes. He said, "Zoe!" like he couldn't believe this was happening. Then he hugged her again.

"It's good to see you," she said, dancing a little on her feet, seeing him.

"Can you believe it?" Gordy said. "I wasn't sure you'd come." He put her back out at arm's length, his hands on her shoulders, dipping his head to look at her, like he was checking for something.

"I'm so completely here," she said.

"I can feel that," he said. His voice was rich, like a purr. He said, "You're the here-est you've ever been. How was the trip?"

"So good," she said. And it had been. Ever since the bus crossed from New Hampshire into Maine on I-95, the landscape had simplified; there had been no big signs, no billboards—just plain, trees-y September on all sides, a strip of ordinary green for a median. Nothing was expressing itself at her. Even the guy that had been sitting next to her on the bus ever since Boston—he was very big and was sleeping, a combination that Zoe believed was Greyhound policy for seatmates, but he wasn't leaning on her. He was very big and sleeping in his own seat. If he'd been a Philadelphia guy, he would have been passed out in her lap, and he would be waking up every once in a while to spit and to give her his loud and spitting point of view about how she shouldn't be moving to Maine at all. But not this guy.

Gordy smiled at her again, which Zoe held onto for a while, almost the same way he was holding onto her shoulders, except hers wasn't literally. Then she became aware of the people moving around them, off into their Portland lives. To think that she was one of those people. Well, standing still for the moment, but metaphysically moving into her Portland life. She was going to be one of them. A little bit more excitement found its way out; she said, "Did you bring Taylor?" Taylor was his five-year-old daughter. A month earlier, when Zoe came for a visit, they didn't get to meet; his ex had their daughter the whole time.

He shook his head. "I thought it'd be good to spend the day together, the two of us. Also, Janine has Taylor this weekend."

"You and me—that's a nice idea," Zoe said, buttoning up the emotions on the not-seeing-Taylor-yet news. It was okay to do that buttoning—good to do that, in fact, for the sake of the calm, no matter what her therapist would say about it, who wasn't going to be her therapist any more.

"Good. Good. I thought we'd meet my parents out for dinner, but that we could spend the day together first." He looked at his watch, a big dial on a thick, hand-woven band, poking out from underneath the sleeve of his jean jacket. "Well, the afternoon."

"It's a very nice plan," Zoe said. Meeting the parents!

They took his truck—no traffic on the way, really, and no honking or yelling at all, whereas in Philly there would have been a riot or something—took it down to the Old Port, a part of town she'd first seen when she came through on the way up to that childhood vacation all those years ago. The Old Port—the fancy restaurants where you didn't have to dress fancy, the stores with their hanging shingle-signs, the cobblestone streets sloping down to the water, the growing ocean smell as you got closer—well, it was pretty much textbook charming, and it hadn't lost any of that since Zoe was last there. It was a cool afternoon but they parked and left her luggage in the truck-bed—no crime to worry about in a place like this—and walked around a while, side by side, holding hands. Gordy pointed out all the different places. They stood on the edge of the water and looked at all the gray-green water wobbling. Then they had coffee and a late lunch at an outdoor table on Exchange Street and talked. "We're all set up for you," Gordy said over the steam of his coffee, over his portabella sandwich.

"Great," Zoe said. She noticed the *we're*—his trailer was on his parents' property, which she had the idea was kind of a Maine thing.

David Ebenbach

Everyone sticking together, without it being a big, colossal deal. With her own parents, it would have been a big, colossal deal, all the way around.

"It'll be cozy in the trailer, but it'll be our own space, and we'll eat up at my parents' place sometimes, if you like."

"It'll be fine," Zoe said. She touched his hand. "I'm just really happy to be with you."

"I'm so transported that you've come," he said, in that warm voice of his that sent her right into an alpha brainwave state. "Transported with delight. You're beautiful."

Zoe looked at him—so clear, so together, so handsome—and then she looked down at herself—loose flannel and jeans over her slightness, a kind of L.L. Bean effort to blend, and her hair hanging in dry, brown curls over her chest. "Really," she said.

He squeezed her hand, smiling serenely. "Really. Zoe, you're radiating health."

They had met at a mindfulness retreat at Kripalu, down in Massachusetts—Massachusetts was now down rather than up, she realized, a sign of how her life was flipping over the way it needed to. And the retreat, which Gordy led so powerfully, was about how meditation could help you find the life you were supposed to be leading, which she already believed, of course, but the way he talked about it made it seem so *possible*, that was when she felt things begin to flip. It started there in his serious eyes, or maybe it started in his bed, but now it was enormous.

"I do feel healthy," she said. She looked at her fiddlehead salad, felt like she didn't even need it. And she didn't want to give her stomach too much to work on anyway.

"I can see it," he said. "So much better than you sounded on the phone. Before you decided, I mean. So much better than when we first met."

She nodded. She hadn't been at her best over the last couple of months.

"So many people," he said, looking down the street. She twisted in her chair to see what he was seeing. Couples holding hands. The clamor of families. "So many of them radiate, well, un-health. Anger. Limitation. Pushing. Do you feel it?"

She stared at the people, at gangly teenagers and older people in thick-knit sweaters, at the occasional lone person on the street, waiting for their auras to appear to her. And in a way so many of them seemed extra-bright, somehow, like the light in them had been turned up to a glare. Of course, that was normal, and there had been times when that glare had made her envious. But on this afternoon she put her chin up. The smell of the ocean—humid, saline, fishy—made her sure she was in a different place than she had been.

Of course her parents had fought her on this.

"It's just such a radical move," her mother had said.

"You have a *good job*," her father said.

Zoe rolled her eyes. This was why she ducked their calls, didn't generally agree to to lunches or dinners. "I'm a *drone*," she said. Technically she was an Associate Coordinator for Parent Engagement in the Office of Parent, Family, Community Engagement & Faith-Based Partnerships of the School District of Philadelphia, which to her sounded even worse than *drone*. And maybe even *was* worse.

"You have a good, *stable* job," her father said. He had not grown up during the Great Depression, obviously, was actually a baby boomer who'd just turned seventy, but you wouldn't know it from talking to him. In his view of the world, Zoe and her little brother were always one step away from selling apples on the sidewalk.

And sure—it was not nothing, quitting a job with a regular paycheck and benefits and everything. In fact, it was actually a pretty big deal. A very big deal, really. But that just showed how urgent this move was; she wouldn't be doing it if it wasn't completely urgent.

"It's just such a big, radical change—can't you take it slowly?" her mother asked. "You don't have to give up your whole life here."

"Slowly?" Every time she talked to her parents she marveled at how much they didn't get it. "Mom. Dad. I'm miserable here. I've always been miserable here." She felt a little bad saying that, since they raised her in Philadelphia, but it was true. "Why would I go slowly when I've finally found what I need?" The line went silent then. And Zoe knew what was coming. All the things she'd tried over her thirty-four years. The therapies; the mysticism; that commune that she barely escaped; et cetera. Not to mention the hospitalization, which was so long ago. The list of what her parents persisted in seeing as failures, as *episodes*. "Don't say it," she said, through almost-gritted teeth. "This is *not* the same thing as those other things."

"Oh, Zoe," her mother said.

"Please," her father said. "Just—promise us—you'll stay on your medication."

That night—if you could call it night, since it was only 5:30—she and Gordy met his parents at the Miss Portland Diner for the meal that his parents apparently called *supper*. The diner was an old train car, or looked like one, attached to a more ordinary restaurant, all of it located on a broad, warehousey street, one without any of the charm of the Old Port. Zoe imagined that this was where real Mainers would eat. And indeed inside were quiet people that to her seemed too solemn, grave even, to possibly be tourists. Gordy led her to a table in the ordinary restaurant part of the diner and they sat down with his parents, who were already there. Zoe was meeting them for the first time; they'd been visiting family upstate the last time she came to Portland.

"Mrs. Boucher," she said, shaking hands, maybe a little vigorously. She was nervous. "Mr. Boucher."

They didn't offer up their first names, but Mrs. Boucher, a solid, steel-haired woman in her sixties, said, "It's a pleasure to meet you, dear."

"I bet we'll be able to fill our bellies here, won't we?" Mr. Boucher said, though he didn't really have a belly to speak of.

The two of them were missing all their r's, in good Maine style. It was like they had a few marbles in their mouths while they were talking.

"Honestly," Mrs. Boucher said, looking at Gordy, "I don't know why we couldn't have just eaten at home. This seems like a bit of a fuss."

Zoe was about to add something—she wasn't sure what, was just going to see what came out—but then Gordy put a hand on her leg. He smiled. "This is a special occasion," he said, almost shyly. She hadn't seen him shy before. It was cute on him. "I think it calls for a bit of a fuss."

"We're happy to have you, Zoe," Mr. Boucher said, smiling affably over his menu, like a host. "What's good here, son?"

"Well, they've got all the usual breakfast things. And the burgers and so on." Zoe was struck by the fact that he mentioned meat as an option. At the retreat he'd called meat *ingestible spiritual death*. "Fried scallops?" he said now.

"Health food, is it?" Mr. Boucher said, in what Zoe recognized as deadpan Maine humor.

The table then settled, sort of abruptly, into a silent study of the menus—several minutes of study. Zoe noticed it when she opened her mouth to say something—she was going to point out the "post-gym omelet" as an example of possible health food—and suddenly realized that it would be weird if she did say something. So, back to the menu she went. Once she'd settled on french toast because the carbs would be easy on her stomach, Zoe sat back into the quiet—nobody in the whole room was talking above a murmur. She was aware that, by now, many parents-of-a-boyfriend would have asked her something about herself, or about her trip up to Portland, and that that wasn't happening in this case. It was actually kind of a relief, though, not having to talk about herself. Who wanted to talk about all that stuff, which she had left behind, anyway? She had had enough of people being all invested and loud and worked up all the time.

In Philly everybody had an opinion about everything, and it was always slathered in emotion. She'd been in a drugstore the other day, loading up on meds for the move, and when the cashier told another woman that her coupon had expired, the man in between Zoe and the coupon woman stepped out of line and started fighting with the cashier, and not even really on the woman's behalf but just out of a general rage. He got so angry that at the end he said, "I oughtta shit in your fucking mouth," and he threw his shampoo bottle, ricocheting it off the counter. That was how Philadelphia was. Whereas in Maine, when she visited Gordy a month ago, she'd seen a similar kind of let-down in a grocery store, and it had gone totally differently. The cashier, a matronly older woman, had said, "Dear, now, I'm sorry to tell you this isn't on sale anymore today," holding up a blue box of crackers she'd lifted from the conveyor belt. And the customer had said, "Oh, my. Is that right?" and the cashier nodded regretfully and then the two of them shared brief smiles and moved right past it—the woman bought the crackers anyway—while the man next in line did and said absolutely nothing at all, his eyes steady on his hand-basket of food. That was Maine. Maine was a place where people kept neat gardens and fences and tidy houses painted in quiet colors, and where the people were just the same as their homes—little well-contained houses that didn't feel the need to spill themselves all over the lawn.

And so there in the restaurant Zoe just watched the rest of the people at her table as they read over their options and thought it all through. At one point Mrs. Boucher leaned over and asked Mr. Boucher a whispered question, pointing at an item on her menu, and he answered in a whisper, and Mrs. Boucher resumed her pondering, her mouth set in a small, efficient line.

"Well," Gordy eventually said, "I think it's the mac and cheese for me." For some reason, that made Zoe second-guess her own choice, but she decided to just go with her idea, and she took his warm hand and they sat and waited. Her stomach felt reasonably settled, which was unusual, and she tried to remember when she'd last taken those meds of hers. Traveling had thrown the daily rhythm off.

"Fried scallops," Mr. Boucher said, putting down his menu.

"Chicken pot pie," Mrs. Boucher said, putting hers down as well. "I never could turn that down." After a moment, turning a sort of brisk expression toward Zoe, she added, "Well."

Zoe balked; she wasn't sure what that "Well" was supposed to trigger, and the moment, vacant, started to stretch out. But then the waitress arrived and they got to the business of ordering.

After that, after the food had come and they'd started into it, ultimately the Bouchers did ask Zoe a few things. Gordy's father wanted to know how the traffic was on her trip, and he'd nodded ruefully as she described the couple of knots between Philadelphia and New York, and again around Boston. "Oh, I can't stand the roads down there," he said. "That's no kind of life for me." And Gordy's mother wanted to know what she was thinking about in terms of work. Zoe glanced at Gordy, then, to see if he would say anything about the mindfulness center they'd been talking about non-stop over the phone, but he looked at her blankly in a way that seemed to say *no*.

"Well, that's the next step," she said. "I guess I don't want to leave any stone unturned. I'm going to settle in and then start looking." Zoe couldn't quite get herself to say she would look into options in the school system; she was really hoping it wouldn't come to that. Though of course she did need to have something soon—something ideally with health coverage. The insurance she got through COBRA was temporary and not a legitimately affordable thing.

"Well, I'm sure that's the best approach," Mrs. Boucher said. That set another pause into motion.

"These are mighty good scallops," Mr. Boucher eventually said.

Zoe considered her own food. The french toast was a little stiff. It wasn't what she'd call mighty good. But this, too, was what it meant to be in a place like this. Less flash, less dazzle. And she knew that sometimes flash and dazzle was just a stimulus to dizziness. She thought about days in bed where the world out her window seemed like a fireworks show that wouldn't stop. Just outside the window—bursting, exploding, detonating. Sometimes you'd rather have a little stiffness in the french toast.

The Bouchers lived not in Portland but outside it, on an up-and-down country road past Westbrook. There was hardly anybody out at all. Zoe just settled into it—the night, the rising and falling. "It's nice out here," she said.

"It's the Garden of Eden," Gordy said, smiling as he drove. "Right in between a paper mill and a correctional facility."

Zoe felt a small pulse of fear. "A correctional facility?" she said.

Gordy looked over, saw her face. "Oh—no. Don't worry. It's minimum-to-medium security. It's nothing serious at all. And it's way down the road. Miles. Trust me. I was just trying to prepare you that this isn't Park Avenue. Was that an unfortunate joke?" He reached out and held her hand.

Zoe had kind of a thing about prisons—she was phobic about getting stuck in one somehow, and then the idea of other people getting out wasn't so great, either, or even the idea of them being stuck in there in the first place.

Really the whole thing was a problem. But she pictured Mrs. Boucher's composed face back at the diner, and said, "Oh, don't fret about me. Everything's fine." She liked that she had said *fret*—that was brand new.

He smiled over at her.

After a few more minutes they got there, and Gordy swung the wheel like an old, easy habit. They took the driveway past where the Bouchers' cars were parked, and the couple of junked ones that Mr. Boucher worked on sometimes, and the main house as well—it was hard to see in the dark, but she remembered it as a small, square place—and further back behind a few trees until they got to the trailer. Zoe had been there before, during her last visit, when his parents were away. It had felt like a high school date, except in a trailer.

They got out of the car and lugged her suitcases out of the truck-bed, and Zoe listened. Because there it was—it was quiet out. Barely even crickets. It was Maine for real right there. And up above were all the stars. Oh, the stars. A lid coming off the pot: finally Zoe was going to be out from under the low, glaring lights of the city.

The trailer was set up like a house, going right down to the ground— you couldn't tell it had once been on wheels. Or maybe there were still wheels under there somewhere—Zoe didn't know. In any case it looked like a home, a narrow one with a pretty big garden in front. Gordy grew his own medicinal herbs, and also regular herbs, and also she thought she remembered he said kale. It was all fenced in against the deer.

"Do you want to go inside?" Gordy said from the top of the couple of front steps, holding her heavier suitcase. He was wiry, but strong. When he held her, she felt like nothing could move her or throw her.

"Sure," she said.

And he opened the front door and went right in. Of course it wasn't even locked. She was going to go in, definitely, obviously, but just for a moment she wanted to absorb the scene a little more. She thought she could smell an herby smell coming up from the garden, and maybe a pine-tree smell from elsewhere. The windows of the trailer lit up behind curtains, warm yellow-brown light.

It had been a long road for Zoe, a long road to this version of her life, and there had been plenty of bad stops along the way—the groups she'd joined, well, she could barely think about them. And the diets never calmed her stomach, not really, and neither did the body work. The things that came up in repressed-memory therapy had been like dark, flapping wings, and she didn't even know if they were real, or what they were if they were real. And regular psychiatrist therapy was basically about telling her that she was stuck being who she was. But the thing about a road is that it takes you somewhere—and now here she was.

The door of the trailer opened again, and there was Gordy, in the light.

"Do you know how it is," Zoe said, "when you spend so many years doing the wrong things?"

He nodded very seriously. "You had to do those things," he said. "You needed to do those things first."

"I did?" she said, and it wasn't that cold but instead of calming in the quiet she was shaking.

"That was your path," he said. She shivered with how close their minds were. Gordy came down the steps and took her hands. "Close your eyes," he said. "Come to stillness."

Zoe tried to do that, standing on the path through Gordy's garden, holding his hands. She tried to come to stillness.

Gordy spoke again, his voice purring. "Why is this the right choice? Why is this the answer?"

"I had to leave the city because cities have been toxic for me," she said. In the darkness of having her eyes closed she felt the darkness of the night, too. And the stars.

"Right."

"I had to leave my job because that job was the opposite of my creativity," she said.

"Good," he said. His voice seemed to be all around her.

"I had to leave therapy because I am not described by those labels."

"Right."

She cleared her throat. "I had to go somewhere calm. Because I need to be calm."

There had been so many un-calm moments. The time she burned her journals and food logs in her kitchen sink and caught the curtains on fire. The multiple times she was half-sobbing, half-choking on the phone to a friend or her brother, and them trying to keep up with her as she ranted through the crying. That spontaneous vacation last year, which was exciting but which also left her stranded in a dead car somewhere in Indiana. The hysteria after she broke her bathroom mirror by punching it, and then she couldn't stop thinking that the glass was under her skin, maybe with some of that silver, which had to be toxic, and maybe that it was all going to go to her kidneys. That one had been so unlike her, at least the punching part, though the rest was probably like her, and there were more times than just those. And so she needed to calm all of that way down for sure. Right as she thought of that, she found herself also picturing Mrs. Boucher's face again. Her face was like a Buddha, a vision of what was possible.

Zoe opened her eyes and looked at Gordy. He was also a vision. "Because I never knew what was wrong before and now I know. Because now I know how to be different from how I was."

Gordy smiled his vivid pleased-ness at her. "There you go," he said. He stroked her hair, and she wasn't shaking anymore. "Now let's go in. I'll get you reacquainted with the place."

He picked up her other suitcase and she followed along behind him, stealing one last look at the soft spray of stars overhead.

Two

The next morning, Monday morning, Zoe woke up to the sound of Gordy making smoothies in the blender. Or *got* up, anyway; she hadn't really been sleeping. Sleep for Zoe was a timid woodland creature, easily scared off. In her experience, you could scare it off just by thinking too much. And she almost always thought too much.

What she usually did when she was stuck awake was to try to just relax her body as much as possible, get her alpha waves going, and hope that that would rest her enough to face the coming day. It wasn't sleep, but it was something. And that's what she'd been doing when Gordy climbed over her to go out of the little trailer bedroom, and that's what she'd been doing when the blender started up. At that point she opened her eyes, and looked over at the clock, which was in the late sevens.

Zoe levered herself up on her elbows. Next to the clock was a picture of Gordy holding his daughter in his arms, from back when Taylor was a baby that looked like most other babies, bald and wrapped up in a blanket, like a thumb poking out of a hole in a worn glove. You couldn't really see his face, either, because he was wearing a baseball cap and looking down at Taylor. It was a picture of a private moment, from the point of view of an outsider. Zoe wondered if even Gordy must look at the picture and feel that way; the father and daughter in the picture couldn't ever be recaptured, really. Even by him.

Zoe shook her head. It wasn't a good idea to start the day thinking negatively like that. Impossibility, inevitability, irredeemability. Those were some of the nasty i-words that she had to avoid. That was actually a concept from Gordy, from the retreat. It was one day when he had them all gathered together, sitting on their mats, and he asked them to contemplate the *I*, to ask themselves what the *I* was for, in their lives. Did it stand for some of the nasty I-words? Which he listed; there were a bunch of those—too many even to remember. *Ignorance* was another one. And others. Or, he suggested, was their *I* maybe for *iridescence, ideas, imagination, insight, interconnectedness?* Or could it be?

Yes.

Zoe flipped the covers—brown, heavy—up off of her, and stood up in the little carpeted walk-space that surrounded the bed. Around her were the birch-veneer cabinets and bookshelves that were on all the walls. The bookshelves were full. Full as in, with books going from end to end and piled sideways on top. Yoga and meditation and somatics and mysticism and nature and alternative medicine and everything she cared about and believed in, right there on the shelves. These were the kinds of books that would make her father go into that worried face that he would sometimes go into—actually, pretty much any time he was with her. And then he would ask if she was taking her medication, might edge toward the word *episode*. But here, here in this safe space of Maine and Gordy and her new life? She could have almost started crying with happiness. Oh, to be in a place where it wasn't crazy to be the person she was!

In fact she did allow herself a quick tear or two.

Then—Maine demeanor restored—she opened the bedroom door, which put Zoe right into the kitchen. Gordy was there, standing in sweatpants and t-shirt, kind of resplendent in them, and she didn't even know until that moment that you could be resplendent in sweats, pouring smoothie into two glasses. Thick, thick beige smoothie. Beige with speckles of something. "Just in time," he said. "Our inner clocks must be synchronizing."

"That and the blender," Zoe said. "*Vrrrrrrrr.*"

Gordy blinked. His hair was wild, hanging down all over the place. "Right. Of course," he said. "Sorry about the noise." He handed her a glass.

"Don't worry," Zoe said, wishing she hadn't mentioned the blender. "Wow—this looks amazing." She checked out her smoothie, which smelled like a lot of things all at once.

"Yogurt, bananas, strawberries, almond butter, and a little flaxseed," he said. "And the bits of green are spinach. You won't really taste those, but they're there."

Zoe's stomach made itself known. "It's awesome."

He nodded.

"I just—"

Gordy's face descended slightly.

"I mean, I'm definitely going to taste it. It sounds amazing," she said. "But it's more like a lunch thing for me. I can't take much in the morning besides coffee. Remember?" They had eaten breakfast together at Kripalu, and they had had breakfast together when she visited.

Gordy took the glass and set it down on the little table that was opposite the sink, built into the wall. Then he took her hands, sat them both down. They were sitting so that their arms were resting on the table, on either side of the smoothie. "Zoe," he said.

She said, "Yes." It felt like something big was happening.

"I meant what I said about you looking healthy yesterday." His t-shirt had a recognizable picture of a cornucopia on it, though it was a little faded. "It's so good that you got yourself away from that life."

Zoe felt a flush of pleasure at that. "Yeah," she said.

He squeezed her hands lightly. "But mainly what I was talking about was, primarily, your inner health."

"What?" she said. She could feel the flush go over to a blush.

"Hang on. Hang on," he said. "What I'm saying—" He paused. And then: "How much do you weigh, Zoe?"

"What?" She looked down at herself, at her arms and legs, which were, she knew, on the pretty skinny side. "I'm like a hundred and ten pounds," she said. Probably it was more like a hundred and five, really. But definitely it wasn't the lowest it had ever been, by any stretch of the imagination.

Gordy breathed in and out once. "What I'm saying is that you were living in a toxic environment before, and so of course your body didn't want to consume anything around it. But now you're in a healthy environment. And you should open yourself to that." He took her hands and put them on the glass in front of her. "It's okay," he said.

"Okay," she said, eyes wide. She took a sip of the smoothie while Gordy watched, and then—he nodded—a gulp. She willed her stomach to be calm. Really this was very tasty.

"Okay?" he said.

"Okay," she said.

His voice turned brisk. "So what's your plan for today?"

"Plan?" she lifted her face away from the glass, feeling the definite feeling of a smoothie mustache on her upper lip.

"Do you want me to drop you in town?" he said. "I have to work." Gordy taught a couple of classes at a Portland yoga studio and also worked in the studio's boutique—yoga gear, CDs, crystals, etc. Zoe had seen it on her last visit, and it was a serene little place.

"Wow," she said, taking another sip. "Do you have to go soon?"

He checked his watch. "Pretty soon. I mean, it's a good thing it isn't one of my teaching days or I'd already be gone. But I should definitely hit the shower in a few minutes."

Zoe contemplated the day. She didn't have any plans at all. She didn't have any plans and she didn't particularly want to have any plans. But if she stayed there she wouldn't have any options at all. Mr. Boucher, she knew, was in heating and cooling repair and sales, and he worked out of an actual shop, so he'd be gone, and Mrs. Boucher worked in the post office starting early. The only cars left behind would be the junked ones.

"Boy," she said. "I'm realizing right this minute that I need to get me some wheels."

"I'm more than happy to give you rides. And there's a bicycle," he said, pointing over his shoulder toward some outdoors location. "You can use that whenever."

"Maybe a ride into town would be good for today," she said.

He nudged the smoothie toward her for another sip.

Once they were both ready—they got a little delayed because Zoe had some gastrointestinal distress, with Gordy on the other side of the door saying, "You know, it's going to be a period of adjustment, even for your body"—they climbed into the truck and drove back along the same curvy, up-and-down country road, and by the paper mill, and on into Portland. While they were driving Zoe realized she'd forgotten something.

"Oh. I didn't take my meds," she said, her hand on her mouth.

Gordy glanced over at her. "You're not still on those, are you?" His face was squinched up, like he was smelling something rotten.

Zoe shrugged.

He sort of *Hmmphed*. "I would ask yourself if that's why your stomach is upset."

"It definitely is a side effect," Zoe said.

"I bet."

"I haven't taken any for the last two days," Zoe said, her eyes wide again. "Or three?" There was a mix of small emotions in her—mini-horror and mini-giddiness, for starters. "I've just been thrown off, with all the traveling and everything."

"Maybe you haven't been thrown off," Gordy said. "Maybe you've been *thrown on.*"

"Huh," Zoe said, struck. Gordy smiled over at her, and she smiled back. She spent the rest of the trip contemplating that idea: thrown-on.

The yoga studio was on Congress Street, over in the West End, which seemed as good a place to explore as any, so she told him he could just drop her there.

"Do you want to have lunch together?" he said. He held up a big brown paper bag. "I made enough for two."

"That sounds good," she said, giving him a tight little hug and stepping back again. "You know what? Can we talk about the mindfulness center idea then?"

His face went a bit blank again. "Sure," he said. "We can talk about that. Say, 12:30?"

She waved goodbye to him as he went into the door to the studio. It was sort of like the night before, standing outside his trailer; the big front window of the boutique faced out onto the sidewalk, and after a minute she could see him moving around in there. And then she realized she had a little more GI distress to work through.

Luckily there was a coffee shop across the street, and Zoe sped right in. She didn't get a look at it until she got out of the bathroom, though. A cute place—the kind where the furniture was all different kinds and colors and the list of beverage options was handwritten on a big blackboard that was hanging on top of a chaotic mural—bodies leaning and heads on long necks pulling in various directions—covering all the walls. Actually, it was a little crazy in that coffee shop, even with hardly anybody there. Zoe considered whether she wanted to stay or not. But just at that moment her phone rang, some very ominous classical music that she'd picked for these particular callers. Parent-identifying music. And so she let the drums and the horns build for a little bit—from behind the counter the barista woman, dressed in all black except for a pink winter cap, a pink winter cap with a pom-pom, looked at Zoe with raised eye-brows—before Zoe sighed and took the call.

"Hi," she said. "I'm safe."

"Well, that's good," her mother said.

"We could have used a safe-arrival call," her father said.

The barista had gone back to staring at her hands. She had splayed them on the counter and she was looking down at them, maybe at the tattoos; in addition to the ones up and down her arms—small, separate ones—there was also a tattoo on the back of each hand. A tattoo and lots of various rings.

"Listen," Zoe said. "Yesterday was a little, you know." She sat down in the nearest chair.

Her mother stepped in diplomatically. "How's Portland?"

Zoe looked around automatically, like she could see the city that way. Instead, just those leaning, stretching bodies. "It's beautiful," she said. "It's a beautiful place. I'm happy. Listen—"

"Will you stay in touch with us?" her father said.

"Larry," her mother said, her voice a little tremulous. "We're in touch right now."

"Okay," he said. "Okay."

Zoe could feel her whole body tensing. "It's not like I'm in Syr-ia," she said. "This is Maine. It's like, maple syrup and lobster bibs and, and—" she flailed for a second.

"Whoopie pies," said the nearby barista, without looking up from her hands.

"Right," Zoe said. "Whoopie pies." She was pretty sure that was some kind of dessert. Though it could also have been cow poop.

"Are you with someone else?" her mother said.

Zoe saw an escape route. "Yes," she said. "I was actually about to have a kind of important conversation when you called."

"Is it a job?" her father said.

"Sure. It's a job," Zoe said. "Everything's a job. Listen—I'll talk to you soon." And she hung up as her mother was saying goodbye and her father was starting a new sentence with "*Promise* us."

"Jesus." Zoe said. "Wow." She got up and walked the few steps to the counter.

"Was that Holst?" the barista said, looking up now. Her black hair spiked out from under her pink cap.

"Holst?"

"The ring tone," she said. "I'm pretty sure that was Gustav Holst's *The Planets*. The Mars movement. *The Bringer of War*."

"Really?" Zoe said.

The barista nodded. "Yup." Her voice was incredibly deadpan.

"Cool," Zoe said. She noticed that although the young woman was wearing a couple of silver necklaces plus those rings on her fingers, there wasn't a single piercing anywhere on her. And the tattoos were all mon-sters—cute, cartoony ones in bright green and blue and red—and they were all a little shiny and wrinkly.

The woman had more to say. "The funny thing is nobody knew about Pluto when he wrote *The Planets*, so he didn't do a movement for Pluto. And then they discovered Pluto before he died, but he didn't want to write anything for it. He was done."

"And now Pluto isn't a planet anymore anyway," Zoe said.

"Right," the barista said. "So, the win goes to Gustav Holst."

"I like your tattoos," Zoe said. The monsters were downright kid-friendly.

"Yeah?" she lifted her arms. "They're temporary."

"Really?"

"Needle-phobic," the barista said, her hands back on the counter. A moment passed, and then she added, "Maybe this is the part where we get all commerce-ish."

There was something amazing about that. As a matter of fact, Zoe hated that transition, that transition from being really friendly and human with someone into business mode. Doing it made her feel like a person falling down a flight of stairs. Socially. And for this young woman to just come out and mark it like that, well. She laughed and looked at the barista with a kind of admiration. "That's awesome," she said. "You know what? I would extremely like a cup of coffee. A large one."

Still deadpan, the barista said, "So I will extremely make you one. Black?" And, once Zoe had nodded gratefully—the young woman knew instinctively just how she liked her coffee—off to the side she went, to make it happen.

"Is it usually this empty?" Zoe said.

"It's usually busier like an hour ago and in another hour from now," the barista said. "I guess."

Zoe turned around and looked at the mural on all the walls. "This is pretty intense," she said.

"I painted that," the barista said.

Zoe spun back to the counter. "Seriously?"

"Nope." She set the coffee down on the counter—a substantial large.

Zoe shook her head, smiling. And then she paid and picked up her coffee. "To Holst," she said, like a toast.

"Screw Pluto," said the barista.

Zoe did end up spending some time in the coffee shop. There was a *Portland Press Herald* on one of the tables, and it had a Classifieds section toward the back. She skipped the apartment listings for now—that could wait. But she looked at the two pages of job openings, or one and a half, anyway, and saw that she wasn't going to be doing any of them, not the clerking or the asset protection agenting or the butchering, definitely, or even the preschool teacher floating. The one that sounded best was a job delivering phone books. She pictured herself on a bicycle with a bunch of phone books on her back. Did they still even have phone books to deliver? Apparently they did. But basically she wasn't ready to start a search, and she did have some money in the bank. Not endless money, nowhere near endless—she felt a scary jolt when she thought about it too much—but enough, she told herself sort of forcefully, that she definitely didn't have to get hyper about this on her first full day in Portland. Plus there was the mindfulness center, which would mean she couldn't really be full-time anywhere else. Zoe folded the paper back up and just stared out the window, stared until she decided she really wanted to get up and go out exploring.

"Bye," she said to the barista on the way out. "I'm Zoe."

"Bye, Zoe," the barista said.

It was a gorgeous early fall day in the city of Portland. It smelled like trees but urban at the same time, and the brisk air made Zoe feel nice in her light jacket. She spent the next few hours feeling that way and wandering up and down Congress Street and off Congress Street with her hands comfortable in her jacket pockets. She took in the brick houses, the restaurants and shops, opening up into the day. She walked by the yoga boutique and peeked in the window but Gordy was busy with a customer and didn't see her. When she got to the intersection where the big sitting statue was, poking out into the middle of traffic on his own parky peninsula, she crossed over to see who was being statued there. And what a pleasure to cross the street in Portland, with drivers in both directions stopping to let her pass, not a sign of irritation or ill-will on any of their faces, whereas in Philly they would have run her over and then gone into reverse to run her over again. Anyway, when she got to the statue she discovered that it was Henry Wadsworth Longfellow, which made Zoe smile even though she wasn't much of a poetry person. Because you had to like a city that made such a big deal about a poet, regardless of whether you liked poetry or not. It was just a good sign.

Longfellow, meanwhile, was a heavily-bearded man, which felt about right to Zoe. Also, there were little lion heads capping off the arms of his chair while he sat back and relaxed, like he was saying, *You don't scare me. I've got my lions*. She appreciated that, and she appreciated that he was sitting in a chair instead of standing up for hundreds of years. Even statues should get to sit down, was how she felt about it. Longfellow, with his one arm resting on the back of his chair, his hand dangling down, seemed to agree. And this, she knew, was the kind of idiosyncratic thinking that would make Dr. Charles nod with that little bit of wince on his face and make her parents worry and make her brother call her *Zoo-head*. Probably affectionately, but. She sat on a bench down below the man's big chair for a while, the two of them sitting comfortably together, until she got jumpy, and then she got back up to walk some more.

Zoe ended up back at the yoga studio a little early, because walking was starting to lose its appeal. At first she didn't see him in the boutique—there was another person working there, a middle-aged woman in a long, willowy dress, plus a couple of customers who looked kind of thick and woolen—but then there he was at the counter. Seeing him again after having been apart for a little while brought on another burst of inner *hooray*, almost like she was stepping off the bus into Portland all over again.

"Hey!" she said, crossing the distance to him.

"Hey." He gave her a big smile. "I can 'clock out' in a few minutes," he said, with air quotes, from behind the counter. "But how's your day been?"

Zoe realized that, in sum, it had been kind of boring. So, "Kind of boring," she said.

"That's a shame," Gordy said. "You know—" And then someone needed help with a purchase and Zoe stepped away from the counter to let him give it.

She poked around the store while she waited. There was a nice smell of incense—not too strong, but kind of pine-foresty—and some kind of tinkling music in the air. She couldn't tell where it was coming from, but it seemed to complement the mini-waterfalls you could buy and bring home. They were like fountains, recycling the water, but these ones let the water crash down on some stones in a basin. Now, this was an idea—having a waterfall in your own home. It made her wish that you could also have a cloud in your home, or a glacier.

"Okay," Gordy said from behind her, clapping his hands a little startlingly. "Do you want to sit outside?"

They ended up back at the feet of Longfellow, eating seitan and mushroom sandwiches on very hearty bread. Plus there was smoothie left over.

"Bored, huh?" Gordy said, chewing.

"Yeah," Zoe said, though not loud. There were other people around, on their own benches, and she didn't want them to think she was criticizing Portland.

"You could go to the art museum," he said. "Or the movies."

Zoe shook her head. "I think I need purpose. I think I thought I needed rest and vacation, but what I actually need is probably purpose."

"Okay." Gordy took a swig of water from a metal water bottle that he kept attached to his backpack, offered it to Zoe. "Did you get a newspaper, look over the want ads?"

She waved the bottle off. "Well," she said, "I'm thinking about the mindfulness center." She waggled her eyebrows at him. "I have all kinds of ideas. Do you want to talk about them? And I bet you have ideas, and you know the area."

"Right," he said.

"Like what neighborhood it should be in. This could be a nice one. If you think it wouldn't compete with the yoga studio, because I wouldn't want to do that. Maybe they could be connected! And, you know, you might also have ideas about what kind of resources we'd need."

Gordy put a hand up. "Hang on, Zoe. I'm happy to talk about this."

"Great," she said, even though she wasn't sure he was finished. "I am, too."

Which he wasn't—finished. "But you sound like we're going to be launching this place next week."

Zoe felt an anxious fluttering in her chest. "Well, I guess I figured we'd kind of get right on it."

They had spent a lot of hours on the phone talking about what it would be like to put together their own center, a place where people could find peace and connection and purpose. There could be yoga, and a restaurant where people ate silently and slowly, maybe some art space. They had considered all kinds of things, late into the night, lying in their respective beds. And Zoe had gotten more and more excited about it with every phone call. When she bought the bus ticket, she halfway thought it would also be a ticket to the door of this place she had been imagining. Which, hey, was not some romantic vision—they had talked a lot about hard-core concrete things, like utilities and number of rooms and how to shrink their carbon footprint.

Gordy said, "Zoe, you've just moved here."

"I know," she said. "I'm a fast starter."

He kept going. "It's a big deal to start a business together. It's a big deal to start your own business anyhow, but to do it together—we need to give it some time, some contemplative time. I'm happy to talk about it, but we have to keep it theoretical for the moment. Don't you think?"

"I guess I see what you mean," Zoe said. Though did she?

"We don't want to put too much pressure on this," he said. "Do we?"

Zoe felt herself blushing. Of course she was being ridiculous again. Of course it was ridiculous, thinking they would just buy a place and open right up. Even if that had been what she was picturing in her bed, not sleeping, a lot of nights. Even if she had basically given up everything in order to pursue this idea. Even if it had seemed so real. And hadn't they been talking about that exact thing, about opening up as soon as possible, for real? Because it had felt the same as talking about her moving, which she went and did, hadn't it been the same?

"How much time?" she said. "How much time do you want to wait?"

"I don't know. You just got here." He looked around, like looking for the answer. "We could at least hold off for a month or two, until you're really settled in."

"A month or two," she said. Panic ripped through her, like an inner cold blast of wind. She needed to do this *now*.

"In the meantime," he said, "you could take some classes. You could sit in on mine. Really do some discernment on the whole thing. We want to be sure it's even the right thing."

"But didn't you—" She was going to say that she thought he'd said something like, *We'll get started when you get up here*, but she wasn't sure whether she could trust her memory, especially with her mind going fast like it suddenly was. Her lease in Philly was broken; her job was quit; her stuff mostly gone. What was she going to do about money? Health insurance? Retirement savings? The flutter in her chest was getting loud and wild, her breathing quick. "Gordy, didn't you—didn't we—" she said. "I just—" She was looking all around Longfellow Square, but not seeing anything.

He took her hands, moved his face until he caught her eyes and held them. "Zoe," he said. "Are you okay?"

It felt like a bunch of birds inside her, was what it really felt like, flapping frantically around and trying to get out. "I don't know," she said. "I don't know." Looking all around; looking everywhere.

"Zoe," he said, from a distance. Everything was trying to get out of her.

"Zoe," he said. "Zoe, come back."

She heard that he was saying that; she felt the birds and at the same time she distantly heard his voice.

"Come back," he said again.

His eyes and his voice—she started to take them in—they were good. His eyes and voice were good. Were they an answer? Were they like a perch where the birds could settle?

"Come back," he said. He was holding her shoulders now. "Come back."

Zoe settled into a lotus position on a yoga mat. She was alone in the room. Gordy had pointed out that there were no classes scheduled at the studio then, and so things were open; he suggested she take some time to get mindful. And although that rankled a little in the super-vivid context of the mindfulness center conversation, she felt that he was probably right anyway. And so, after she spent a little time in the bathroom, she'd climbed the stairs and stepped into the space—bright, smooth wood floors, lots of light from the windows facing south over Congress Street—and closed the door behind her, turning off the little sounds following her up from the store and leaving her small but significant in the bright, open space where now she had settled into position on the mat, facing the blank white wall opposite the windows.

She had been doing meditation for years. There was a good place in Mt. Airy—that was the neighborhood she should have been living in back in Philly, really—and she'd been going there for so long that her teacher had looked sad when Zoe told him she was leaving. He—his name was Jonathan—had smiled sadly and said, "May you leave in peace and arrive in joy." Which she would treasure for sure. Though she had already messed it up, maybe. Because it seemed like maybe she had left in joy instead of peace, and now hadn't even *arrived* in peace.

Which reminded her—she hadn't ever told Dr. Charles she was leaving. She'd just skipped the last two therapy sessions—told him she was on vacation two weeks ago, once she'd made the decision to go to Maine, and she called in sick the week after that. There was another appointment on the books for this week, which she was pretty much just going to miss. And not call. The hope was that she could slip away noiselessly, undetected, without a trace. Which Dr. Charles would have had plenty to say about, of course, if she'd run the idea by him.

Zoe closed her eyes and tried to relax the frown off her face. She used her visualization.

She started by picturing herself in a dense fog. Sitting like she was on the mat, but in thick, thick fog all the way down to the floor and pressing on her from every side. It was easy to picture; there had been times in her life when the fog just wouldn't lift. In meditation, though, in good meditation, she could often move it. First it lifted a few inches, so that beams of light from the windows behind her—she allowed herself to become aware of it—started to warm the floor underneath her. Not even her directly; just the floor. And when she could really feel that—it took a while—she breathed out and the fog raised a few more inches, allowing the light to reach as high as her tailbone. She let the warmth come in from that. Then up a few more inches, and a few more, each time pausing until she really could feel the sunlight on her lower back and then middle back and then upper. All the way up the body she saw the fog dissipating—or, in fact, she saw the light coming, because really there wasn't any fog, which she realized anew each time. Really the fog was just a manifestation of being closed off, about not-seeing. And the light—well, you needed light to see. When she felt the warmth touch the back of her head, she savored it for a few minutes, very quietly. Then she allowed herself to ask, in her mind, *What do I need to do?*

The answer couldn't come, though, until the final step. Zoe allowed beams of light to touch her face, even though her face was pointed away from the window. Because it wasn't light. It was understanding. And it touched her face. It reached through her in all directions.

Zoe opened her eyes. She knew what she needed to do.

That night they had dinner—*supper*—in the Bouchers' house. As in, "We've put up some corn and such for supper," said Gordy's mother. "We know you go in for the vegetables, like the boy does." She nodded at Gordy. "Plus the beans—there's no meat in those."

"Thanks, Mrs. Boucher," Zoe said. She felt very peaceful and slow after that meditation session. She felt good.

"Well, we've learned our way around the vegetarian cuisine," Mr. Boucher said, sitting at the kitchen table with a beer in his hand.

"*You* can talk," his wife said. "I'm the one cooking. All you've learned is how to *eat* it."

"Well," he said with a wink at Zoe, "that did take some learning."

When she offered to help, Zoe was waved out of the kitchen and Gordy was told to give her a tour of the little house. His parents didn't know, obviously, that she'd already seen the place on her last visit, or at least they were acting that way. So she re-toured the place.

"This is the living room," Gordy said, a look on his face. Concerned maybe. He'd been sweet and very tentative around her ever since lunch.

Zoe stared afresh at the beige carpet, the flowered couch with the clear plastic slipcover on it. "Nice," she said. It was like light was moving through all of it.

Gordy led her up the carpeted stairs and showed her the upstairs bathroom with its white tile with black speckles, which she thought was a handy thing in case you weren't that clean, though the Bouchers seemed very clean, and he showed her the door to his parents' bedroom, closed—at this point Zoe wondered why he was still pretending to introduce her to the place, but maybe his parents were tracking the location of his footsteps from downstairs to make sure there was no funny business going on—and then the room that had been his bedroom but was now a guest bedroom. Flowers on the comforter and curtains. It struck Zoe, the fact that Mrs. Boucher was so floral in her decorations, but so un-floral in her words and expressions. Maybe there was some kind of lesson there. Probably.

"How are you doing?" Gordy said, sitting on the bed. It looked like a soft bed, the way it gave in to his sitting.

She went over to him and took his hands. "I'm really good," she said.

"The meditation helped," he said, kind of a question.

"Totally," she said. "And you helped, too."

He got that look again, but he didn't say anything else.

"Really," she said, and she cupped his warm cheek in her hand.

Supper was another quiet supper experience. Little things were said like, "Corn's fresh," and "Beans," and Mr. Boucher told a brief story about a customer who wanted to pay for a home job with a credit card, right there on the spot, as though Mr. Boucher had a slot in his arm or something where he could just run the card. And Mrs. Boucher chuckled and said, "New in town, I guess." And Mr. Boucher had said, "You got that right." But otherwise it was pretty quiet. Zoe took in the wood-paneled walls of the dining room, the seemingly-obligatory old timey, maybe thrift-store painting of a sailboat, the low banquette with the family photos on it. There was one photo she stared at a lot, which showed Mr. and Mrs. Boucher in formal clothes, dancing together. It was maybe their wedding, but still it was remarkable to see them dancing, holding each other, grinning. Not just smiling but grinning. It seemed like two completely other people, but it wasn't. She took that in for quite a while. And, finally moving on, she took in the yellow light, yellow like old parchment. And, when she was done taking all that in and still nobody was saying much, Zoe thought about the idea she and Gordy had had about a restaurant inside the mindfulness center, one with silent meals, because eating was one of the times when people were the least present, and she decided this was an opportunity. She saw that there were baked beans in front of her, and green beans, and the corn. She saw the colors. Tasted the molasses and maple syrup on the baked beans, the butter on the green beans and corn, the salt on everything. There was a lot of salt. She felt the husks of the kernels wanting to get in between her teeth, which was a little irritating, and the meal in general wasn't extremely healthy and she would pay for it later, but still—in that moment she was experiencing it, bite by bite. At one point, Mrs. Boucher noticed Zoe and said, "Are you quite all right, dear?" and Zoe, feeling a bit transported, could only nod.

That night she and Gordy made love again, back in the trailer, like the night before. Because she *wasn't* mad at him; in fact, he really *had* helped her, helped her on her own personal mission, which for a short time she had forgotten was hers. As relieved and excited as she was to finally be with Gordy, this wasn't all about him, really. It was even bigger than that. So she wasn't mad and they made love, and he was slow and he made a lot of eye contact, like he was communicating something or like he might suddenly lose her if he looked away for a second. Zoe stared up at him, or into him, or everywhere. There was light all over the place.

Tomorrow she was starting her own mindfulness center.

Three

The next morning Gordy did have a class, so they got up early to go in together. This time Zoe asked him if they could put the bicycle in the truck-bed.

"I might want to zip around a little," she said.

"That's a good idea," he said. "It's a good walking city, but the bike'll give you more range. What are you going to do?"

"Explore," Zoe said.

He nodded. "You sure *you* don't want anything to eat this morning? I think it's more compassionate toward your body to start with something."

Zoe's stomach was a little extra jumpy this morning—there was a lot of light in there, light plus some butterflies—but she accepted some smoothie anyway, because it was nice, him wanting to take care of her. When he got up to change his clothes, she poured a little into the kitchen sink, and that was her breakfast. The coffee part—he just didn't keep it around his place, didn't believe in it—would have to wait until they were in town again. Until after his class. He said it was okay if she sat in, even though she wasn't paying for the class.

"You know," she said in the truck, chucking him on the arm. "Since we're both in the profession."

He looked over at her. "Of course," he said. "A couple of times shouldn't be a problem."

The class was in the same room where she'd meditated yesterday. They were more than an hour past dawn—really it was scheduled so that people could go right before work, instead of being scheduled at a time of maximum Qi—but that meant the sun was already filling the room, and Zoe felt gratitude all throughout her. People began to fill the room, too; there were eleven other people in there—well, women, specifically—by the time he got started.

Gordy sat in his white teacher clothes at the front of the room, lotus, his braid forward over his left shoulder. Zoe, sitting among all the women, beamed at him. She saw again how impressive, how powerful he was. Not to mention good-looking. Like handsomeness and light mixed together. She also saw that everybody else saw that, too. Which brought up a little surge of jealousy, after which she re-focused.

"Find yourself," he said, his voice like a warm weather front moving through the cool room, like the promise of rain. "Where are you?" he said. He took long pauses between each thing that he said. And then: "Are you at home, checking your to-do list?" Pause. "Are you in the car, texting?" Pause. "Where are you?" Zoe could feel everyone in the room breathing. "Find yourself," he said again. And then: "Find yourself heeere." The word *here* felt like it was in just a little bit of slow motion.

Most of his class was guided meditation like that, and she knew what his method was. She had more or less studied it, after all. His first thing, like a lot of people, was to get everybody into the room, which was very helpful considering how scattered life was and how the mind was one of the main things that got scattered by it.

"I want you to open your eyes. I want you to focus on the *eye*," he said, pointing to his own left eye, so that people didn't get it mixed up with the letter. "On what you can actually see, here in the room. It's an illusion, this room, this world, but I want us to see it. We're going to keep our eyes open this morning."

After that, some breathing while everybody looked around. There wasn't much actually *in* the room, but they looked at it anyway. The not-much was one of the things Zoe liked about places like this. Growing up, really she'd only ever been to synagogue—very occasionally—with her family, and a church here or there because of a friend, and those tended to be busier places, aesthetically. Maybe spiritually, too.

"And I want us," he said, snapping Zoe back to attention, "to focus on our other *I*"—here he pointed at his chest—"by which I mean the self. That's an illusion, too, an even tougher one, but I want to make space and validity for us to take it in."

Then he said, "The *I* is false, but we live there. And this practice is for your life. Your actual, lived life. And we live in the *I*, in the *I* of the storm." Which is what he said at Kripalu, too. Zoe knew his philosophy, and she allowed her mind to step back a few paces, to hear things in a summary way, as a backdrop for her focus on her eye and her I.

Gordy—or Gordon, in this environment—kept going, did the whole beautiful i-word thing. Which i-words are helpful and which ones are not. He laid it out slowly. One sentence at a time. Zoe felt it fill up the room, felt the fullness and the emptiness of everything. Gordy's voice was like a cello, playing notes at the frequency of life. And all through this he occasionally had them shift poses. Nothing too advanced because it was more a meditation class than a yoga class, but poses like garland and warrior and even just mountain, and moving between them to keep the body and the mind awake. "Find yourself here," he said. "And find yourself nowhere."

He kept them on that path for about a half-hour. Then he got them into hero pose, each woman kneeling and letting her buttocks settle down on the mat between her ankles. It was a harder pose than it looked—hence the heroic label—and some of the folks had to do rock pose instead, which was also okay, but Zoe had done hero plenty of times, and she was nothing if not flexible. And from there they did Sat Kriya meditation for probably eleven minutes, which felt to Zoe like really the perfect thing, reaching up like that. They only did corpse pose afterward for a few minutes. Zoe could have used more; the butterflies in her were better than birds, but they still flapped. But they did what they did and she received it.

Afterward all of the women thanked Gordy, several of them coming right up to him to thank him and to shake his hand in a mutual two-hand handshake that was pretty close, in fact, to holding hands. Zoe saw again how good-looking he was. Luckily, however, a number of the women were not so good-looking, being squat Mainer-type women. As soon as she felt herself thinking that unkind thought, Zoe blushed at herself and sank right back down into hero pose to do some more Sat Kriya on her own. It was amazing the way the mind could get away from you, and where it would go. She did three minutes of that—her body told her when it was three minutes—and then she laid herself out into corpse pose, intending to stay there for at least five more.

"Zoe," came Gordy's voice. "I think there's another class."

She opened her eyes and there he was. It was okay for her Gordy to be attractive.

"I'm sorry," he said. "But Autumn needs the space."

For a second, Zoe thought that somehow the entire season needed the space, which was a sign of how connected she was to the universe, because of course it was actually just a woman's name, and there was the woman, also in all white—maybe a requirement of the studio—stretching toward the front of the room. She was long and lean, with a bouncy ponytail. Zoe was pretty sure she was going to make the next batch of students work their asses off.

"Oh," Zoe said. "No problem. I was just grounding. But I'm good."

Gordy extended an arm and helped her up. He walked her out of the room and to the top of the stairs. "I have to change back into my regular clothes before I start down at the store," he said, thumbing back at where the bathroom was. "Do you need to get in there first?"

"I'm okay," Zoe said. She patted her stomach. Fluttery, but not in a bad or imminent kind of way.

"You're already purging the toxins," Gordy said, a hand on her shoulder.

"Yeah."

"So, where are you going to explore today?"

"I don't know," she said, truthfully. Zoe hadn't thought about it, because most of the day—this was the secret part—was going to be devoted to getting the mindfulness center started. But she would have to go somewhere at least a little explorey, at least for part of the day, to have some tales to tell Gordy afterward.

"You could check the *Phoenix* to see what's going on," he said. "That's the weekly. I bet there are some on one of the corners, or in that coffee shop."

"I'll check it out," she said.

This time she looked at the outside of the coffee shop before she went into it. It was called *JoJo's*. And then, inside—she didn't realize how much she was hoping for it until it happened—there was the same barista from yesterday. This time in black and gray—shirt and jeans, respectively—but still with the pink pom-pom cap. "You're here!" Zoe said, louder than she meant to, her arms up in the air.

This somehow didn't startle the young woman, who only said, "So it seems."

But Zoe pulled her arms down and quieted herself. "Hey," she said, "are you JoJo?"

The barista shook her head. "I'm twenty years old," she said. "I just work here."

"Right."

"And the truth is—" She paused, widened her eyes. "There is no JoJo."

Zoe stared back.

"You know, like in *The Matrix*? The spoon?"

"Okay," Zoe said. "Listen—what's your name?"

The barista looked at her temporary-tattooed hands. "Would you believe me if I said it was Arachne, the Spider Goddess?"

Zoe stepped closer. "I would believe whatever you told me," she said.

Possibly-Arachne looked up, and for the first time her expression was not deadpan. "Whoa," she said. "That's pretty intense. My name is actually Brittany."

"Hi, Brittany," Zoe said. "I'm Zoe. It's good to meet you."

Brittany nodded. And then: "We'd better go into commerce now," she said.

Zoe smiled. Everybody was doing whatever they needed to do to survive. "Sure," she said. "Can I have a coffee? Black again?"

"Sure." And off to the side again, to pour it.

"Hey," Zoe said. "Do people ever come in here and, you know, tutor other people, or teach them something, or have business meetings or something?" A couple of young men came in as Zoe asked, ambled over behind her in line.

Brittany's eyes peeped up over the steamer. "I guess so."

"Cool," Zoe said. "That's perfect."

There was a copy of the *Phoenix* on one of the tables. Zoe sat down with it while she drank her coffee. She would have preferred to just get going on her plan—once she had an idea it was hard to wait—but she had a full cup, and she couldn't bring that on the bike, which was probably how she was going to be getting around. It was possible that Gordy was right about coffee; caffeine was probably not a good thing in the long run or maybe even in the short run, if only because it bound you to a habit. She looked up from the paper sharply; Zoe hadn't taken her meds *again* that morning. That made three days straight—or four?—and she hadn't been super-one-hundred-percent-consistent, to be honest, before the cold turkey. She didn't feel different yet, aside from not having been stuck miserable in the bathroom even once that morning. But that could be the food choices; really she *wouldn't* feel different yet. She would feel different if she kept skipping—that was for sure. It had been so long since she'd been off the stuff. Gordy had commented on that more than once over the phone. "How do you know you still need them?" he'd said, which was a good question. "How do you know that the pills don't create their own need?" Which was maybe an even better question.

She knew how Dr. Charles would have answered it, because he had answered it before. He would have said, "It's a disease, Zoe. A chronic disease. No different from diabetes or asthma. This disease is a fact about your life. It's a fact. And that's why you need the medication." But the truth was, Zoe wasn't sure. It had been so long since she'd been medication-free. Why was it obvious that she still had to be on it, after all this time? Her stomach went from fluttering to flapping as she thought about it. It was definitely true that she'd started with the pills because they had calmed her down, evened things out a lot. It was like taking the musty basement out of her moods, which was a nice thing, but it also meant losing the penthouse suite, though. Plus she hated the side effects. And she was at a really good place in her life now, having figured things out, having taken action, action she was still taking today. She was not the same Zoe who had started taking medication way back when.

Her decision about the mindfulness practice was the clearest sign of her well-being. From the outside it might not seem that way—after all, she'd never started any kind of business before, so it could look like she was way out on a limb—but inside everything was clicking. All the years and years of meditation and yoga and mindfulness sessions that Zoe had taken in, how devoted and attentive she had been to those experiences, along with how quickly she picked up on things, and how much of a self-starter she could be, and then, too, all the practical thinking she'd already done with Gordy about starting a center—it just added up. She could feel the way everything was coming together so neatly and perfectly. She could really *feel* that, inside her. Sure, she'd never done anything quite like this before, but her life had quietly been preparing her for this kind of move, and now she was making the move. Her life was orienting itself.

The whole thing was a fresh start, a fresh Zoe—maybe a Zoe who didn't need what the old one thought she did. Maybe a Zoe who could find inner peace without pills.

Zoe shook her head; she didn't have to decide anything about her medications that exact second. She took another sip of her coffee and dug around in the *Phoenix* for things she could do so she could tell Gordy about them later. Theater, which was at night. Music, at night. Comedy, at night. Maybe she could go to a museum or something, or a park. Was there a lighthouse? She couldn't spend too much energy or time on any of it—it was just about keeping Gordy suspicion-free. Which she felt bad about, deceiving him, but the purpose was the most important thing. If he had an outside point of view on the situation, he would agree with that. Anyway, she couldn't get worked up about it because she still just wanted to get started.

Things had picked up at JoJo's, but not to the point of actually hectic, so she could just walk up to the counter if she wanted, which she did. "Hey, Brittany," she said. "How far is the nearest public library?"

Brittany pointed, her arm still spotted with cute monsters. "Like five blocks that way."

"That," Zoe said, "is ideal."

Brittany nodded.

On the way to the library, on foot with her coffee, Zoe got a call from her brother. She had assigned him a normal ring tone.

"Hey, Zo," he said. "I thought I'd completely spontaneously call you and say hello, with no pressure at all from our parents to check up on you, nor to do so as soon as possible."

Zoe yelped out a laugh, right there on the street. She had to stop and step over to the edge of the sidewalk; things were getting more downtowny as she walked and there were some people around. "Hi, Noah," she said, her heart full of affection. "Wow. They are just unbelievable."

"Well, you did just get very beatnik on them," Noah said. "These people grew up in the *On the Road* era, so they know what to be afraid of."

"I seriously doubt they've even read Jack Kerouac," Zoe said.

"Have *you*?" Noah was really into books. Should have been a writer or something, but wasn't.

"Probably in high school," Zoe said. "I don't remember. Listen—can you tell them I'm fine?"

"Sure," he said. And then, after a pause: "*Are* you fine?"

Zoe leaned against a mailbox. "Oh, not you, too."

"I'm just asking," he said. "It's my job."

"Noah, you're my *little* brother. It's not your job," she said, though even as she said it she knew she was saying something untrue. He was the one who took her late-night calls when she couldn't stop her mind from thinking so much that it scared her; he was the one who listened to her ideas when she knew she couldn't tell their parents. He was the one who had talked her down after she punched her mirror and freaked out about the glass. Zoe shuddered, thinking about that.

After a few moments, he said, "I'm just asking." And then, after a few more, "I mean, I need to gather actionable intelligence for Mom and Dad."

"You're worried about me, too," she said.

He didn't respond to that.

"Noah, please—this is what I need to do. I'm taking charge of my future. I'm going to do the things I've been meant to do. I'm finally giving myself the chance to be the person I'm meant to be."

"Okay," he said.

"You have to believe in me."

He cleared his throat. He said, "I got your back, Zo."

"Thank you," she said.

"Your back, your side, your top. Whatever. I got it."

"Thanks, Noah," she said.

"Call me if you want."

Zoe leaned against the mailbox, her phone in her hand hanging down by her side. She felt a little like crying, but she was in Maine and she didn't.

It turned out the library—a big, modern, windowy place—didn't open until ten, so Zoe hung out in in the square across the street, at the feet of another statue. This one was a woman, who had to stand—and there were even some other statue guys, soldier types, standing around on the sides of the pedestal. The whole thing was very military—even the woman on top, with her sword and shield. Zoe finished her coffee.

When the library opened, she moved through the steps of the plan: she arranged for a temporary library card using Gordy's address, and then she used the temporary library card to sign up for a computer, and then she sat down at a computer, and then she began to type.

Zoe knew how to get things done. She had hated her job with the school district, but the weird thing was that she'd actually been pretty good at it. Zoe set up talkback meetings with parents and training meetings and workshops with teachers, and meetings with both parents *and* teachers, and she prepared guidelines and guidebooks and workshop curricula, and she wrote tons and tons of copy. She was glad the word *copy* existed for what she wrote, because that word made it seem alien and strange, which it was. But she'd been good at making it warm, which is what it needed to be if you were going to entice parents to get involved with their kids' education. So here was another sign that it made sense, this mindfulness idea.

In this case it wasn't copy at all, of course; it was more than that. In a half-hour she had some writing that made her want to fly. *Zoe Tussler*, it said. *Private Mindfulness Coach.* It said how clients could come to her by appointment—she was going to use the coffee shop for that—or she could come to them. That was a risky thing, maybe, going to people's houses, but it was also her favorite part of the idea, getting on the bike and pedaling out to whoever needed it. Instead of phone books, she would be carrying peace. And maybe arriving in joy? Maybe? Online, she bought classified ad space in the *Phoenix* and the *Press Herald* for a condensed version, and she put the full version up on Craigslist in the *Lessons* section and also the *Therapeutic* section, even though the latter one cost ten dollars and was mostly skeevy-looking "Asian massage and bodywork" ads. But you never knew. And she made up fliers, another specialty from her years in the school district, using some clip art she found—a cartoon of a serenely smiling face. She thought about using her own face—there were some pictures she could get to online because of her school district job—but she wasn't serenely smiling in any of them. And the clip art was nice.

She sat back and marveled at what she'd done. *Zoe Tussler, Private Mindfulness Coach.* It was almost like she could already feel it rippling out into the world. Although she knew it was too soon for anything, she hovered over her phone for the next half hour after that. But it was, in fact, too soon for anything.

"How's it going today?" Gordy said. They were walking down the street toward Longfellow Square again.

Zoe was actually, among other things, feeling hungry. So, "I'm feeling hungry," she said.

"That's wonderful," Gordy said. He lifted up another big brown paper bag. "Yogurt and fruit. We'll fill that belly."

"Awesome," she said. She took his hand and squeezed it. She was so jazzed up that she pretty much needed to hold his hand or else she'd fly right off the earth.

Gordy smiled at her, a little bemused. It was a cute look on him. "Where did you spend the morning?" he said.

"I went to the library," she said, and she dug her temporary library card out of her pocket. "They're going to mail me the real one."

"You're settling right in," he said. "Where else?"

"Well, just more wandering, this morning." Zoe had spent the last hour or so putting fliers up everywhere it seemed reasonable to put them, including, on her way in to see him, on the bulletin board inside the front door of Gordy's yoga studio. She was banking on him not paying much attention to the bulletin board at his own place. Or maybe she was trying to get caught. Zoe always wanted to be caught, according to a therapist she once had—not Dr. Charles but someone else. Man—Dr. Charles. It was the day before her next appointment. Zoe bet that his office was going to call when she missed it.

Anyway.

Gordy had said something. Zoe processed it after the fact, retroactively. "Anywhere in particular?" she repeated. "No. Just up and down. I'm going to get off Congress Street this afternoon."

"Sounds good," Gordy said. "And perhaps it's time to start thinking about how you're going to want to spend your days, in general."

"There was one interesting place," Zoe said, breezing right past his last comment. "Do you know about that cryptozoology museum?"

It was next to a bookstore where she'd posted a flier. She didn't go in, but she peeked in the window, and right there was a giant Chewbacca kind of manikin, or whatever you would call a display guy in a museum, except that this one looked like Chewbacca. She could see the window now, from where they were, crossing over to the Longfellow peninsula area, and she pointed at it.

"Ha. That place. That place is pretty intriguing," Gordy said. "I took a tour once. It's very small, but you need a tour because it's packed full of stuff, and because they have to do a lot of explaining. It's about Bigfoot and the Loch Ness monster and such."

"Seriously?"

"Yes. 'Cryptozoology' means the study of hidden animals. Undiscovered animals."

"Huh," Zoe said. So, not Chewbacca. It was interesting seeing that she had limits; she considered herself really open-minded, but Bigfoot maybe crossed the line into wacky for her.

She wondered whether a line like that was a good thing. She had a feeling her family, for starters, would say that you need a line.

When they got to the square they sat on the same bench and ate their yogurt, which Gordy had made and strained himself. You could kind of tell.

That afternoon, Zoe got herself off Congress Street. She used her phone to find coffee shops, natural food stores, bookstores, art galleries, gyms—anywhere and everywhere that would let her put up one of her fliers—and then she got on the bike. It was nice to ride around—she'd sold her old bike back in Philly, and already missed it. And Zoe felt like she was starting to get a sense of Portland, just by zipping around a little. Like how the University of Southern Maine—a perfect spot to hit—was just beyond Deering Oaks Park with its little duck pond and how

Brighton Avenue, which they'd driven in on, went right through campus; how Back Cove, circled by runners and speed-walkers, was just east of that; how the Old Port was south of there and east of where she'd been hanging out on Congress. She didn't manage any more than that, and didn't paper any one spot too thoroughly, but she scattered her fliers as far as she could in one afternoon, and maybe that was far enough. She felt like Janey Appleseed.

By that time the day was pretty much tapped out; she put the bike back into the pickup, went into the coffee shop, which was very busy by then, and there was a different barista who was a guy—a baristo?—with a whole Rastafarian look going on but no time to talk, and she got coffee and brought it over to the yoga studio, where Gordy was outside, waiting.

"Big day?" he said, which meant that he'd been waiting a little while and wanted to know why.

"I guess so," Zoe said. She was a little stiff from all the biking; she was certainly not in her twenties any more. "Portland is great."

On the drive back to the Boucher estate, she tried not to think about how nobody had called her yet. It was too soon to expect anything, definitely too soon for the ads and probably even for the fliers, but still—she couldn't help wanting it. Luckily, Gordy had questions. Specifically: "So, what did you see?"

Zoe had meant to get across the bridge to South Portland for a tourist moment—there was something called Bug Light over there—or at least to the Eastern Promenade, but none of it happened. Luckily, she had prepared a back-up. She said, "I went up to the USM campus."

"Really?" he said. "That's my alma mater."

"Really?" She could see the just-out-of-high-school version of his face, shining out for a moment.

"Go Huskies," he said, a loose fist very slightly up in the air. "It's not much of a campus."

It's true that it was no University of Pennsylvania. Now *that* was a good-looking campus, with all the greenspace in the middle of West Philadelphia and the gothic buildings and the modern buildings and that big weirdo broken-shirt-button sculpture. USM was pretty much a bunch of little white houses with USM signs on them plus a few big blocky brick buildings which all looked like parking garages, including the one that was a parking garage, plus a long, low student center. But the campus did have its own sort of broken button.

"There's that one place with the crazy sculpture," Zoe said. "The crazy table and chairs?"

"What's that?"

"From the first floor it looks like a bunch of really tall poles, but when you get to the second floor you see that they're the legs of a table and chair. There's just this very simple table and chairs at the top of them." It was very inviting, actually, like you'd want to step over the second floor railing to climb into open space and take a seat at the table—if you weren't afraid of heights, which Zoe was, a little.

"Huh. Is that in that Abromson Center?"

"I don't know. It was a big place right next to the parking garage. The front was, like, all glass."

"That's the one," he said. "That's new since I went to school."

She sat there nodding.

"Well, that's good," he said, smiling with nostalgia. "Sounds like a fine afternoon."

They went over a bump and Zoe heard the bike rattle around in the truck-bed. She liked the sound. It was the sound of how Janey Appleseed was going to get around.

Then her phone started to ring.

"Who's that?" Gordy said.

Zoe did not recognize the number, but the area code was Maine. Her internal birds got a little rowdy. "It's my parents," she said. "I'll call them back later."

"Wow," Gordy said. "Again?" And then: "I thought you had that sinister music for whenever they called."

"Must be on the fritz," Zoe said.

Once they were parked back at his place, she told him she'd be in in a minute and she wandered back behind the trailer under a tree to listen to the voicemail, because there was indeed a voicemail. Which said: *Hi. My name is Eleanor. I saw your poster and I would lo-ho-ho-hove to meet and have a mindfulness session with you. Because, I need it. Really. I could come to you. Do you have anything, for example, tomorrow morning? Which is Wednesday?*

Signs and signs and signs!

Eleanor left her phone number, and gradually Zoe returned to planet Earth from wherever she'd been floating on massive, puffy de-light-clouds during the voicemail. She returned to Earth and there she was, standing out in the backyard in soft, calf-high grass, under the canopy of an old tree, in front of its solid trunk and its branches, and those branches were spreading, spreading, spreading.

Four

Here's the thing: the whole Portland move—uprooting herself, starting over, re-rooting herself—it was important. Very important. Because even if this wasn't like the other things she had tried in the past, even though it was finally the *right* thing, a little part of her still thought of it as a thing she was trying. And probably Gordy would say that little part was a remnant of old ways of thinking or maybe a relic from her child-hood or bad psychiatrist therapy or something, but still—there it was. Because Zoe really had tried a lot of things in her life.

Zoe had the view that a lot of people were born with some of the dials set wrong. Maybe all people were born like that. By dials she meant, for example, the family you were born into; maybe you were a sensitive, transcendental type, and you were born into a family of worriers and businesspeople, like in her case. Or the dial of your emotional life, which could be cranked too high and needed to be turned down. Or the dial of your reaction to the culture, which was always throwing noise and food at you even if you were a person who would rather not have noise and food thrown at you. And so on. It was another way of thinking about the pile of shoes and laundry that life dumps on you from the start. And maybe some people were tuned right from the beginning, or had the right stuff to carry, and they could just stroll through life whistling, and maybe others could stay set up wrong but just didn't mind somehow or tried not to think about it. But then there were the people who were off and couldn't live with it. And the experience of that—well, if the dial was a thermostat, and the room was set at a temperature that everybody else found comfortable, but you were sweating through your shirt and nobody could understand why, well, that was the experience. Except there were many, many dials, and so you were uncomfortable in a lot of different ways. You were too hot and sweating; the air pressure was too intense and your head hurt; plus, you couldn't breathe, really; your stomach was turning; gravity was too much and you couldn't get up out of bed; there was a constant sound of something that most people couldn't hear but that for you was like someone scraping glass with claws.

And so Zoe tried things. The commune was the worst of the bunch, bad enough that she preferred to put it away into a place in her mind where she never went. At times she had flashes—Samuel's eyes, Phebe's eyes, the disciplinary meetings, the rough sheets on the bed where they took everyone, took her. Their rough hands on her. The months of recovery, almost catatonic in bed. But she shoved those thoughts out as fast as she could and only reminded herself that the impulse had been right, even if it had been directed wrong. She'd tried it because those were people who wanted to re-set things. Them and, later, the mystical Judaism people. That one was also a cult, it turned out, but not as bad as the commune, and the idea was good, the idea that we were these broken vessels full of divine sparks, and it made sense that you had to take their classes to open yourself up, and really take on their whole system, even if it was pretty expensive, because why shouldn't they get paid for their life's work? The guy who had been her kind of guru seemed to be an entirely enlightened human being. Lior moved like a ballet dancer, but slowly, and he was always, always calm. Well, almost always. He would look at you with his slow-blinking blue eyes and you had the sense that he already knew everything you would ever say or do. And they worked together on raising her sparks up and understanding the *sefirot* and the other stuff from the *Zohar*, which was the ancient book of Jewish mysticism, and by a certain point she was there several times a week. Every day, pretty much. But things kept getting more expensive and they were asking her to cut off the people in her life, even the good ones, because they were *spark-hoarders*, and, even setting that shady stuff aside, she had a major emotional crash in the middle of all this, right at a time when Lior was telling her she was full of light. She remembered a day in bed when she realized that none of that stuff was helping her at all. It was like realizing that she was hanging from a rope that couldn't hold her weight. When she finally told Lior she had to leave—that was the one time he wasn't calm. He'd actually said, "You're going to regret leaving," his voice a growl, almost a snarl.

Part of what Zoe had realized recently—part of the reason that Portland was the answer and not just another thing—was that you couldn't get yourself right by depending on another person. It had to be you.

But you doing what? That was the question.

Zoe had done a lot of work in her life, and most of it she'd gotten herself into very intentionally. Except the school district appointment— the Associate Coordinator of Blah Blah Engagement Blah Blah Blah; that one she'd started pretty much just because she met a woman at a party who knew about an opening. At the time, Zoe was trying to not be destroyed inside by temp work—all that administrative assistant work would turn out to be handy when she went for the drone job—so when this woman frowned and said, "You'd be perfect for that engagement position," Zoe made a mental note and later applied, even though it hadn't exactly sounded like a compliment, the way the woman had said it.

The temp stuff that came before the drone stuff had been an experiment, basically—an experiment creating a life where she would think of a job as just a job and not anything more than that. Because Zoe had always seen work as an enormous thing, as connected to everything else and as a way to sort her life out. Even her first babysitting jobs seemed like an opportunity to be connected to what was young and untroubled and possible. Or her first official job, which was at a bakery even though she wasn't good in the kitchen; it felt obvious to her that people spent too much time in their heads and that you had to work with your hands if you wanted to get out. Or the data entry thing later on so she could get her mind into order, or the desk gig at the free clinic, for ethical reasons. So all the jobs were like that, but the problem was that none of the jobs actually sorted anything out. Whether it was because she really, really wasn't good in the kitchen or because she took the clinic visitors' struggles too much to heart, or how her mind stayed disorderly despite all the data entry, it just didn't change things the way she hoped. The last thing in her late twenties was training to do massage, for intimacy, and when she discovered that all that touching was *too* much intimacy, she decided that she was trying too hard to turn work into something more than what it was—and that maybe the actual thing to do was to do work that was totally meaningless so that you could focus on the rest of your life. That's where the temping came from.

Though that was a disaster, too.

Basically temp work was like being forced to go on a geographically complicated family trip with an extremely stressed-out family of strangers, and then, after two weeks where you ended up full of misery wondering about how people ended up the way they did, you got shipped to a new family. It was like the foster care of the employment world. Zoe knew it wasn't as bad as that, truly, but she thought thoughts like that on her worst days. As in, for example, the day where her supervisor at the time, a trembly woman who was as skinny as a stick, right in the middle of all the cubicles got into a screaming match with the Vice-President's wife, who was not an employee but had showed up because she seemed to believe that Zoe's supervisor was sleeping with the VP, even though Zoe was pretty sure they were just *wanting* to sleep together, and maybe talking about it a little. Or the day where a different supervisor at a different assignment, a guy, sat on Zoe's desk with his legs kind of open and told her about his workout routine for forty-five minutes. Or the day where another supervisor looked into Zoe's face and said, "Well, I can see why you ended up doing temp work."

Boy—that day. There was a keening in her ears for the rest of the day, a keening that was louder than the subway she took to get home and that continued into her apartment—it actually was a version of the claws on glass, she realized—and she stared over her getting-cold microwaved veggie burgers at the walls of her apartment and thought about how people were angry and cruel and how maybe her life was falling apart and that maybe that's what her life was designed to do. She could sense her various neighbors in the units above and below and on the sides, moving through their evenings. Or possibly they were staring at their walls, too.

Realistically, Zoe couldn't just stop taking the temping assignments; her medications were too expensive—her medical stuff in general was too expensive. So she kept doing it, trying to punch in and punch out and not give work so much importance, trying to not let it annihilate her soul. She listened to music on headphones on the subway and while walking and sometimes at home, too, so that she wouldn't hear that sound so much. Though it was hard to block out the fear that she would never work anyplace long enough to contribute anything to the universe or even build up a pension or—there were just increasing fears in general. Then, as it happened, she went to that party and met that woman and applied and more or less fell into the school district job. And Parent Engagement had some real pluses. She got to help people feel connected to their kids' education, people who might not have even felt that connected to their own education—sort of like Zoe, as a matter of fact—and she learned some Spanish and even a little Vietnamese, and she sometimes got to be around kids. She'd always loved kids. If she didn't have any of her own, with this job she at least got to be around them sometimes. But most of it was meetings and organizing meetings and debriefing about meetings and planning new meetings and even meeting about past and future meetings. She remembered, too, one occasion, where she was at a meeting in a small basement room and someone—Reggie, it was Reggie—was shaking his head and squeezing his tie, saying none of this was going to work unless they scheduled a meeting-planning meeting. And she saw that jobs, these jobs, weren't family vacations. They were families getting together to do their taxes, and this particular experience in the schools wasn't even going to be temporary.

At that point in her life she was also trying another thing, which was staying with something for a while. Because her parents were always on her about that, about changing jobs or other things all the time, and even though they were usually wrong, it seemed like—especially given that she could still hear that claws-on-glass sound pretty much continuously—it was worth a shot to just stay in a job for a while and see what happened. Because maybe that would give her job less importance in her life, if she wasn't always worrying about whether she should stay in it or not. Plus there were long-term economic concerns. In general, there was something to be said for stability. At least that way you weren't forever figuring out some new place's lunchroom microwave.

Looking back, though, Zoe couldn't believe she'd lost four years to a job like that.

And still there was that sound. And sometimes it wasn't just about stopping it—it was about stopping it before the glass went ahead and broke.

Five

Gordy didn't teach Wednesday morning, and the yoga studio's class spaces were all busy with other classes that Gordy didn't think she could just pop into, plus she didn't have time anyway, so Zoe couldn't get any of her own calm going before heading over to the coffee shop, which was where she was meeting her first client. It was all happening very fast. In fact, she'd had to get Gordy to come in just a little early—she told him she wanted to get a jump on exploring—so she actually could get herself settled in by 9:00, which was the appointment time. "It's great to see you so excited," Gordy said.

"Totally," Zoe said. She was trying to not say very much, to stick to the letter of the truth as much as possible. Meanwhile she felt like a rubber ball pressed against a spring, ready to launch and ricochet around the universe. Luckily, she was able to zip off from Gordy without too much discussion—a quick kiss and a mention of her needing coffee and a promise of lunch and then she was off like zoom. Though, while she was zooming, she was simultaneously very aware that she did need to get at least a little calm. Nobody wanted a scatterbrained mindfulness coach. Luckily again, Brittany was at JoJo's again—turned out she was there most mornings, "Because, you know, nobody else wants them," she said, "and I just don't care at all"—and she was predictably deadpan about Zoe's announcement that she was going to be meeting with her *first client ever* right there at JoJo's. "Cool," Brittany had said, with a small nod. Which sobered Zoe right up, at least a little. And this time there was a mini-line of customers, so they went to the commerce thing early. *Business*, Zoe thought. *Right. Business.*

She was wearing her loose, white blouse and her linen pants, even if it was a little cool for it and she'd had to find a way to explain to Gordy why she was dressing like that—"It's just a mood," she said, hoping he'd chalk it up to womanly something-or-other, which he completely did. Gathering two of the most muted and brown chairs from among the unmatched many, she set them up at a table in the corner of the coffee shop next to a window, and where there was some ivy hanging down from a hanging plant pot. It wasn't exactly secluded, but a corner was not a bad start. Plus she could seat Eleanor facing the wall instead of the rest of the room. There would still be the mural to deal with—it seemed more insane than usual that day—but mindfulness was a challenge, after all.

And so was waiting. Nine o'clock found Zoe frozen in a position of anticipatory joy at her table, her elbows on the table and her hands clasped together so tightly they were almost quivering, a grin on her face that she could feel in her neck. But nobody came into JoJo's at that particular moment, or in the subsequent moments up through 9:05. And then, when the door opened—Zoe almost flipped out of her chair and over the table—it was just a cluster of furry art students looking like they were on their way to bed instead of from it. And then nobody for the next five minutes or so, and then—the opening door like getting shocked with heart-paddles—a man and a woman came in talking very intently, mid-meeting, and then nobody, and Zoe was clasping her hands like she was crushing coal into a diamond between them, talking silently to her not-hearing-it self about the Maine demeanor, and then 9:15 went by. She felt it go by. She felt it in the way you would feel everything slow down right after you stepped into a tar pit. After you stepped into it, knee-deep, and started sinking. In a way, it was a kind of calm. Her hands unclasped. She pulled out her phone—dragged it out, actually—and looked for messages that weren't there. The sounds of the coffee shop faded, along with the colors tearing through the mural. And the real problem was that this was only a temporary calm. Doubts—maybe she *was* way out on a limb with this; maybe she *didn't* have what it took to start a practice like this— started to crowd in close. Zoe knew that there was that change in her breath coming, that panicky fast breathing.

Before that could happen, she sat up straight in the chair and closed her eyes. She put her palms flat on the table, her feet solidly on the ground. She told herself that she was perfectly still, and that the panic couldn't live in a perfectly still human being, that it was like electricity looking for somewhere to go. Zoe felt it zapping around in her, wanting to jerk her into pieces, but she told herself she was still, and she stilled herself. The next part was harder. But she did it. Zoe thought about the palms of her hands, the soles of her feet, turned them into unblocked gates, into points of contact, and gave the electricity paths through her arms and into the table, through her legs and down into the floor. With some effort, some real effort, she opened the gates, let it all pass out of her mind and through those points of contact and also into her hair and out, buzzing into the air. She sat like that, letting the charge run out of her.

Still, she did jump a little bit when someone, right in front of her, said, "Oh, wow—" and her eyes opened as the woman continued, "I am *very* sorry."

"That's okay," Zoe said, even before she realized who this probably was.

"I'm Eleanor," the woman said, extending her hand.

Zoe took it. She said, "I'm Zoe."

Eleanor nodded. "I knew it. I could tell as soon as I came in." She was a woman in her fifties, with short, probably-dyed brown hair, but a really good dye job if so, and wearing not yoga clothes but the very expensive kind of regular clothes that you could buy from a yoga clothes catalogue. Oatmeal-Heather-colored tunic and so on. "You were so peaceful in your little corner," she said.

"Right," Zoe said.

"Listen," the woman started, sitting right down, "I know I'm awfully late. Murderously late. If you can't fit me in, I com-*ple*-tely understand."

Zoe shook her head. "No, really, it's all right. Let me just—" and she pulled out her phone, feeling ridiculous as she pulled up her blank calendar that she never even used, and studied it, thumbing the total blankness up and down. "It should be fine. It shouldn't be a problem," she said.

"Oh, glorious, glorious," Eleanor said, taking Zoe's free hand in both of hers. "Because I'm so looking forward to this. Like a gift in an enormous box. I'm just a mess this morning. I couldn't even begin to tell you."

"Don't worry," Zoe said, finally fully arriving in the moment. "You're here now." She squeezed Eleanor's hands in hers.

"Yes," the woman said, her eyes very intense. "I'm here now. Oh, I'm so glad." She let go of Zoe's hands. "You wouldn't believe the morning I've had. This, that, and the other thing. I don't even know if you know, but I drove down here from Falmouth."

"Falmouth?" Zoe said. She didn't know where/what that was.

"Oh, boy," Eleanor said. "I mean, it's not such a bad drive—it's not—but, well, I don't know. Something about it. I don't even know why I'm talking about that. Where are you from, dear?"

Zoe was feeling very off-balance in this conversation. Which was better than almost a panic attack, but still not the best. "I'm from Philadelphia," she said.

Eleanor smiled. "I would have said New York. From your accent. But it's the City of Brotherly Love—perfect! Though we're sisters. Have you lived here long?"

"Not too long," Zoe said. "Um."

"Oh. Well, you're going to love it. I mean, it does take a while to find your place, I think. Some people never do. Mainers are very tightly-knit. I'm sure you've noticed that."

Zoe trod carefully. "I've seen a little bit of that."

"A little bit? I mean, woo hoo. Do you know that, a few years back, the newspaper—the Portland newspaper—had a poll asking Mainers to vote on the best advice for tourists? And of course 'You can't get they-yah from hee-yah' was the big one," she said, exaggerating the accent, "and I think some business owners wrote in with 'Try our famous lobster rolls' and so on—capitalism thrives here!—but do you know what the winner was? The most popular choice?"

Zoe shook her head.

"It was 'Go home.' Really. That's what won. 'Go home.' Isn't that some awful?"

"Well—" Zoe started.

"Awful," Eleanor said, frowning, almost in a huff. "Sometimes I just want to throw people out the window. Into a ravine." Then her face cleared in a sudden blast. "But you have to admit it's beautiful here. I mean, the beauty!"

Zoe hadn't seen that much since she'd gotten into town, but she'd seen lovely things on her last visit. Not that this was a visit. This was the destination. Anyway, she said, "It certainly is. It's a wonderful place to live."

Eleanor glowed. "You'll fit right in, dear," she said, taking her hands again.

"Thank you." And there was a tiny pause, which Zoe decided to go ahead and seize. "Well, maybe we should talk about—"

"Yes, yes," Eleanor said. "Absolutely. Nevermind me. Don't worry about me. Let's get started. Let me just get some tea." She let go of Zoe's hands again and stood up. "Can I get you anything?"

"Me? I'm okay," Zoe said.

After Eleanor left, saying, "I won't be a minute," Zoe reminded herself that this was the point. Anybody could stand in place on a day when the air was calm. What was impressive was standing in a windstorm, if Zoe could manage it. And of course the palm tree, which bent with the wind, had the best chance in the storm. She watched this woman, her first client, line up behind another person and give a little wide-eyed wave back at Zoe, which Zoe returned. And then, while the person ahead of her worked through the process of placing an order with Brittany, Eleanor bobbed her head back and forth, offered Zoe an apologetic stage grimace because of the wait. Zoe smiled and shook her head as if to say, *Don't worry about it.* And the funny thing was that they were only like fifteen or twenty feet apart, so they could have just communicated by speaking, but they didn't.

Zoe decided the professional-looking thing was to mess with her phone again as though carefully considering and maybe even rearranging upcoming appointments in order to better accommodate Eleanor. Professional plus it meant she didn't have to navigate the whole miming thing that was going on.

After a couple of minutes, Eleanor got back and put two cups of tea on the table, one of them in front of Zoe. "I know, I know," she said. "Just in case." Some kind of flowery, herby smell steamed up.

"Oh," Zoe said. "Okay. Thanks."

"It's rooibos," she said. "Swahili for '*Oh, my God.*'"

"It smells very nice."

"That young woman," Eleanor said. "Isn't she striking? All that black?" Zoe looked over at Brittany, who was actually eyeing Eleanor from her distance, a little warily. "I have to say," Eleanor continued, "I so prefer the all-black to the green and the pink, all those hair dyes. But that was the eighties, really. How old are you, dear?"

"Oh," Zoe said. "Thirty-four." The palm tree was getting a workout, though it was still upright.

"I guess the eighties were about diapers and gumming your food and Teletubbies for you, weren't they? Or, did you have Teletubbies?"

Zoe shook her head.

"Oh, well, you didn't miss much. Or at least that's what I understand," Eleanor said. "I haven't seen them, really."

And in the breath before Eleanor said something else, Zoe leapt in. "I wonder if we should talk a little bit about what you're hoping to get from this session," she said.

"Oh." Eleanor seemed a little startled. "Of course. You're right. Let's get down to it. I'm kind of a talker. Don't let that stop you from going right ahead."

"Great. So—what are you hoping to get from this session?" Zoe said.

"Exactly," Eleanor said. "I knew this about you from the first minute I saw you meditating over here at your little table. I knew you were going to be able to whip me into shape. Believe me—I need it."

Zoe was not so easily going to let go of the reins this time. She smiled and said, "It's probably not going to feel like a whipping."

Eleanor waved both her hands in front of her face. "No—of course not. That's not the kind of language you would want to use here. Don't even listen to me."

"The most important thing is *you* being here to listen," Zoe said, feeling pretty much inspired. She really did know her way around a mindfulness session. "To the moment. To yourself, in the moment."

The woman sat back in her chair, a hand on the top of her head. Blown-away pose. "Yes," she said. "That's it. That's it exactly." And then: "Can I tell you something?"

"Okay," Zoe said, despite herself.

Eleanor launched into a description of a yoga teacher she once had who was just brilliant, just a miracle, just a guru, but the teacher moved to the Pacific Northwest—the *other* Portland, Eleanor was pretty sure, saying *other* with some disdain—and from there it had just been a string of teachers who didn't know the difference between inner peace and brain death, if Zoe would excuse that kind of language, but terrible, just terrible. Then she said a few more things about that, or connected to that, which Zoe did not actually catch, because she was, in fact, drifting away. It felt like she had a choice, either to dance around with Eleanor and try to keep up, or to float off. Except she didn't really choose it so much as it chose her; she only knew she was drifting away, but in the way you would know it if you were in a hot-air balloon that had suddenly become untethered and you were not a trained balloon pilot and were kind of in shock. As in, *Well—would you look at that thing that's happening.* It wasn't a terrible feeling. The mural floated loose all around her, like clouds. As she bobbed off into the air, she was vaguely aware of the herby smell of the tea next to her, and Brittany stealing glances over at the table—more wary glances.

And so: Eleanor got her tea warmed up and Eleanor had to use the bathroom and Eleanor told stories—about her short husband, about an unbelievable Pilates class, about what she'd eaten for the last week, breakfast, lunch, and dinner—and Eleanor had to check her phone and she talked about both of her children and asked Zoe about where she'd gone to college. When the answer—Zoe answered from a distance—reminded Eleanor of someone she'd known whose daughter had gone to the same place, Eleanor had been delighted by the appropriateness. "And look at you," she said, "running your own portable temple. The alumni association would be proud of you." Which led right into her theory of coincidences, which was that there weren't any, though explaining it took more time than that. Zoe—Zoe floated. This time it was more on purpose. Maybe palm trees would be better off if they could float, she thought.

And then, when some indeterminate amount of time had passed,

Eleanor abruptly said, "Should we meditate or something along those lines?" And Zoe crashed down and crawled out of the balloon-wreckage. She grabbed Eleanor's hands. She said, "Yes. Yes. Let's close our eyes." She closed her own. Peace was attainable.

"Okay," Zoe said. "Let's think about our breath." And she walked Eleanor through a few minutes of breathing and paying attention to the breath. "Feel your lungs take hold of it," she said, "spreading life through your body. Your whole body." She talked about life being one thing, all around, about allowing it in. She could feel her own breath becoming slow and regular, the whole world settling down. Everything was one thing. And, in a way, all of it was light. She talked about that light, too—light pulsing like soft waves from the center of the heart.

She heard the sound of a sob. Her eyes snapped open, the coffee shop springing back into existence. That and Eleanor, in front of her, crying with her eyes closed.

"Oh," Zoe said. "Oh—are you okay?"

Eleanor kept her eyes closed. "I'm okay. I'm okay. Nevermind me. Keep going."

Zoe hesitated but then continued. She'd seen people cry in mindfulness situations before; she just really wasn't expecting it this time. "Let yourself be aware of the light," she said. She talked about light for a while, about seeing light and feeling it on the skin. About allowing it into the breath. She was feeling flustered, but she tried to settle things down, tried to open herself to that. She made a drop of light and then a puddle of light and finally a pool of light for them to dwell in. They were soaking in light! The sobbing escalated. Then, just before Zoe was going to shift to a few words about peace, talking about the feeling of that, Eleanor's phone made a text-message sound and Eleanor jerked her hands free. It was a little like being in a very small hot tub and the other person just suddenly jumping out, leaving everything—in this case the pool of light—sloshing all around. Eleanor was checking her phone, her face wet. "Oh, no," she said. "I really do have to go. Look at that," she said, without showing Zoe anything.

"Okay," Zoe said. "Do you really—"

"One sec." Eleanor jumped up and dashed over to the counter—where Brittany looked positively nervous—to grab a napkin, giving her face a thorough pat-down on the way back to the table. "Oh, wow," she said. "You are wicked good, as they say."

"Okay," Zoe said. "Great. So—that was very powerful for you."

Eleanor nodded. "It certainly was. It certainly was. I really do need to go—you wouldn't even believe what time it is, and I know you've got other appointments—but, I mean, I can't tell you. I can't *tell* you how important that was for me." She smiled a teary kind of smile.

"That's really good," Zoe said. She was feeling a surge of a kind of love for Eleanor, who, she now saw, turned herself into a moving target because standing still was so intense for her.

"So," Eleanor said, suddenly crisp and brisk again. "How much do you charge?"

The commerce part, in other words. Zoe nodded. Luckily, she had thought about that in advance. "It's forty dollars for a session," she said.

Eleanor dug into her purse. "Okay. That's good. I'll give you fifty. Well, I only have twenties, so here's sixty." She put three crisp bills onto the table.

Zoe flapped around like a bird, at least internally, saying, "Oh—you don't have to—that's not—"

Eleanor patted the money firmly into the table. "No, no. I was late, and I was difficult. Per usual. That's hazard pay." She stood up. "Is this time good for you next week?"

Zoe understood palpably now why business owners would frame

the first dollar they ever earned. If she had a frame, she would have gotten down to some serious framing herself. She would have bronzed the bills if she could. Lacking those options, she spent a while gathering her wits—they were scattered around on the floor and caught in the hanging plant and so on—and staring around at the very bright coffee shop. It seemed extremely bright. And then, not much quieted down, she picked herself up out of the chair and went over to Brittany, who was unoccupied for the moment.

"Who. Was that?" she said, all staccato.

"My first client," Zoe said, grinning big again, "ever."

Brittany shook her head. "Yeah, well. I hope you can do something for her."

"Oh, you," Zoe said.

She was fairly buzzing as she left JoJo's and walked around to the truck to grab the bicycle from the back. The outside world was extra-bright, too, though Zoe had a feeling that not everybody could see it. Mostly the people outside had on these very understated Maine facial expressions, and she was an advocate for that, definitely, but it seemed like it would have been okay for them to stop short of *dour*, anyway, and maybe even to show some contentment. She soaked in the brightness, the almost super-Technicolor brightness, out there.

Today was going to be the East End. She got on her bike and headed that way up Congress Street, practically whistling. And she did hit this hill right as she passed a cemetery, a hill that just kept going up for like half a mile, and she did notice that pretty much everything around her after a certain point was un-flier-able houses. Still, she kept going, feeling it in her thighs but brimming with more than enough bonus energy to handle it. Because she was zooming internally, basically, and was maybe too distracted to do any fliering anyway. Zoe was thinking about clients and more clients and more clients and people crying and getting to very deep places and the soulful look on their faces, the Buddha nature rising up, and eventually her own space, her own place, big and open and bright, lots of windows, where people would come in from a scattered world outside, themselves very scattered and struggling and maybe even frightened, and they would come into her place and all of that would stop. Hers would be a place where people could be finally whole.

She stopped abruptly at pretty much the top of the hill, because—well, because there was a lighthouse there. A lighthouse, but—she looked around—no ocean on any side. It was just a lighthouse in the middle of a residential street. Completely crazy and exciting, is what Zoe thought about that. Also, *Why not*? People were always doing amazing things, just because they could do them. And so there was a cemetery at the bottom of the hill, but there was a lighthouse if you pushed yourself to the top.

Maybe she should even live in this neighborhood when she got her own place. On this street, next to the lighthouse!

From there, feeling almost like she was in love, Zoe really coasted—it even went downhill for a while—and, aside from one convenience store that she hit mainly out of a sense of wanting to be diligent, and where the owner didn't say anything when she entered and asked about fliering—he just nodded—aside from that, she forgot about businessy stuff, and instead zoomed along. The air smelled sharper now, and it smelled sharper because, after a few blocks—yes—there it was: the ocean that lighthouse had been missing.

Zoe got off her bike and walked it up over the curb and onto the grass. This was the Eastern Promenade. A park—grass and a trail and trees and, sure, parking lots, and the ocean. Big and actually blue and continuing onward and outward and the sunlight all over it. And the world was covered with water, and air, and life, and Zoe, standing there in the grass, her shoes already off—she was connected to all of it.

She was late for lunch. It was hard to even say where the time had gone—she'd spent the rest of the morning walking the Promenade and lying in the grass and thinking about how enormous the future was, and somehow that took up a couple of hours or so, and then she had to hop on the bike and push up the hill and race down the other side to get back to the Longfellow statue, where both Longfellow and Gordy were sitting in a kind of stony fashion. Except Longfellow was made of bronze, and Gordy was made out of irritable.

"I only have about a half-hour left," he said.

Zoe was pretty sure it was more like forty-five more minutes, but still. "I'm sorry," she said. "I guess I just got caught up." Everything was still very bright. Maybe even like there was a corona around Gordy's head, around the statue, everything. She sat down.

"I feel that you weren't being thoughtful of me," he said.

"I'm sorry," Zoe said. He was right. "Totally."

Gordy nodded a few times. "Okay," he said. He made a visible internal effort and a stiff smile to go with it. "Well, I made you a sandwich," he said, holding up the paper bag.

"I remember," Zoe said, because she did. And, when more of his face stiffened at that, she added, "Thanks." She really hadn't meant anything by that; she just did remember him making the sandwich, standing in the little trailer kitchen, leaning over the laminate counter.

He handed her a sandwich, which she knew had veggie lunchmeat in it. "I had things I wanted to tell you about," he said. It sounded like he *had* wanted to tell her, but now maybe he wouldn't. Off on another bench she saw another couple, or what looked like a couple, and it seemed like they were having a super-easy time, smiling and nodding about everything.

"I'm interested," Zoe said. She took a big, enthusiastic bite of the sandwich.

"Did you do something exciting today?" he said. He was trying, the sweet guy. She wasn't sure why it was taking so much trying, but she could see that he was trying.

"I went to the Eastern Promenade," she said. "I've been there for hours, actually. It's so nice, looking out at the ocean."

"That's Casco Bay," Gordy said.

Zoe could feel her stomach tightening. "I don't want to fight," she said.

"We're not fighting," he said.

"Okay. Listen—I really want to hear about what you wanted to tell me."

He smiled a little. "You're right. It's just been a kind of long day, and you were late, and everything." Gordy shook his head. "But it's okay. I'm okay with it." He ran a hand back over his hair like he was wiping it clean, and took his braid in his hand, and then let it go. "I'm content," he said. "It's just been a long day."

"Did you want to tell me those things?" Zoe said, this time taking a sandwich nibble, because she had to defer to her stomach, too.

"Sure," he said, slowing down. "Surely. Well, first of all, Taylor."

Zoe's eyebrows shot up. "Taylor?"

"I have her this weekend," he said.

Zoe set down her sandwich and clapped. "That's great!" she said.

It really was, too. One of the things she had been picturing about Maine, if she was honest, was a kind of family life. Her and Gordy and Taylor. It wasn't *about* that—that wasn't the *reason* she moved up here—but being in her mid-thirties had made the countdown clock of possible motherhood tick louder, and sometimes before she left Philly she would picture herself in something like a real picture, a family photo, with two adults standing happy behind a child.

Gordy smiled. "It'll be good," he said. Then he wrinkled his nose. "We'll probably have to adjust the sleeping, though."

"Adjust it?"

"Well, I'm thinking you could sleep in my parents' house. Just for the weekend."

"Oh," Zoe said.

"Just for the weekend," he said. "I want to be sure that it's not weird for anyone."

"Totally. That makes total sense," Zoe said. "I don't want Taylor to be weirded out."

"I know I'd hear about it from Janine."

Janine was Taylor's mother. Zoe didn't know that much about her, aside from the fact that she and Gordy had met about six years ago, also at Kripalu, and that she was an artist of some kind and was maybe kind of crazy and got pregnant on one of their very first dates. There weren't too many dates after that—pregnancy seemed to be a kind of you're-in-or-you're-out decision moment—but they'd stayed in each other's lives for Taylor's sake. Zoe didn't really feel the need to think about her a whole lot.

"Okay," Zoe said.

"Do you want to hear the other thing?" Gordy said.

Zoe squinted at him; she was noticing that the light, the extra-bright light, was actually getting a little glarey. "Sure."

"Autumn told me there's an opening at the studio," he said, his eyebrows up high with expectation.

Zoe's mouth fell open. "What? Seriously?" It was like everything was coming together all at once. She looked around the little Longfellow peninsula as though she was going to see people approaching from all sides, bearing gifts. Though mostly it was just people eating on benches, and one possibly homeless guy.

He laughed, a hearty whole-grain kind of laugh. "Complete seriousness."

"What is it?" she said.

"Well, it's part-time, first of all," he said, "and it's not glamorous. It's a caretaking position."

"Caretaking?"

"Basically that means keeping the studio spaces clean," he said.

Zoe pursed her lips. "Huh," she said.

"You don't sound too excited."

"I mean, there's nothing wrong with that," Zoe said. "I just thought you were going to tell me it was a teaching position or something. Something with yoga or meditation in it."

Gordy set his sandwich down and put his hands in front of him like there was a crystal ball there, but he kept his gaze going into her eyes. "You could look at it this way. In quite a few temples, people apprentice with masters through just this kind of caretaking. You get to know the space intimately. You treat it reverently. You create the space, in fact. It's the foundation of the whole temple, the whole studio. Do you remember the part of *Siddhartha* where he becomes a ferryman? Where he talks to the river?"

Zoe shook her head. "I haven't read that book."

"Oh—you have to. Well, there's a part where he becomes a ferryman. You know, that's pretty basic work, being a ferryman, but he learns that it's sacred work. Right? It's what you see in it, Zoe."

"That's actually a pretty good point," she said. Though it wasn't exactly on topic for her. It wasn't that she saw the work as beneath her; it's just that she really, really wanted to be specifically a teacher. But maybe that was only ego talking. And maybe this was a way of reaching people, too. She thought about how bright and open the class spaces were, and how that helped to open her up. Making the spaces that way—it would be teaching, kind of, if she did it mindfully. "You think I should take it," she said.

"It'd give you something to do," he said. "And we'd even be working at the same place."

It was only part-time, which on the one hand meant no benefits, which meant staying on her temporary COBRA insurance, but also meant she could still run her private sessions quietly in the background. And the fact was that she hadn't gotten any other calls yet from potential clients anyway, so it's not like she was already full-time busy. Not that that was a bad sign, but just that realistically it was going to take a while to build up. Zoe looked up at the sky. It seemed like everything was trying to tell her something, and like maybe she should try to hear it. She found herself nodding.

Six

The next couple of days, Thursday and Friday, went by mostly uneventfully. She interviewed for the position at the studio—it turned out the two owners were Melanie, who was the woman she'd seen working in the shop that one day, and Autumn, the hardcore ponytailed yoga teacher. They were a little like good Buddha, bad Buddha—well, that was too strong, but just meaning that Melanie was very soft and said things like, "I really feel like we're making a connection here," and Autumn sat straight in her chair and said things like, "What experience do you have?" She was pleasant, but not exactly warm. Gordy had said she was the one who really kept the place running. Anyway, Zoe got the job, even though she didn't have any relevant experience, in fact, and she started right away. Mostly it was sweeping and dusting and taking care of the floors—sweeping and washing the classroom ones and vacuuming the store ones. And there was a fair amount of bathroom-cleaning, too. It wasn't a piece of cake, getting super-mindful about the work, but she focused as best she could and she did it all very slowly and carefully and thoroughly, and at times it did feel sort of meditative.

Zoe did her work mostly in the afternoon those couple of days—between classes and also when the store closed at the end of the day—but she still came in early with Gordy and spent the day in town. She spent some of her time out on the bike—fliers went up in new neighborhoods, even across the bridge in South Portland—and sometimes she sat in the coffee shop, trying to read. Gordy had given her his copy of *Siddhartha*. She liked what she'd read of the book so far, but often she was too jumpy to get into it. Too jumpy to write anything in her journal, either, for that matter—she hadn't touched it since she got to town. It felt like an almost physical jumpiness, like one of her dials had gotten cranked to a new position, and it made it hard for her to focus on things like pages. But she read enough of *Siddhartha*, anyway, to give progress reports. Gordy especially lit up when she had questions, like, *Why is Hesse so worked up about how good-looking and lovable Siddhartha is, anyway?*

There were also a couple of steps forward in her project. On Thursday she got a text from a woman named Rose who had seen one of her posters, and they went back and forth with texts instead of phone calls, which was a little impersonal for Zoe's taste, but they ended up with a session scheduled at Rose's apartment downtown for a week later, and on Friday she got a call from another woman, Mary, who wanted to meet on Tuesday. Plus Eleanor was still on the calendar for Wednesday. So things were actually coming along pretty well. She was having fewer surges of panic about needing to get her life on track.

The other thing that happened on Thursday was that she missed her therapy appointment back in Philly, and she was aware of it going by. She was aware during, when she felt it pass like a shadowy stranger that she was successfully avoiding, and she was aware after, when Dr. Charles' office called and left a message on her voicemail. The surprise was that it turned out to be Dr. Charles himself on the voicemail. "Zoe, I'm concerned," he said. "You've disappeared." That's how he sounded at first—clipped, serious. But then there was a pause and he said, "I just want you to remember that this is how it happens. Something takes a hold of you, not because it's a good idea but because you do get swept away. And, while you're in it, you can't see that you're in it. That's the power of a manic episode." She winced at that word, *episode*, and there was another pause, almost as though Dr. Charles was giving her a little space to have that reaction. "Please give me a call, Zoe," he said. "I'd like to talk to you. Call me anytime—day or night. And please remember." He paused again. "The medications help you. They've always helped you."

In point of fact, Zoe had been off them the whole week, and things seemed basically fine. Maybe the world was a little glarey, and maybe she was a little jumpy and excited—but there was plenty to *be* excited about. And, even if she'd needed the medications in the past, it was a known fact—a *scientific* fact—that sometimes people took them for a while and then their internal stuff got rearranged right and they didn't need them anymore. And that's even *if* they actually needed them in the first place. She did feel a little bad about the fact that she didn't call Dr. Charles back—he meant well, even if he was trapped in a very traditional medical model, sort of like his own manic state that he couldn't see—but she couldn't deal just then with calling him, and she decided that was okay. You took things on when you could, and her life was pretty busy.

And then on Friday they got Taylor. In the early evening Gordy dropped Zoe off at Taylor's favorite restaurant—Denny's—and went to pick up his daughter alone. "We don't want a scene," he said. And even if it wasn't totally clear why there would be a scene—Gordy and Janine hadn't dated for years, and if it was about Taylor's feelings, well, she was about to hang out with Zoe anyway—still, Zoe actually didn't want a scene, herself, so she accepted the drop-off and settled into the booth where the waitress had directed her with a "How about over there, dear?" in a robust Maine accent. So robust that it startled Zoe a little.

Zoe was next to a window and she had a view of Brighton Avenue, which right there was basically a busy four-lane semi-highway lined with strip malls, and that evening was gray with a light rain. It wasn't really a view, unless everything was a view. Which maybe everything was supposed to be. But she mostly wasn't even looking at it. She was thinking about her vision of the family photograph and also the new client that had called earlier in the day and partly thinking about how probably the only safe thing for her to eat at Denny's was the pancakes, and how even that would be too much unless she removed the huge ball of butter they usually scooped on top. The first time she'd ever seen their pancakes she thought for a second that they'd accidentally made them a la mode. She was somewhat aware, waiting for Gordy and Taylor, that her knees were bouncing a lot under the table. It was a big deal, meeting Taylor.

"Can I get you anything in the meantime?" came a voice, and Zoe jumped again, in her seat. The waitress had sidled up noiselessly despite being a very large woman. "Sorry, dear," the waitress said. "Didn't mean to scare you."

"Oh, that's fine," Zoe said. "I startle easily. It's not your fault."

The waitress patted her on the shoulder. "So—can I get you anything, or are you just going to hold down the fort?"

"Maybe water?" Zoe said, like making a guess on a game show.

"Sure thing," the woman said, smiling briskly and moving off again. On the way, she went by a man sitting on a stool at the counter, and she clapped him on the back. "You good, Mikey?" It was the kind of clap that would have been powerful enough to knock some people right off their stools, but this guy was also quite big. The general largeness said something about the food in the place, obviously; Zoe had an impulse to stand up on her booth seat and start speechifying to everyone—there were a couple families in other booths, too, everyone big or on the way to it—speechifying about the way we use food as a weapon against ourselves or the way we use it to try to nourish things that can't be nourished that way, or even just how we don't pay attention to what we put into ourselves, and wasn't that incredibly strange? If you were to ask someone to just put any other random thing into their body without checking it out first, wouldn't they freak out? And yet that same person probably did that every day, with food. Of course, Zoe didn't stand up, even though she had a very clear image of doing it, didn't share what she knew about any of those things; she knew that, if she did, she would be the crazy one. Which showed you how upside-down everything was.

It took a while for Gordy to get back to the restaurant with Taylor.

In the meanwhile, Zoe tried reading a little more of *Siddhartha*; she was still at the part where Siddhartha and Govinda were traveling around together, before they even got to the Buddha. But she couldn't really take it in. She was too preoccupied thinking about everything. It really did feel like that, like she was thinking about everything, about all things, though she knew it was actually just a subset. Zoe wondered if one's mind could become big enough to do that—to encompass all possible thought. You would have the mind of God in that case, she supposed.

The door opened, and there they were. Zoe could feel her heartbeat, like her heart, too, had become enlarged—too big for her body, even. She smiled a little toward the door, maybe to stave off the possibility that Taylor would come raging in, attacking Zoe with fists, yelling, *You're not my mother!*—but instead they seemed sort of stuck in the door. She could see Gordy bent over, whispering to his daughter, pointing toward Zoe, or at least toward the table where Zoe was. They did that for a little while, Taylor holding her father's hand and nuzzling at his side, a thumb in her mouth. It was an extremely sweet portrait kind of moment. Among other things, it frankly made Zoe swoon a little over Daddy-Gordy. Finally he reached down and pulled the thumb loose—Taylor seemed shocked, but didn't make a sound—and then he led her over to the table.

"Say hi, lovey," he said to her. Taylor only stood there, wide-eyed, her head all asymmetrical pigtails. "Can you say 'Nice to meet you'?"

"It's okay," Zoe said. She had been planning to give her a lot of space early on, anyway. "We can meet each other without saying a word. People do it all the time."

Taylor put her thumb back in her mouth. Zoe looked at Gordy instead, just so she didn't overwhelm the girl with too much eye contact.

"Well, let's at least sit down," Gordy said, waving his daughter into the booth. "Sorry," he said. "She fell asleep in the car. That usually brings out the shyness." Then, to Taylor: "Do you want to tell Zoe, let's see. Do you want to tell her about school?" She shook her head silently. "Or about Rufus?" Zoe thought that was probably a pet, or a stuffed animal; either way it got another shake *no*. "Or how you're…three years old?" Being actually five, of course, she shook her head again, more violently this time. But it didn't provoke any words out of her.

Zoe said, "It's no problem. Really." She almost asked Taylor something about her t-shirt—there was a cartoony pony on it—but thought better of it. "Maybe we should look at the menus. I bet everybody's hungry, right?"

Taylor wordlessly picked up her kids' menu and stared at it, turning it from right-side up to sideways. After a minute she leaned over to her father and whispered something, even going so far as to cup her hand around her mouth, possibly in case Zoe was a lip-reader or something.

"The Oreo *Blender Blaster*?" Gordy said slowly, an *I-don't-think-so* expression on his face.

"Did you read that?" Zoe said to her, impressed.

"She has the menu memorized," he said. And then, to his daughter: "You can't get a milkshake for dinner."

Taylor squeezed up her face and whispered some more.

"You know how this works," her father said. "If you eat something good for you, we can talk about dessert afterward."

Taylor hunched down in her seat, arms crossed, in a total *humph* posture.

"When I was a little girl," Zoe said, "I used to go to Friendly's with my grandmother. And she was usually really strict, but whenever we went to Friendly's, she would let me get a sundae for lunch, as long as I got something healthy with it."

Taylor didn't say "Really?" or anything, but she raised her eyebrows. So Zoe nodded. "And the best part was that *french fries* counted as healthy. So I could get a sundae as long as I also got french fries. It's weird because usually she was so strict."

Taylor's eyes were wide.

"I know," Zoe said. Then she caught Gordy's eye. He was staring at her significantly. "I mean," she said in a hurry, "they're not good for you." And, "Your Dad's right."

Taylor re-*humphed* herself. Zoe could almost feel that physically, the withdrawal of the child's attention and interest. Almost a physical pain.

Gordy reached over and tipped his daughter's face his way. "Don't be sullen. It's not okay to be sullen." He didn't raise his voice, but the way her face was held in his hand—well, his hand was remarkably big in a relative sense. Zoe focused on her own menu as Taylor nodded a tiny nod.

Things got even quieter after that. Zoe noticed that there was silence at a lot of the tables in there. When the waitress came back—she said, "The gang's all here, huh?"—they ordered. Zoe got the french toast, Gordy the veggie omelette, and for Taylor—having received her order via another whisper—he asked for grilled cheese with apples on the side.

"Isn't she a cute little newt?" the waitress said with a big smile. "You two are lucky ones," she added, to Gordy *and* Zoe.

Gordy said, "Oh, she's mine," but he also reached over and squeezed Zoe's hand, and the whole thing was still sort of nice. He said to Taylor, "That was a healthier choice."

But Zoe missed her menu as soon as it was gone; without that prop, there wasn't any avoiding the fact that they weren't really talking. Or only one of them was; Gordy had a little more to add to a story he'd been telling her earlier. It was about a strange customer from earlier in the day, a woman who spent forty-five minutes in the store, moving slowly from one side of the shop to the other, almost like a performance piece.

But Zoe wasn't listening to him, not a hundred percent, because a lot of her was looking at Taylor without looking right at her, doing it peripherally, taking in sideways the blonde askew pigtails and the smallness and the pink pony shirt. She pretty much was a bundle of sweetness, even if Zoe hadn't heard one syllable out of her yet that evening.

After a while, maybe kind of abruptly, possibly in the middle of one of Gordy's sentences, Zoe said, "So what are we going to *do* this weekend?"

Gordy looked startled, but Taylor latched on, bouncing a little in her seat, chewing on her upper lip. She leaned over to her father and said something that was almost audible this time.

"Really?" he said. And then, to Zoe: "Did you bring a bathing suit?"

"A bathing suit?"

"She wants to go to the beach."

"Ooh, yes," Zoe said. She looked out the window at the gray. "But is it too cold for the beach, already?"

Taylor whipped her head back toward her father.

"There's nothing wrong with a little cold," Gordy said. "As long as the rain stops. And the water would still be warm. By Maine standards, anyway."

His daughter visibly relaxed.

"Let's do it," Gordy said. "As long as the weather clears up."

Zoe raised her water glass to the prospect, and Gordy clinked it, a plastic clink, with his. Taylor even raised her own glass, with both hands, and almost added her own tap. Zoe felt the thrill of it—of being a team, a group, a tribe, almost even a *family*, like that—she felt it all through her. Never mind the gray out the window, or even the little bit of rain that was falling; she could practically sweep that away with her hand.

After dinner, which was more of the talking-adults and mute-child routine, they all drove back to the Bouchers' property—*home*, Zoe allowed herself to think—and Gordy parked the truck at his parents' house. Mr. and Mrs. Boucher were waiting for them inside.

Taylor ran right up to her grandmother in the living room and bounced in front of her.

"Now, aren't you all excited," Mrs. Boucher said.

Taylor continued to bounce.

"Well, if you've got something to say," Mrs. Boucher said.

"It's me," Zoe said. "She's shy around me."

Mrs. Boucher turned toward her son. "The child needs to be able to speak in public."

Gordy shrugged. "I agree. But she's also her own human being."

"Maybe I should go off to the bathroom or something," Zoe said. "Give you guys a little space."

Gordy shook his head. "That's not necessary. Taylor," he said, "It's time for you to speak up."

Taylor shot Zoe a look—not hostile at all but deeply anxious—and it was like her feelings poured right into Zoe, churning up some other ones along with them. Specifically, guilt, compassion, and a substantial wave of briny rejection. Zoe broke eye contact first, looking down at her nervous feet.

Then a tiny voice said, "We're going to the beach, Granny."

Zoe snapped her eyes back on Taylor, though surreptitiously, with her face still pointed toward her shoes. Taylor was actually looking back at her. It was hard to read that little face—but anyway she had spoken.

"See, now—there you go," Mrs. Boucher said. "That wasn't so hard."

"You going to go down to Cape Elizabeth?" Mr. Boucher asked.

"I thought we might," Gordy said. "If the rain clears out."

"Nice down there."

"It shouldn't be that crowded this time of year, I wouldn't think,"

Gordy said.

"Not if it keeps raining."

Zoe smiled. The two of them, standing together with their arms crossed, like a pair of old farmers discussing the advantages and disadvantages of different fertilizers or debating the Almanac's predictions for the growing season.

"Well, the truth is that we probably shouldn't visit too long tonight," Gordy said. "We've got to get this little girl to bed."

Taylor developed a scandalized expression, and pointed toward the kitchen.

"You've already had dessert," Gordy said. Indeed she had gotten a bowl of ice cream with chocolate sauce on it, back at Denny's. A little spot of chocolate was still on one of her cheeks.

"I don't have anything, anyway, dearie," Mrs. Boucher said, and, in response to her granddaughter's hangdog look, she added, "Maybe I just might have to bake something tomorrow for after the beach. We'll see."

Somehow Zoe hadn't pictured Mrs. Boucher as a baker—they hadn't had any dessert either of the suppers they'd had together—but it was a nice surprise, and it certainly made Taylor happy, even if Mrs. Boucher had to caution her with, "Now, I haven't promised anything. I said *maybe*." Taylor bounced on her feet all the same.

And then she and Gordy did go off to the trailer. The goodbyes were hugs between the family members, a chaste one from Gordy to Zoe, and, from Taylor to Zoe, a pretty much squeezeless handshake with a little shy eye contact as well.

It was going to take time. At least time.

"We'll come scoop you up in the morning," Gordy said. "I'm sure you're up for a little much-needed beach vacation, huh, Zoe?"

Vacation? Zoe didn't know what to make of that. She just waved.

And now it was her and the Bouchers, standing in the living room.

They stared at each other for a moment, and then, just as Zoe—still wondering what Gordy had just meant—was about to say, *Well, what now? Are you guys card players?* or something, Mrs. Boucher got down to it. "We've set you up in Gordy's old room," she said with a clap, "Your bed is made, and there are towels and a facecloth. Is there anything else you'll need?"

"Um," Zoe said. She could suggest tea. She wanted to suggest tea. They could have tea together. But instead she said, "No, that's everything," and they both spent a little time nodding. The sound of the TV came on—Mr. Boucher had put himself in a chair, and was watching maybe some kind of fishing show, it looked like. What the Bouchers were about, Zoe saw, was a quiet evening of not very much. And maybe that was the right kind of evening to have. Certainly it had to be better than a few hours of total drama right before bed, which at some points in her life was what Zoe had been prone to. Maybe the Bouchers used to be prone to those nights, too, back when they danced. Though probably not.

"I guess I'll go upstairs," she said.

Mrs. Boucher nodded.

Zoe went upstairs and closed the door to the little guest bedroom and sat down on the very neatly-made bed. Flowers were on every bit of fabric in the room. Not bright flowers, but like quaint wallpaper type flowers. She was aware that her slight snuffly allergic-feeling reaction to all the bloomage was probably psychosomatic.

Now, when a person says *A little much-needed vacation time, huh?* it could mean several things. It could mean that Gordy knew she'd been in Maine for a week and had been hoping to get to a beach and now it was finally happening. It could mean that Gordy thought she was mostly lazing around all day and he was finding a way to sort of critique that with an ironic *much-needed*. Or, probably not, but maybe it could mean something bigger; that maybe he'd even seen one of her posters advertising her mindfulness work and thus knew she really *was* working and he was revealing that her secret was out, but not whether he was okay with it or not. And that maybe he wasn't okay with it.

Zoe's mind started to get hectic. Which she didn't want.

What would really have been perfect, to calm herself back down, was going for a walk or a bike ride or something. Those long, hilly Maine roads slaloming alongside fields and woods. She had a feeling that that would make her look a little odd in the eyes of the Bouchers, though, and that maybe they'd have a point in seeing her as odd. After all, it was dark out, and still rainy. Presumably there'd be cars just flying by on those roads, which would not only cut down on the pastoral aspect of things but also could possibly run her over and kill her. And where would she walk to? The prison? The paper mill? Zoe went to the window, which faced toward Route 25. Yup—rain. Her elbow, which she'd once broken, felt it, a tiny dull ache. And when she put her face up to the glass, she could see outside, which was basically darkness. Then, sure enough, just then a set of headlights tore by, tires hissing on the wet asphalt. She wondered where that car was going. She wondered where she herself was going. Though of course she wasn't going anywhere; she was staying. Zoe put her hands on the glass, both of them, and waited for another car to go by.

Seven

In the morning the sky was perfectly clear. Zoe could tell even before her eyes were open; she drifted up out of sleep and, just as she crossed that gray line between basically asleep and pretty much not asleep, she knew that there was sun and clarity. And then opening her eyes was like throwing open the door to a loved one.

After a quiet breakfast—white, buttered toast plus Mr. Boucher reading the newspaper and Mrs. Boucher puttering around in the kitchen—Zoe got herself together and headed out back to meet up with Gordy and Taylor. Resplendent Gordy was already outside, hefting a couple of beach chairs into the bed of his truck, and there was Taylor on the steps up to the trailer, watching him quietly. She was wearing her bathing suit and only her bathing suit.

"Click," Zoe said, pantomiming like she was taking a picture. Because if there were pictures, this was a picture. And just like a real one, afterward her two subjects were frozen in surprise for a second, staring at her. "Capture the memories," she said.

The trip down to Cape Elizabeth took about a half-hour. Gordy drove, Zoe was at the passenger-side window, and in between them, on a portable car seat, one for big girls, was Taylor, still sort of bouncing about the whole beach thing. Zoe didn't know whether it was legal to have a child's booster seat in the front of a pickup truck—there was no back seat—but she didn't want to second-guess Gordy, who obviously knew what he was doing, or risk scaring Taylor, by asking about it. Instead she just readied herself to dive between child and dashboard if something went wrong. Meanwhile Gordy tried a few conversational angles, work and food and things, but Zoe couldn't concentrate on them—being ready to save a little girl took up a surprisingly large amount of mental space—and of course his daughter was quiet, so at some point Gordy turned on the radio. Classical music.

And then, after a while, they were there. They were there and they parked the truck and got out and gathered their stuff, their awkward armfuls, and went to the beach. *The beach!* Zoe thought. *Dunes and sand and water.*

"Oh, ocean," she said out loud. "It's you."

Gordy went by her with chairs and towels, brushing her arm with his in a flirty way. "It's Saco Bay, really."

Saco Bay. Unbelievable—it was just one bay after another. Zoe shook her head. There had to be some ocean somewhere around here. This was Maine, not Montana, wasn't it?

Anyway, the place they'd gotten to seemed to be functioning like a beach, with the sand, and water lapping up on that sand, and people lounging around here and there. As they walked into the middle of it, Zoe could have practically been a kid again, going to the Jersey shore, which had been a regular thing for the Tusslers. Maybe it was a little colder than Jersey, but not that much, only kind of breezy, and everything else was perfectly familiar. In fact, it wasn't just that she could have been a kid again but that she could have been a way-back ancestor of herself, because for how long had people been slowing down on a beach somewhere to sit where sun and sea and land all joined together three-wise? Probably as long as there had been people. And still they were doing it, even with all the televisions and video games and everything to distract them—people were still coming to the joining place. Zoe helped Gordy get everything set up, like a real Mom and Dad together, and she sunscreened herself while he sunscreened Taylor—but inside she was thinking about how they were participating in something ancient and primal. When she sat down in her beach chair, she sat into it deep.

Taylor, on the other hand, had no interest in sitting. She dragged her father down to the water right away, such that he had to take off his t-shirt in the midst of the dragging, and fling it back to the area they had staked out. It landed next to Zoe, more or less. She was glad it landed next to her and not on her; she once had a boyfriend who would throw cloth things on her in a playful way—like she would ask him to toss her a blanket and he would toss it in such a way that it landed on her head and covered her all up—and it always made her feel like garbage. Like that she was actual garbage. It was practically a criterion for her now, not to date anyone who did that.

Gordy and Taylor messed around in the water. Splashy stuff in the shallows, him holding on firmly to her hand; it was clear she couldn't swim yet. That was amazing, too—the water was a potentially dangerous thing for kids but still that's where they wanted to be. Amazing.

Zoe watched them from afar. She wanted to work her way up to the water. Bay or ocean, it was big, and she wanted to approach it with reverence.

Also she knew, watching Gordy pick Taylor up and swing her around, drops of water flying in an arc, that this was a father-daughter moment. What she didn't know was whether they would all be father-daughter moments, or whether eventually—maybe even that day—there'd be some room for her to get involved. A threewise joining—here was an epiphany—like the elements of the beach. Which one would they each be? Seemed like Taylor would be the sea—children would always be the water—but would Gordy then be the sun and Zoe the sand, or the other way around? Or was it not even a very good analogy? Zoe shook her head again, this time to clear it; basically she just wondered if she'd get to be involved, whether sea or sand or sun or girlfriend. And wondering made her feel a little jittery, like her nerves were extra sensitive. She dragged her hand through the sand and the pads of her fingers tingled all the way through, almost electrically. Plus the sun was again very bright.

Zoe looked around the beach. Families and couples, basically. There was suntanning going on, and reading under umbrellas, and people dripping their way up from the water to towels and chairs or sand-kicking their way down from the towels and chairs to the water. A couple of guys were sending a Frisbee back and forth. There were always a couple of guys doing that at a beach—maybe even cavepeople did it, with bark Frisbees—and here they were now.

Though what she remembered from her childhood was paddle ball. A rubber ball that was pink like an eraser, and two wooden paddles. She and Noah would try to get volleys going and end up repeatedly face-down in the sand. She laughed thinking about it. It would be nice to talk to him, really.

Almost before she even knew it, Zoe had dug her phone out of her bag and was calling him.

"Zo? Hey, Zo," Noah said. He sounded happy. And then he sounded a little concerned, with, "How you doing?"

"Guess where I am," Zoe said. She took the phone off her ear and held it in the air, in the direction of the ocean for a minute.

When she put it back on her ear, Noah was saying, "Zoe? Are you there?"

"I'm here," she said. "Did you guess where I am?"

"It sounds like you're next to a highway or something."

She rolled her eyes, though of course he couldn't see that. "Hint," she said. "Paddle ball."

"You're playing paddle ball?"

Zoe sighed. This was sort of not fun after all. "I'm at the beach, is my point," she said. "In Maine. Do you remember how we used to play paddle ball?"

"Oh," he said. "Sure. That was fun. The beach, huh? Isn't it too cold up there?"

"It's perfect," she said. Maybe it was breezy, but more or less perfect.

"Sounds like you're having fun," Noah said.

"You know what I was thinking about?" she said. "I was thinking about the fact that human beings have been coming to the beach for *millennia*. For, you know, hundreds of thousands of years, probably. I mean, everything we do is some kind of replaying of something we've been doing just about forever—but this, this is so primal and basic."

After a moment, Noah said, "You're getting pretty deep for a Saturday morning."

Zoe laughed. "I'm serious."

"I know," he said.

"Because it's profound, isn't it? It seems to me that we spend most of our lives trying to do new things—see the new movie, eat the new food, go to the new place. That's what our whole culture is about. Invention, replacement, everything new—you know?"

"I think so, yeah."

"I mean, that's America right there. The *New* World. Not because it was actually new—there were people already here, obviously—but because it was a world that only cared about being new. The white people, I mean. Like a religion about being new. America."

"Okay."

"And then it turns out that we're not really *designed* to be new. We're designed to be ourselves, the way we've always been. Here at the beach, or in love, or eating some warm food or something."

Zoe paused, frowning in thought. The whole beach seemed to be glowing. Gordy and Taylor were splashing and so were other people and light was everywhere. She herself was kind of panting. She felt like she was close to something important and unexpected.

"Zoe?" Noah said.

"Yeah?"

"Are you okay?"

All of a sudden the exhilaration felt wilder and angrier. "Why would you even ask that? Don't you hear what I'm telling you?"

"I do, Zo, I do," he said. "It's just—you sound, you know." He stopped there.

Zoe's mouth set. She wasn't going to finish his sentence for him, wasn't going to say the word *manic* for him. Oh, how people loved to throw that word around—as though it had ever defined or decided or solved anything.

After a moment, Noah said, "It's just."

"It's just *what*, Noah?"

"I don't want to get into anything," he said.

"You might as well say whatever you were going to say." She looked off at the ocean, or the water, or whatever, which was too far away.

"I've—I've heard you sound like this before."

"No," Zoe said, feeling just a footstep away from tears. "You haven't. You're not even hearing me now."

"Listen," he said. "When you said you were moving to Maine, I was supportive, right?"

Zoe shrugged, unseen.

"I tried to be," he said. "Except all along, I was thinking, what if this is just another one of those things?"

She knew what he was getting at. After the experience with the mystical Judaism cult—she could admit it was a cult, which was proof of how clear her head had gotten—Noah had sat down next to her, there on the bathroom floor where she was crying that one night, and once she was done crying he said to her, "Zoe, this keeps happening." He said, "I don't know if you see it, but this keeps happening. You get excited about one thing, really excited, and then it goes wrong and you fall into a funk and then you forget about it, and—and then you get excited about something else." She remembered looking up—she'd been holding her face in her hands as though otherwise it might not hold together at all, and suddenly there was a stranger in her bathroom. The one person who she needed to not be a stranger.

"Because," Noah said now, "this seems like it could be just another one of those things. You know, it all happened pretty fast. This guy, this move…"

Zoe stood up, started to walk in circles around her chair. "Okay," she said, feeling very shaky. "Okay. Okay. I'm not saying you were wrong before, about that one thing, that one time—but you're wrong *now*. This is *different*. This is not about some *guy*," she said, looking at Gordy, there in the water with his daughter. He wasn't looking in her direction. He had to keep his eyes on Taylor, for sure. "And it's not *manic*. I *planned* this. I just. I just, I mean, I don't know why you would think what you're thinking."

"Zoe, I—" he started.

"This is *different*," Zoe said, probably too loud. "This isn't some *dream*. I'm not here so that some impossible thing will happen. This is completely different from how those other things happened. Completely. I'm here because I wanted a fresh start in a better place, and I'm working on a business, a career, something I could actually be interested in, and honestly I'm having a lot of realizations here. That stuff about the ocean—I don't know why you can't appreciate that. You would appreciate it if someone else said it."

"Hey," he said. "That's not fair."

"What's the big deal if I moved, anyway? You *know* I never liked living in Philly."

"I know," he said. "I know."

"You know that. People are c-crazy there," she said, the word *crazy* sticking in her throat a little. She was crying. "I couldn't stay there."

"Okay," he said. He was doing that thing where he agreed with her without actually agreeing with her. Everybody did that to her.

Zoe could feel the anger in her throat. She wanted to scream. She said, pretty much yelling, "And besides—what are you saying, anyway? Really—what are you saying? I mean, just because some other things didn't work out doesn't mean that nothing will ever work out. Does it? Because, does it? Like, nothing ever changes no matter what you do? I mean, are you saying to me, are you saying, Zoe, don't even try anything, don't even try, don't try anything, because nothing's *ever* going to work out?" She gasped. Tears were all over her face now, her voice hiccupping. It seemed like other people were paying attention to her from their own towels and chairs. She couldn't keep her voice down. "Does it mean that, Noah? Does it?" Her breath kept hiccupping.

There was a long moment where no voices went either way through the phone. It was just an object.

And then, finally, Noah said, "Oh, Zo," he said. "That's not—that's not what I'm saying."

But it was. She was not stupid, and she knew when her brother was lying. Lying was the kind of thing that made her burn inside. "I'm going to go," she said, furious. "You're just like everyone else, and I'm going to go."

He said something else, but the phone was back to being just an object, and Zoe, burning, made it stop talking, chucked it down so that it landed in the sand. And then she tore off her shirt and shorts, bathing suit on underneath, and ran for the water. There was no more working her way up to it—she needed it now. She ran for it, splashing right by Gordy and Taylor, pushing herself further out, and, when it was deep enough to cover her, she dove in.

Oh, suddenly, suddenly. It was very cold. All around her, the shock of a very cold ocean. Or she was a finite, overheated thing within it. It was her temperature that needed to change. She was a small, finite, overheated thing. And the ocean? The ocean was bigger than anything that had ever happened to her or ever would. It had been here since forever. She felt herself arriving into her place in the ocean. Or bay, or whatever it was. How many people had been in this vast space before? Looking at the green or the blue or the sandy-foggy or the clear of it, depending? The cold braced her on every part of her body. She stayed under. She stayed under as long as her lungs could manage it, or maybe a little longer.

Eventually Zoe came back to the surface, bursting out like a water-spout herself up into the air. Gordy was staring at her, a couple of feet away now, Taylor in his arms. He looked worried, like he had maybe lost her for a minute. Lovey guy. While the little girl—the little wide-eyed, open-mouthed girl—was clapping. Clapping for her.

Zoe grinned—she could feel herself grinning. "Ta-da," she said.

They spent a while in the ocean after that, sloshing water around, going under, holding hands—all three of them. They chased each other; they floated; they faced the waves. Taylor was squealy the whole time, as though things were almost dangerously wonderful. Zoe knew that feeling. And they were together around it. Taylor held hands with her, too, not only with her Dad. So hopeful now, Zoe encouraged everyone to dunk their heads under—there they all were, in that enormous space— and they all came up gasping. It was magical, honestly, with ocean spray playing the role of fairy dust. Gordy seemed to get a little bored of it all after a while, but that happened sometimes, Zoe remembered, and it didn't change the basic fact: by the time he led them all out of the water and back onto the drying sand, who knows how much later, something had changed. Taylor, for one, was still holding Zoe's hand, even though she was safe on land again. And she was talking.

"Do you think there are sand crabs in the sand?" she said—to Zoe.

Crab-type things were not Zoe's favorite, but she for sure wasn't going to miss an opportunity like this one, so she said, "Let's find out."

Gordy did look tired or something. "I'm going to go sit for a while," he said, giving Zoe's shoulder a warm squeeze. "You guys dig away."

Zoe turned to Taylor. "Maybe we'll dig to China," she said.

Before he turned away to head off, "Right here? I think if you went straight through you'd end up in like Australia. Or the Indian Ocean."

Zoe stared after him, all his wet hair running unbraided down his back. Anyway, she turned to Taylor and said quietly, "That's only if we go right through the center. Which would mean going through a lot of boiling magma. So I'm thinking we'd be better off digging at an angle, toward China. That's more traditional anyway."

Taylor smiled shyly, like she was getting away with something. She didn't say anything, but she giggled.

Zoe didn't usually let herself think too much about having kids. First of all, she was getting to an age where that would be tougher and tougher and more dicey, in terms of making a baby that was healthy. And then there was the feeling that, with her own experience the way it was sometimes—well, she was honestly a little scared of the idea of introducing another life, a fragile life, into her own. In a way, it was like a race; could she pull things together before it was too late, biologically, to have a baby? But now—Zoe shook her head to refocus herself—here was this beautiful, sweet child in front of her, and maybe this moment could just be itself without anybody needing to think any more about it.

So they dug for sand crabs in the borderland between dry and wet, wherever they saw the tiny air holes in the sand after the water pulled back. And they found sand crabs. Little gray shelly things that were probably freaked out by the exhumation, but who hopefully didn't have the memory capacity to be traumatized for the long-term. Zoe let one and then another and then another crawl pretty much disgustingly across the palm of her hand. She did it so that Taylor wouldn't be scared of them. It felt very mothering, doing that. And Taylor did let them crawl on her palm, too, squealing, with happiness as far as Zoe could tell. Whenever they put the creatures back down, they burrowed themselves gone right away. Maybe they wondered why they hadn't been eaten.

Gordy was asleep in his chair by the time they got back to their home patch of sand. The two diggers were hungry—Zoe was a little surprised to discover herself hungry, but she was—and so even though it wasn't quite lunchtime they dug into the bag for their sandwiches. Cashew nut butter and jelly on some whole grain kind of bread—that and thermosed water was, in this context, about the most satisfying thing in the world. Taylor and Zoe sat together eating and drying off in the sun and watching the ocean. They didn't say anything. They didn't need to.

It was an idyllic day. Eventually Gordy woke back up and ate his own sandwich, and he joined them in some more digging and water play, though even then he retreated a few more times to his chair. "I just feel so lazy today," he said. "Well, that's the unkind way to put it," he added thoughtfully. "I just mean I'm in the mood to replenish." For her part, Zoe didn't leave Taylor for a second, not even when nature called the little girl. That was some mothering stuff right there, taking her to the public restroom where inevitably you have to think about contagious diseases.

And they talked, too—not endlessly, not continuously, but here and there. Between one thing and another, Zoe learned that Taylor *hated* eggs, which Zoe could relate to somewhat, depending on how they were made, that Taylor had a friend named Brittany—"So do *I*!" Zoe said— and that sand tickled the palms of Taylor's hands. And Zoe told her a long story about the ocean, a story about whales traveling long, long ways just to find other whales to be with, which they always did. They always found each other.

On the way back in the car a few hours later, it was Taylor's turn to sleep, there in her booster seat between the two grownups, wrapped up in a towel. Zoe still sat at the ready to dive between the girl and the dashboard, but it wasn't as tense as on the way down, because now everything felt safer and more sure. She mostly didn't think about her brother, and things felt fine. Some things obviously *could* work out, whatever anybody else said.

"You and Taylor really hit it off today," Gordy said quietly.

Zoe drew in a big, satisfied breath. "I think so," she said. "I think we did. You know? Something about being in such a primal place, maybe. It just makes so many things possible, I think."

"I knew you would," he said, though Zoe wondered if there was an off note in his voice, his smile, at all. Probably not. Probably she was imagining it.

"Did you have a nice day?" she asked him.

"Oh, sure."

"You seemed kind of tired."

"I think I was," he said. "I really did need the replenishing."

"So it wasn't that something was wrong or something."

He looked over at her. "Zoe, I said I was fine."

She couldn't tell whether that was befuddlement or exasperation or even him being charmed by her concern, but she decided to let it all go and just enjoy the road and her skin humming with the sunlight it had absorbed that day.

That night they ate dinner with the Bouchers in their dark-ish dining room—baked ziti—and a little quiet back-and-forth about nothing much. Taylor seemed to go back into her shell a bit, keeping to herself throughout the meal unless she was asked a direct question. Zoe took the opportunity once again to be mindful about eating. One ziti (maybe zito, in the singular?) and then another. One and then another. She didn't get through a ton of the meal that way, but that was probably for the best, anyway.

Dessert was apple pie. Zoe had been wondering whether the ziti was what Mrs. Boucher meant when she said she might bake something for after the beach, but no—there was also apple pie with that lattice top and everything. It was pretty good, too. Not as sweet as some other pies, but Zoe appreciated that; desserts were insane sometimes. Total sugar bombs. She said as much to Mrs. Boucher, who responded, "Apples are fresh." Not as a general statement about all apples always, Zoe gathered, but about at this time of year. Taylor seemed to like the pie a lot, her eyes wide as she forked her way into it. And Gordy had a slice and a half. Zoe didn't want to push it, so she just ate a good chunk of one slice, but she did appreciate that it wasn't over the top. Then, afterward, Gordy announced another vanishing act with Taylor. He stood up and gestured for his daughter to stand up with him. "We'll just head back to the trailer and get this little girl to sleep," he said. .

"Do you want me to come over later to hang out?" Zoe said, trying to keep her eyes from darting nervously at his parents, but in any case picturing another lonely evening in the little bedroom upstairs. "Once she's asleep?"

"Definitely," he said, flooding her with relief. "Give it an hour or so."

She nodded, and then she got up—everybody was getting up now—and went over to Taylor, squatted down to her level. "I had *so. Much. Fun.* With you today," she said.

Taylor seemed almost embarrassed by that, the way she squinched up against Gordy's side, but she nodded, too. She definitely nodded.

The door closed behind them, and Zoe turned around. The Bouchers were already in position—Mrs. in the kitchen cleaning up, and Mr. in front of the TV. Okay, then.

Zoe was halfway upstairs to the little bedroom, intending to just wait the hour out, when she turned herself around and took herself into the kitchen, where Mrs. Boucher was washing dishes.

"Could you use some help with drying?" she asked.

Mrs. Boucher turned around, a little surprise on her face. "Well, sure," she said, and she nodded toward a dishtowel that was hung over the over door handle.

And, just like that, Mrs. Boucher was washing and racking and Zoe was drying. No conversation or anything, but this was another obvious opportunity to really inhabit the moment at hand. To think about how Mrs. Boucher was putting water on the dishes and Zoe was lifting it off again—not destroying water, not eliminating it, but moving it to another place once it had done its part in making things clean again. What a thing water was! Zoe, meanwhile, didn't know where anything went and she didn't want to disrupt the smooth machinery of their working together, so she made an executive decision to stack things on the counter once she was done with them. The putting away part could come after.

Which indeed it did. Once Mrs. Boucher had finished racking the last of the clean, wet dishes, she went around Zoe to grab the plates and glasses and silverware and got them to their proper places. Only once or twice did she have to touch up Zoe's drying job.

"Thanks, dear," Mrs. Boucher said with a smile.

"Oh, it was my pleasure," Zoe said. "Doing the dishes is sort of meditative for me."

"Well, it does go quicker with two," Mrs. Boucher said.

After that, there wasn't much to say, so they went off into the living room, where Mr. Boucher was again watching some type of fishing show. There was a boat and a man with a beard talking into the camera about "line." The two women sat down in available chairs, no two adults on the same piece of furniture.

"Do you fish, Mr. Boucher?" Zoe thought that catching and killing animals by hooking them in the mouth was kind of a horrible thing to do, but you had to make conversation somehow.

"What's that?" he said. He had maybe been a little bit asleep, she now realized.

"Do you fish, yourself?"

"I have been known to sit on a boat a while, sometimes," he said.

"Sit and not much else," Mrs. Boucher said.

"Sitting is the best part." He grinned loosely and Mrs. Boucher gave him a wry look. Zoe saw that she was witnessing marital affection.

They settled into quiet watching, which Zoe spent thinking about what she might do with Gordy and Taylor the next day. There was probably a children's museum, in town, or they could go to a park. Or do a crafts project without ever leaving the house. Looking at the Bouchers, Zoe understood that love didn't have to be flashy.

Maybe a little less than an hour after Gordy had taken Taylor back to the trailer, Zoe made her way across the back lawn herself. At the front door of the trailer she hesitated and then decided not to walk right in but to knock instead. It seemed like the right thing to do.

Gordy appeared at the door, which he'd opened a hand's-width. The light was all around him and he looked beautiful. "Hi, Zoe," he said, quietly.

"Oh—is Taylor still awake?"

He nodded, and then squeezed himself out and closed the door behind himself, putting the light back into the trailer. "She's close, but sometimes it takes a while. She slept a lot in the car."

"That's true."

He nodded back toward the trailer. "So I should probably stay in there."

"No problem," Zoe said. "You can call me on my cell when you're all set." She was pretty sure it was still working after throwing it into the sand that day. "Or we could just plan to meet up tomorrow morning. What do you want to do?"

Gordy was nodding, and kept nodding after she'd finished speaking. It was a thinking kind of nodding. "You know," he said, taking her in his arms and holding her close, "Zoe."

"Yes?" she said, as though roll was being called.

"I think Taylor and I could use a day to nurture our relationship," he said. She could feel his voice all through her body. "To get back in touch."

Now Zoe was nodding—a trying-to-catch-up kind of nodding, against his shoulder.

"I think we could use a day to ourselves," he said.

Zoe's mouth opened in the shape of the word "Oh," though she didn't actually say it.

"Just a father-daughter thing," he said, letting Zoe go again. "No worries—everything is fine. She's already fond of you, and I'm especially fond of you. Everything's fine. It's just a delicate relationship, the father-daughter relationship, with us living apart. It's so hard sometimes. It takes extra attention, extra work to build and maintain. And given that you're living here now, you'll have plenty of opportunities to join in from now on. Right?"

"Right," Zoe said. And then, after a second, "Oh, totally. Of course."

"Right," he said. "Thanks. I knew you'd get it."

He sealed it all by bending over and kissing her, and giving her a grateful smile before slipping back into the trailer.

Zoe stood there for maybe even another whole minute. And then she turned slowly back toward the house, and the little bedroom.

Eight

There was no reason to get up early on Sunday morning, so Zoe didn't. She woke up somewhere in the eights—but then she just lay in bed after that, very very heavy on the mattress. She lay there a long time. Time filled her body. It laid itself on her body, like she was under the mattress instead of on top.

She lay there a long time, long enough to study the light shifting across the walls and ceiling, except she didn't study it. She just saw it. It was the same way she saw the flowers on the curtains, one by one, all the way down the length of the curtains. The flowers were all exactly the same, except where some of them were cut off by hemming.

The only thing she did was blink. And it felt like a dozen years passed every time she blinked. A dozen years. A dozen years. Five dozen. A dozen dozen.

When, at some point, she felt the sensation of hunger, remote but recognizable, Zoe just lay there feeling it distantly, the same way she distantly felt how hard everything was, fundamentally. How fundamentally difficult.

A hundred dozen years. Four hundred dozen years. A thousand. Fifty thousand.

At some other point she heard the sound of Gordy's truck as it drove by and out onto the road. And then also the Bouchers' cars. One and then the other.

Everything was very far away.

Also remote but not completely missing was something else. There was Zoe's awareness that this, this unmoving place, was a place she had been before. When she was in this place it was like all the normal assumptions of life lost their hold. You didn't *have* to get up. You didn't *have* to produce things, or work, or eat. You didn't even have to move at all. In this place she understood: we just *told* ourselves that we had to do those things. The truth, the truth as she saw it from this place, was that the default was nothing. The default was nothing—and each action, if you were going to do one, had to be decided and then it had to happen. And it took significant effort on your part. The default thing was to be inert. Was nothing.

A million years.

But—

A dozen years.

But...but being in this place and knowing that she was in it was different from being in it unaware—and this morning she saw, distantly, that she was in it.

She saw it.

Through her blinks she saw it.

And with that came the gradual recognition—it felt like it approached from a long way off, and on slow feet—the recognition that she could decide to move.

That it might be good to make the decision to move. To put in the requisite effort.

Because she knew, she knew that this got very ugly if you let it just go.

She started to talk to herself, silently, through the heaviness. The words floated up in her like through a thick syrup, but they eventually came. It wasn't even true, she reminded herself. It wasn't true about how we didn't have to move. We were always moving. While we were alive we were always moving. There was the blinking. That was something, she told herself. Blinking was actually something. And then the lungs pulling in air and letting it go. The lungs. And the heart sending blood to every part of the body. Including the brain. The brain firing away.

Even if we didn't get out of bed, didn't even shift an inch in one direction or the other, we were moving. We were, we were abuzz with movement.

Zoe knew this. She did.

Get up, she told herself. *Get up. Get up right now.*

And it wasn't right then—it took a while—but it did finally happen. With a great oomph finally she sat up in bed, shocked at being partly upright again. It was now in the early tens. Zoe kept it going: she swung her legs out and got to her feet. And then, for sure, found the bathroom.

Then Zoe changed into daytime clothes—she felt like things were speeding up now, though still not at normal speed—and went downstairs, where nobody was. And as glad as she was to have made the decision to move, she could feel that resolve threatened by the fact that there was nothing to move toward. She could easily just sink into the couch as into the bed. Still—she made herself eat a piece of toast, looked out the window at some birds who were doing their usual bird activities, which were amazing, she pointed out to herself, and tried to think as bravely as possible about how to spend a day trapped in an empty house in the middle of nowhere in particular. Wait—unless—

Zoe got up and washed and dried her dish—things were definitely speeding up—and went outside and over to the trailer where—yes—it was there. Zoe felt almost a sob in her throat. Gordy had left her the bike! She ran right up to it. There was even a little note attached. *Have a good day*, it said.

You see? That was the thing about that place she went to sometimes. It was a mood; it wasn't inherently truth. And it was gone now. *Gone*, she said in her mind. *Gone*!

Because that was the choice—to be heavy and inert or to be light and full of electricity. She saw them right in front of her, those options, like two different levers, and everything in her reached for the electricity.

So—with a brand-new sense of possibility, Zoe got a bag together and a jacket and then before she knew it she was on the bike on her way into town. By car, she remembered, it was only like ten or twenty minutes, with a lot of stoplights, so it couldn't be too many miles. And she was really starting to be tuned up after a week biking all around town with her fliers.

She felt good, genuinely good, going down and up hills, breathing vigorously, the country on both sides—or at least she felt good when cars weren't racing around her. But even they began to slow down as she worked her way into the towny feel of the outskirts of things, and there was the mill, and then the strip-mall area—hi, Denny's—and then cozy residential stuff, each thing coming like a natural stage of life. Zoe paused a couple of times as she biked, but more to appreciate the distance she was covering than to rest. Well, maybe to rest a little. At one point—she was pretty sure she was in Portland proper by then—she stopped next to a hospital and had a drink of water from a bottle she'd packed. It was up a little grassy slope, the hospital, and surrounded by all kinds of parking lot, and it looked sort of like a castle that way—not the building itself, which was of course one hundred percent box, but the general situation. Raised up and moated. Zoe couldn't know the stories that were playing out in there, but she wished all the unwell people well. She had had one of her lowest moments in a hospital—she would never forget that feeling of sedation, the white-gray ceiling that seemed to press down on her to break her more than she was already broken—so she knew how things could get. She wished these people well.

Zoe took off on her bike again. Again it felt good to move. Though the thing was, she realized, where was she going, anyway? She hadn't checked her newspaper to see what was going on in town, and she didn't really know where things were, except vaguely and mixed-up from her fliering of town. For a moment she felt a spike of panic and, right behind it, the syrup wanting to ooze down into her, threatening to fill her up again, that syrup that made her inert. Oh, God, what would she *do*?

That's when Zoe saw it. She squeezed the brakes hard, made them squeal. A couple of people on the sidewalk nearby—there were a few, dressed up nicely—jumped a little at the sound. But Zoe was only half-noticing them. Because she was busy, busy being in awe and not understanding how some people were atheists. Not that she believed in some big, bearded man in the sky in a fancy chair, throwing light-ning bolts, but there had to be something, something arranging things, making things happen. There had to be. How could anybody think otherwise? Because right there next to her was this beautiful, white, super-New-Englandy building, this classic steepled kind of deal, right there on the other side of these well-dressed people, who were in fact headed right up the sidewalk and turning onto the path and right into the front door. A church. Right there. Oh, God, exactly!

Zoe got off the bike and leaned it up against a tree. She didn't have a lock, but she doubted anybody would be stealing the bike around there. She also didn't have nice clothes—she was in jeans and a long-sleeved t-shirt that said *Weaver's Way Co-Op* on it—but she couldn't imagine anybody would turn her away, whatever she was wearing.

Zoe clapped her hands twice, as though to get the dust off, and took to the sidewalk herself. She, of course, was not Christian—she'd been raised in a sort of vaguely Jewish household, the kind that went to the synagogue for the major holidays some of the times and that sent its kids to Hebrew School with no expectations that any of it would really stick; that did a Christmas-sized Hanukkah every year, sometimes on not ex-actly the right dates; that preferred that everybody would marry Jewish people; and that maybe had some thoughts about the lurking ever-read-iness of anti-Semitism; but that otherwise went along to get along. So, pretty assimilated but nonetheless not Christian; mostly these days she was in Buddhist or approximately Buddhist environments. But what it all boiled down to was that now Zoe was a grownup who believed that something big was making the whole world happen, and that that something could be found anyplace if you were looking for it with an openness, and that people had made beautiful places of worship so that it would be easier to be open. And that here she was heading for one such place.

At the door the line of nicely-dressed people bunched up a little as they worked their way in. Zoe, standing out in her casual clothes, smiled a kind of *Hey, what can you do* smile at an older lady in a gray-blue dress. The lady did smile a polite smile back, which Zoe chose to interpret as her answering, *I'm with you, dear.*

There were only a few people, really, so pretty soon Zoe found herself inside. It was bright white inside, and it was basically simple. Not a lot of stuff, decoration-wise. In that way, and because of the light and the whiteness, it was sort of like the yoga studio—except that there were pews, obviously. Long wooden ones. Zoe chose one toward the back in case there was any kind of unspoken or even spoken hierarchy about where people sat. In terms of crowded, it was medium, and it was just about eleven o'clock, which she was betting was the start time. A few more congregants filtered in. As it happened, nobody else sat in her particular pew, because there was enough room ahead of her. But she didn't change seats. This one was as good as any of them.

It was exactly eleven when the minister or pastor or reverend or possibly priest took his place at the front of the room behind a podium. He was a white-haired, older man in dark robes, with something like a white scarf or a prayer shawl over his shoulders. Older or not, there was something very solid about him, not quite football-solid, but sturdy and like it wouldn't be easy to move him from his spot if you wanted to try. He looked up from the lectern—there was a flash of sunlight off his glasses—and looked out with palpable seriousness at the congregation.

He said, "The Peace of Christ be with you."

Zoe sort of jumped at the word "Christ"—she wasn't closed-minded about different religious faiths, but something in her Jewish innards made her a little jumpy around the word "Christ." And then the congregation all responded, in unison, "And with you," unexpectedly. It became a thing between everybody, everybody saying, "The Peace of Christ be with you," to the point where a man a couple rows ahead of her twisted uncomfortably around in his seat—he was elderly, too—and said it to her, too, glancing just a glance at her informal-wear. Somehow Zoe blew the response; she said, "Thanks," instead of "And with you." She added, "That's really nice of you," but he was already turned back around.

After that was another sort of back and forth. The pastor-minister-priest-deacon-vicar said, in a kind of oratorical voice, "A psalm of David. Give ear to my words, oh Lord. Consider my meditation." And then the congregation came back with "Hearken unto the voice of my cry, my King and my God, for unto thee I will pray." Zoe started looking around, wondering how everybody knew what to say, and then she saw that they were looking at programs that they'd gotten from somewhere and that she didn't have. Well, really she was there to listen, anyway. Which she wasn't doing, because she was thinking about the program—so Zoe snapped herself to attention, just as the—she was going to go ahead and call him a minister—just as the minister said, "The foolish shall not stand in Thy sight," and she found herself a little put off by that as she listened to the rest. At the end, he said, "In Thy fear shall I worship toward Thy holy temple," which was intense in its own way.

Luckily, the next thing was a hymn, and there was a book of hymns, so even though she didn't know the tune she could stand up with the rest of the people and read it to herself. It was, not really too surprising, about praising God always. The voices of the people around her were solemn and calm. Not, like, gorgeous, but soothing. Zoe closed her eyes and swayed along a little.

And then there were more prayers, and the minister read some Bible verses along the way. Something from the Book of Isaiah—"*Seek ye the Lord while He may be found*"—and although Zoe wasn't too big on calling God *He*, still it was a thing worth hearing. And the minister said it with a firm, certain tone, as in, *As you know, people, you'd better seek God while God may be found.* Also something from the Book of Mark, which was New Testament stuff, and had Jesus being pretty stern with his followers. The minister read, "*Whosoever will come after me, let him deny himself, and take up his cross, and follow me.*" The sunlight flashed off the minister's glasses as he looked up and down, consulting notes and fixing the congregation in his view.

Zoe saw the service's theme building as it built: she saw that it was all about seeking God. She could abstract that from the happenings even if she was an outsider. And it was a pleasing thought, since she was in there specifically in order to do some spiritual seeking. *Check,* she thought. *I'm on it.* And then she reminded herself to be humble about the journey.

Things got quiet then, and Zoe realized that the minister was about to go into a sermon; you could feel it. Everybody was sitting still and watching the man as he looked down at his podium, shuffling things around.

"Humility," he said suddenly, looking up with that flash again. *Whoa,* Zoe thought. She had *just* been thinking about that. And then he repeated it: "Humility." Zoe was trembling a little.

"I suppose it's an old-fashioned idea," the minister said, looking down again, reading from his notes. "We are not taught humility anymore. Not in our schools, not on television, certainly, and not in our homes. These days and in this country what's expected of us is self-satisfaction and self-aggrandizement. We are becoming a world where you can be famous for nothing at all—not for accomplishments or good deeds—and where fame itself is the trophy we're after."

It would have been more dramatic if he'd been speaking it instead of reading it word for word, but Zoe was still locked in.

"This is the cult of the individual," he read. "The word 'idolatry' was at one time considered a negative word, but now we have 'American Idol'"—Zoe could hear the quote marks on that one—"and it's something young people aspire to. They line up down the block just for the chance that they might get to be an 'idol.' What they want is the spotlight. 'American Idol.'"

Zoe was struck by the way he talked about a show that had been on TV for more than a decade, as though it were a recently-launched attack. It was hard to gauge his face from the back pew and with him looking down, but he seemed relatively worked up. Still solemn, sober, measured, but maybe a little louder. The congregants, meanwhile, sat very straight in their seats and listened in perfect silence.

He kept going. "And of course it's not just young people. The grownups want their promotions, their expensive automobiles, their accolades. But Jesus said, *Whosoever will come after me, let him deny himself, and take up his cross, and follow me*. He told them not to revere themselves but to *deny* themselves." That one would have been especially good spoken off the cuff instead of read, Zoe thought. *Deny* themselves. Bang. She chose to hear it in her head that way. "Mm," she said quietly to herself in appreciation.

"What does it mean to deny yourself?" he asked nobody in particular, though Zoe took it as a personal question. He answered before she could formulate her own thought fully. "It means to set yourself aside, to stop idolizing yourself and to start following God."

"Yes," Zoe said softly. The people a couple rows ahead of her shifted slightly in their pews, maybe starting to get into the spirit.

"Proverbs: *Pride goeth before destruction*," he said. "*A man's pride shall bring him low. Jeremiah: Woe to the crown of pride.*"

"Mm," Zoe said again, a little louder, maybe regular talking volume. There was more movement a couple rows ahead of her.

"But Jesus told us to deny ourselves," the minister said.

"Deny ourselves," Zoe repeated. And at that, two people turned around in their pew to face her—the man who'd wished Christ on her at the beginning and a woman from another row further up. They didn't say anything, but Zoe saw that they definitely wanted her to be quiet. The face can be very communicative on its own. She felt her own face blush and she looked down at her jeans-wearing knees.

The sermon kept going, unpaused—Zoe hadn't bothered the minister, at least—and she listened to him talk more about following Christ with a cross on your back and no ego, basically, which was a Buddhist kind of principle that she could appreciate, except that she felt pretty abashed and also alone, so she was having some trouble. It wasn't like anybody had yelled at her, but it just—she was just having some trouble, and it felt like the kind of trouble that could spiral downward.

When the minister finished—people were silent in response—everyone stood up for another hymn. On her feet again, Zoe decided that she should probably take it as a segue into walking, as in, walking right out of there again. The experience was definitely souring for her, and maybe it would be good to quit while she wasn't too far behind. And so she did. With the steady voices singing in the rows ahead of her, her own breath getting ragged, she sidled her way down the length of the pew and out into the aisle, and then to the door, which made a little noise, but at least everybody was singing, and then she was out.

On her bike again, crying only a little bit, Zoe tried to figure out what to do. It was the same thing as before the church—she had no idea what to do with herself—but this time there wasn't anything appearing suddenly like a sign telling her what to do. Still she pulled over again, to think. What would she do if she were back in Philly and it were Sunday? Well, she might do yoga or meditation at the place in Mt. Airy, and then she might get coffee with a friend. Grace, maybe, or Brenda. She pictured Brenda's calm face, her short dreads. Zoe could call her. Except—she shook her head—Brenda had been kind of skeptical about this move to Maine, too. Like everyone. It had been more gentle, coming from her—it was more a look in her eyes than anything—but it was clear enough anyway. Zoe shook her head. Besides, what she needed wasn't old friendships but new ones. She needed friends in Portland.

The problem was that she didn't have any.

Zoe pulled up with the bike in front of the yoga studio and stared at the building. It felt a little weird, being there, what with it being Gordy's studio. Though it was hers, too—she cleaned up part-time, after all. So she leaned the bike against a pole and went to the front door. Which was locked. Zoe checked out the schedule that was taped there: the Sunday morning classes were over already, and the one mid-afternoon one wasn't until three o'clock. Even the gift shop wasn't opening until one.

Probably there were other places she could go. Zoe took out her phone to do a search, but she wasn't even sure it would work right since she had chucked it into the sand the day before and left it there for a while. More to the point, she was actually getting hungry. Maybe the thing was to eat something. All she'd had that day was a piece of toast, and it was about noon already. Zoe looked around as though trying to spot a place, but really she was casting around in a different way; she didn't want to eat alone and, even if it was ridiculous, it was like she was looking around to find someone to eat with.

Except it wasn't ridiculous. The coffee shop, she thought as she saw it.

Brittany. Brittany worked mornings, and got off around lunchtime. Zoe snapped her fingers in a *Eureka!* kind of way, and set off across the street.

And there, just as Zoe was going in, was Brittany, coming out from behind the counter in her pink cap and an olive-green military jacket over the regular black and waving good-bye to the next barista. It was unbelievable. Zoe wondered at people who didn't believe in signs and kismet and divine provenance and karma, all of it. She stood at the door so that she was there when Brittany got there.

"Brittany," she said. "You're leaving."

The young woman didn't show any surprise at all. She was just ready for whatever. "A-yup," she said, a variation on the traditional Maine *a-yuh.*

"Have you eaten lunch?"

Her eyebrows went up very slightly. "I have not eaten lunch."

"Then listen—let's have lunch together," Zoe said. "I'm hungry and I don't know anything about where anything is, and you probably do. And I feel like having lunch with a friend."

Brittany looked at her sort of impassively. Not irritable, not happy. Disinterested. "You do realize that our relationship is driven by relatively circumscribed, culturally-defined roles."

Zoe blinked at that. "You mean, you're a barista who's doing a job and I'm a customer."

Brittany nodded. A couple came in through the door and weaved past them, into the open space of the coffee shop.

"Plus I'm way older than you," Zoe said. "And plus you were probably just going to go back home, to eat something at home."

Brittany nodded again, but there was something apologetic in it.

Two levers. Inert or electric. Zoe grabbed the electric again. "I don't believe in circumscribed," she said. "I think we can be friends, too."

Brittany narrowed her eyes, studying. Finally she said, "That's too much for me, all of a sudden. Here's what I can do. I can have a back-and-forth conversation standing here in the coffee shop for a couple minutes. A miniature version of having lunch, but without food."

"Okay," Zoe said. "Is it, like, a test run or something?"

"It's getting to know each other a little," Brittany said.

"Okay," Zoe said again. They stood there in silence for a few moments, until, "So," she said, feeling like an idiot, "are you a student?"

Brittany nodded. "Mecca," she said.

"What?" For a second she had a vision of this goth girl being a student in a Muslim madrasa.

"Maine College of Art," Brittany said, tipping her head off to the side as if to say, *It's down the street that way.*

"Oh," Zoe said. "M-C-A."

"Well, M-E-C-A, with the Maine postal code. M-E."

"Ah," Zoe said. "So you're an artist? I should have known you were an artist."

"Metalsmithing," Brittany said.

"Wow—seriously?"

Brittany nodded. "I made these," she said, holding up her fingers and, along with them, her rings. Rings that were all pretty different—one a fat, featureless, dark and shining silver; another one that was a whiter but more matte silver, finely-detailed, made to look like a string of tiny leaves; another in bronze that looked pitted and scarred. "And these," she said, lifting her necklaces up off her chest, pendants with strange patterns on them, like there were layers exposed under other layers.

"They're amazing," Zoe said.

"The pendants are *mokume gane*," she said. "That's what I'm really into now."

Zoe shook her head in amazement. She thought about how cool it was, being able to make metal move and take shapes; in her experience it was only solid and hard. "You're very powerful," she said.

Brittany gave her a somewhat quizzical look at that point. "Thanks?" she said.

"What you can do with metal—it's powerful," Zoe said.

And then there was a moment of silence, or two.

Brittany finally broke it. "And you're, like, a—what, like a life coach or something?"

"Basically. I'm calling myself a Mindfulness Coach. It's about being present to the moment instead of being scattered all over the place." A person went by them on her way out the door. They really were blocking the entrance.

Brittany nodded soberly. "Sounds interesting," she said.

"Well, I'm just getting started. I've had one client so far. You remember her."

"Sure do," Brittany said. "Why do you want to do that?"

"Why do I want to do that?"

"Yeah."

Zoe felt like a long answer would be the truest, but this was supposed to be relatively quick, so she just said, "Because I think people really need it and I can help them. I know it's helped me."

"Makes sense," Brittany said, nodding again, but this time kind of decisively. Just before Zoe was about to go on, Brittany continued: "So, now we know each other a little bit."

"I guess so," Zoe said. "It's nice."

Brittany nodded seriously. "Well, I'd better go. Oh—and there's a noodle place like a block down that way." Brittany lifted a be-ringed hand to point and then wave goodbye, and she went out the door. Zoe noticed that her tattoos were starting to wear off.

"Bye," Zoe said.

Zoe spent the next hour or so eating take-out rice noodles very slowly, one at a time, with Henry Wadsworth Longfellow. The noodles were good—something Thai, specifically un-spicy—but mainly she felt off, sitting there alone on her bench. There were people on other benches, but they were on other benches, and they didn't count as company. She found herself wishing that the base of the statue at least had some of Longfellow's poetry chiseled into it, so she could get to know him a little, and have something to read. Though generally she didn't like reading and eating at the same time. It was anti-mindful. So she sat there and just ate the good noodles, until she was done. And then she tried her phone to see if she could look up some poems by Longfellow. She didn't have anything else to do.

Her phone worked fine—it felt a little hot, but it seemed to be working fine. Of course there were a lot of his poems online—one website had pages and pages of his stuff, alphabetically by title. It was overwhelming. Zoe stuck with the letter A just to narrow things down, and picked out one called "Autumn." It seemed like a good choice, since it was in fact Autumn right then in Portland, and it would be like she and Longfellow were making small talk about it.

Except it seemed Longfellow wasn't much for small talk. *Thou comest, Autumn, heralded by the rain,* he wrote. *With banners, by great gales incessant fanned,/Brighter than brightest silks of Samarcand,/And stately oxen harnessed to thy wain!* Zoe looked around at the calm of the day, no great gales getting fanned anywhere, and no stately oxen either. If this had been an actual back and forth, Zoe might have said, *Well, so far it's actually pretty mild, don't you think?* Of course, she knew he was going for the drama, and that that was his job.

She read quite a bit of his poetry after that, all the way until it was time for the yoga class, or close enough, and then she made her way over to the studio, which was open. She poked her head into the gift shop, because it wasn't quite time to go upstairs. Melanie was there, arranging some display things on the counter. There were no customers just then.

"Oh, hi, Zoe," she said. "I didn't know you were in today."

"Well, not for work," Zoe said. "I thought I'd see if I could sit in on the yoga."

Melanie smiled a warm *That's a good idea* smile, and moved to a table that had some bright woven scarves on it, straightening them.

Could Melanie be a friend? Maybe. But Zoe wasn't sure she wanted to risk trying for it, just at that particular moment. "I'll see you," she said.

And again Melanie smiled. *That's a good idea, too*, she seemed to say.

Zoe spent the yoga class focusing on her inner resources. The class was led by a stout woman she'd seen once or twice before in the studio, with short, red hair, a slight Spanish-speaking accent, and always barefoot. In the class she spoke very little, aside from naming poses. By the end they were hard poses, but she named them calmly, like they were no big deal, and Zoe was able to do them. As Zoe folded out of plank and lifted into crane, her knees tucked into her armpits, her feet off the ground, all of her balanced on her hands, she reminded herself: *You are strong*, she said. *You are strong. You are the universe, and you are strong.*

After class, Zoe got her bike and went back out to Longfellow Square, not wanting to start yet into the more-or-less grind of a trip back to the Bouchers'. She read some more Longfellow poems for a while, and then she called Gordy. It was almost five o'clock by then, and she decided it was okay to call him if she wanted to. Pretty much whether he liked it or not.

"Hey, Zoe," he said. He sounded happy to hear from her. "How's it going?"

\

"Good, good," she said. "I biked into town, read some poetry, did a yoga class."

"That's really lovely," he said.

"What have you been up to?"

"Oh, the basics," he said. "The Portland Children's Museum and junk food." Zoe didn't hear any complaining from Taylor on the other end, but she must have given him a protesting look, because Gordy added, "Well, it *was* junky, kiddo."

"That's fun," Zoe said, unable to stop a note of longing from slipping into her voice. "Where are you now?"

"Well, we're about to head out to Janine's place. I said I'd get Taylor back before dinner."

"Are you in Portland?" Zoe said.

"Yeah—why?"

"Well, my thighs are pretty tired," Zoe said. "Could I get a ride back?"

"Hm. Well, I'd have to pick you up now, because I've got to get Taylor back. I don't know about bringing you by Janine's."

Zoe felt herself get a little angry. "Right," she said. Who *was* this guy?

But Taylor must have made another protesting face, because Gordy said, clearly not to Zoe, "Well, it's complicated. It's a grown-up thing." And then, "Okay, okay." And then, back into the phone, "Yeah—yeah. Of course. You shouldn't have to bike back from there, anyway."

Zoe was kind of flipping. Gordy was being a weirdo, but Taylor had pushed him on it—for Zoe!

And finally, more quietly, maybe turned away from his daughter for privacy, Gordy said, "Would you be okay with staying in the truck when I bring Taylor inside?"

"Sure, sure," Zoe said. "Whatever is fine."

It was only a few minutes before the pickup pulled up next to the square. Zoe bounced off the bench and over to them, grinning through the passenger window. Still—even in her excitement she remembered that she had to have a soft touch with someone so shy. She lifted the bike into the bed of the truck, and then she gave Taylor a small wiggling-finger wave before opening the door. Part of her felt like she was approaching a woodland creature who might skitter right past her and up a tree and away. "Hey, guys," Zoe said.

They both smiled at her. "Hey," Gordy said. He looked different somehow. Like the light on him was different.

Checking Taylor's pretty eager body language to make sure it was okay, Zoe squeezed in next to her booster seat.

"Right before we got here," Gordy said, "Taylor asked me, 'Are you guys going to kiss when you see each other?'"

Taylor, horrified, wrapped her arms around her face and head.

Zoe laughed. "What did you say?"

And Zoe hadn't decided whether she felt kissy yet or not, but Gordy leaned past his daughter and gave Zoe a kiss—a really chaste one, anyway—on the lips. "You can look now," he said to his daughter. "It's all over."

"Do you think that's icky?" Zoe asked her.

Taylor hesitated, and then shook her head *No*.

"Well, why don't you guys tell me about your day?" Zoe said. "What was your favorite part of the museum?"

Gordy looked at Taylor with his eyebrows up, and then he pulled away from the curb.

Taylor thought about it and said, "We saw a fairies play."

Zoe put her own eyebrows up, and Taylor kept going. "There was a really mean guy who wanted to cut all the trees down. With a mean face. Fairies live in trees. And but the queen—" and so on. Classic stuff that Taylor was very, very into. But she could have been saying anything, really. Zoe was blissed out regardless, and every once in a while as she listened she snuck a look up at Gordy's handsome profile. He was smiling, too.

"That sounds amazing," Zoe said at the end.

Taylor nodded very seriously. It *was* amazing, is what she was saying.

They drove through Portland and out of it, though not exactly toward Gordy's place. For a while they went that way, but then they turned off, and they wound around past more houses and trees and into a little residential area with very small houses, some of which were the kind that were trailers that had been permanently grounded, like Gordy's. Zoe was remembering to be nervous by then. The things she had heard about Janine—that she was angry, so angry, that she liked to yell and scream. Her I-words were *Irate* and *Indignation*. Maybe *Irritable* on a good day. Having finished describing the play, Taylor was now playing with her own hands in her own lap, like she had discovered some new toy, and Zoe was thinking about how explosive this could all get.

Finally they parked in the driveway of a little brown house that kind of leaned to the side as though trying to eavesdrop on the next house. Gordy looked over at both of them for a moment, sizing everybody up, and then said to his daughter, "Do you want to say goodbye to Zoe?" Taylor offered another one of those soft handshakes—such little hands! how did she even use them?—and then the two of them got out, father and then daughter out of the driver's side. At the open door of the cab, Gordy leaned back in and said, "Thanks for understanding about this. It's just awkward. I'll be out in a minute."

"Sure," Zoe said.

Gordy smiled maybe sadly and then led Taylor off to the front door. She didn't look back, which made sense—she was probably thinking mainly about her mother, which why shouldn't she be?

Zoe put her head back against the headrest, the hard headrest. She tried for a position of calm because, inside, her brain was zapping around. Zapping from what she wanted from Gordy, to what she wanted from Taylor, to what she wanted from those people in the church or Brittany, what she wanted from yoga, what she wanted from Henry Longfellow, and then, too, zapping toward that earlier mood hovering in the not-far-enough-distance, and also her nervousness about Janine and whether this was a pretty bad idea, being there. Zoe closed her eyes, defensively, as though not being able to see the house would reduce the danger. She breathed. She breathed some more. She talked to herself. *You are the universe*, she said.

"So—you're the girlfriend."

Zoe's eyes snapped open. There at the open door of the cab was a woman, a woman with an awful lot of curly blonde-brown hair and a hand on her hip—there was dried clay on that hand—and an eyebrow raised archly over the round wire rim of her glasses.

Zoe was still gathering herself when the woman said, "Janine," sticking her hand into the cab for a shake. Zoe took it—not a small hand, not a soft shake, and crusty—and said her own name.

Janine crossed her arms over her clay-smeared black t-shirt, which said *Black Flies* on it in white. "He told you to stay in the truck, didn't he?"

"Well," Zoe said. "I mean, it seemed like it would be awkward."

Janine shook her head. "Awkward. That guy's approach to *life* is awkward."

Zoe didn't know what to say to that.

Anyway, Janine had more. "So what's your deal?"

"My deal?" Zoe looked around, back over at the house, checking for maybe an escape route, maybe for Gordy.

"Don't worry—I've got him upstairs looking at some papers. He likes it when you turn to him for advice. You've probably already noticed that. But yeah. What's your deal?"

"My deal?" she said again.

Janine eyed her closely. "Your story."

Zoe took a deep breath. "I just moved here from Philadelphia."

"Why?" Janine said. "Just to be with Gordy?"

"No," Zoe said, and it was the truth. Why did everyone think this was about him?

"Because I can tell you it's never a good idea to make a big move just for a guy."

"I know," Zoe said.

"Especially if the guy is Gordy," Janine said.

Zoe stared at this woman, this woman that was standing there handing out unsolicited advice. Having been on her heels so far in the conversation, she felt herself plant firmly in place. "I didn't move here for him," she said. "I'm pretty sure I just told you that."

Now both eyebrows went up over the wire rims, and Janine uncrossed her arms so that she could put them on her hips. She was smiling. "Oh," she said. "You're going to be just fine."

Zoe was back on her heels, in a different way, but she managed, "Well, yeah. I am."

Janine smiled a little more. She was pretty, the kind of eyes that could sparkle if things went the right way. "We should go get a beer sometime," she said. "I could tell you a few things. Really I *should* tell you a few things."

"Um," Zoe said.

"Hey," came Gordy's voice from over Zoe's shoulder. She looked over that way, saw him standing confused at the open front door of the house. "Are you—is everybody—?"

Janine let out a big laugh. "You caught me, Gord. I told her she has until midnight to get outta Dodge. Or else." Then she ducked her head into the cab and produced a little object she'd dug out of her jeans pocket, held it out on her palm toward Zoe. It was a tiny ceramic bear, brown. "I'm into bears," she said.

Hesitantly, Zoe took it, held it in her own hand. Janine gave her a wink, said, "Be safe," pulled out of the truck, and headed back to the house. At the front door, she clapped Gordy on the shoulder and went inside. Gordy glanced over at Zoe and then followed Janine.

The bear in Zoe's palm was unglazed, rough, and very bear-like. It looked like the thing had been alive, lumbering right through a miniature woods, when Janine suddenly froze it in clay.

Be safe?

A few minutes later, when Gordy got back to the truck, the bear was in Zoe's pocket.

"I'm sorry about that," he said, frowning.

"It's fine," she said. "No big deal."

"Yeah, well," Gordy said. Then he patted her leg, put the truck in gear, and backed them out of the driveway. Zoe watched the house as they went. Even though there were no curtains on the windows, she couldn't see anybody inside. But she could feel the bear in her pocket.

Nine

And so began the week of worrying about Gordy.

Zoe couldn't help it—meeting Janine had shaken her somehow. Or getting shut out of daddy-and-daughter day plus meeting Janine had shaken her. Or Gordy saying no to the mindfulness center plus getting shut out plus Janine. Or plus those smoothies she never wanted to drink but that he kept making her drink in the mornings. But definitely, she thought as she lay in bed on Monday morning, gearing herself up for the day to the sound of the blender in the extremely-nearby galley kitchen, a switch had been flipped, and meeting Janine was part of what did it.

Gordy had told horror stories about his ex. There was a story where she screamed accusations at him in the middle of a yoga class, another story where she was giving birth to Taylor and when he showed up she cursed at him to get out, *get the fuck out* of the delivery room, which he did. Gordy told her about battles over when and how he could see their daughter. Stories where Janine was controlling and hyper-reactive and paranoid. There was even a story where she threw one of her clay pots at him.

But Zoe pictured Janine's face and, sure, it was a little intense, but it actually wasn't the face of a crazy woman.

And Janine had been right about Gordy liking to give advice. Maybe she was right about his approach to life being awkward, too. And so maybe there *were* a few things Janine knew, things that she should be telling Zoe.

One thing she actually *had* told her was to be safe.

Zoe shook her head. That last one was too much to think about. She tried to mute that area of her busy brain and instead stared over at the picture of Gordy and Taylor and thought about the advice-giving thing. It was relevant, because he had given her advice—they shouldn't open a mindfulness center—and there she was sort of going ahead with it anyway. She had been wondering all along how he'd react if he found out, but now she was extra wondering. She didn't know what to expect, but she had a feeling it would be bad. Sometimes his eyes—well, they had a look. It was hard to pin down, but sort of like there was something waiting behind them. And there she was thinking about it. *Be safe.*

The blender whirred to a stop, and Zoe sat up, slid out of bed, stood there for a moment, and then put on her jeans. As she did so, she could feel it in her pocket—that little ceramic bear. A little poke in her thigh.

Monday she mostly spent at the yoga studio, cleaning. She wasn't sure why they had given her weekends off, because there were a bunch of classes on the weekends, but anyway the place was a little less spotless than usual by the time she got there on Monday morning. She started in the store, dusting and vacuuming the carpet before they opened the doors—Gordy was actually drinking tea across the street at JoJo's coffee shop, which somehow felt a little odd to Zoe as she made her way through the store, like they had swapped something. Maybe something important. From time to time she stared out the window at the coffee shop, but it was opaque from where she was.

She was just finishing up—a last wipe of the counters around the cash register—as he came back. Zoe had kind of timed it that way. That way they could pass each other, him coming into the store and her going out, and they wouldn't have to talk. She didn't really want to talk. That morning he'd said to her, "Why so quiet?" and she'd shrugged, said, "Just quiet." She didn't for sure know the real answer herself.

Now, this morning, he said, "Looks great," as he came into the store, smelling like tea.

"Thanks," she said, making her way toward out.

"Hey," he said. "Do you want to go out for lunch together today?"

"Why?" said Zoe before she could get a hold of her mouth.

Gordy laughed a strange little laugh and shook his head. "There's a nice vegan place a few blocks away that I thought you would want to check out."

Zoe nodded. "Okay," she said, trying to sound natural. "Sure." And then she went out the door.

In her right pocket was the bear. In her left was the crumpled ball of the poster for her mindfulness practice, the one she had posted on the bulletin board just inside the front door the previous week, and which she had taken down this morning. It seemed like the online stuff was reaching people, anyway, and anyway it just didn't seem like a good idea anymore, taking the chance of Gordy seeing it. She wasn't ready right then for the conversation, or whatever, that would come out of him finding out.

Then it occurred to her, heading up the stairs to the first yoga place: What if he had already seen the poster, though, and just wasn't saying anything? Was that possible? What would it mean? Was the lunch thing about that somehow? Zoe shook her head to clear it out, but the clamor kept on clamoring.

The lunch place turned out to be a kind of order-at-the-counter place, mostly a bakery but with this lunch menu, too. Interesting things—huevos rancheros that were of course not eggs, a totally vegan Reuben sandwich, a lentil salad. That kind of thing.

Zoe stood at the counter, distractedly considering. Gordy had already ordered the Reuben, but Zoe wasn't sure. The woman behind the counter, who had bright, dyed-orange hair, like a little fluorescent fire on her head, waited very patiently.

"What's the mildest thing?" Zoe said, touching her stomach. "The easiest on the digestion, I mean." Her stomach had been extra off all morning. Her hands had been a little shaky and her stomach off.

The woman looked over at the menu and thought about the question with evident seriousness. "Hmmm," she said. "Well, you know, I guess I'd stay away from the beans and that kind of thing. Maybe the Elvis? We could take the tempeh bacon off. Then it would just be peanut butter and bananas. Well, and a little bit of agave syrup." She turned back to Zoe. "People really love that sandwich. We make the bread, we make the peanut butter."

"Perfect," Zoe said.

"Still having stomach issues?" Gordy said as he paid. Possibly there was a note of disappointment in his voice.

Zoe nodded. "Still adjusting, I guess." She was wondering why she hadn't even offered to pay for her own sandwich. Was she becoming dependent on him?

He nodded, too, and then pointed out an open table by the window where they could sit.

They got there, and sat down, and Gordy said, "So."

The thing about Zoe was that, once she got an idea in her head, it was hard to shake it. And therefore she was feeling weird about Gordy, and therefore she couldn't help reading into every little thing he said. As in, was that a *Well, what's new?* kind of "So," or was it a *We've already run out of things to talk about and I don't know what to say* kind of "So" or was it even an *I'm really angry* or an *I have something terrible to say to you* kind of "So"?

"So," Zoe said. As neutrally as possible.

"I feel like I owe you an apology for yesterday," Gordy said.

"Oh." Zoe sat back in her chair.

"I mean, I'm conflicted," Gordy said. "Because my relationship with Taylor is special, and it needs special space. But on the other hand I think I hurt your feelings, and I didn't want to do that. I really don't want to hurt you at all."

"Right." Zoe fiddled with her silverware—it was all mismatched—but kept her eyes pretty much on him. That sentence *I really don't want to hurt you* was a weirdish one.

"But also because I'm still thinking about whether hurting your feelings was really about being thoughtless on my part or maybe about you just still getting used to my valid needs."

"Huh."

"So I don't know," Gordy said. "I don't know." And then, after a few moments that he spent looking out the window, "Do you have any thoughts?"

Zoe had a lot of thoughts, but it was a little hard to get hold of them. "Well, it did feel bad," she said.

Gordy looked away from the window, which was just facing some empty sidewalk anyway.

"But," she added honestly, "I guess I don't know totally what all the different causes of that were."

Gordy slowly nodded at her. His hands were folded together on the table, a diner-style table. He was thinking.

"I mean, I wanted to be included," she said.

"Right. Of course you did. Totally." Gordy paused. "But you were with us Friday night and all of Saturday," he said. "What I'm trying to work out is how much it's reasonable to ask for time alone with my daughter. I have to think it's somewhat reasonable."

"Well, sure," Zoe said. "Of course."

"Your hands are trembling," Gordy said.

Zoe looked at her hands, which were messing with the silverware, and saw that they were shaking again. "I'm feeling a little off today," she said.

Gordy enclosed her hands in his, held them together, held them still. "We don't have to talk about this now."

"Okay," she said.

"Zoe, listen," he said, and she looked up at his face, which was smiling kindly. "I'm sorry for anything that I've done wrong."

After a moment, she said, "Thanks."

When the food came, she was glad. From there they went on to simpler things. Zoe liked her sandwich; she could see how the savory aspect of the tempeh bacon would have been good, but she was glad, of course, to eat something really basic. Gordy asked her if she wanted to try his Reuben, but—very gently—she said she didn't. They talked about the morning Gordy had spent in the store—there was an interesting recurring customer named Saffron who was a midwife and who'd been there today. While he told the story of her most recent recurrence, Zoe consciously made herself focus on his words, because her mind was still fluttery, grabbing stuff at random to shout at her. *Sandwich!* it said. *Window! Music! Silverware you don't need! Your family! People at other tables! Secrets!* They also talked about the morning Zoe had spent cleaning, about which there was not an awful lot to say. Things started out less-than-clean and then she made them cleaner. Then they talked about what she would do with her afternoon, which wasn't much. This was less simple territory. Zoe wondered (not aloud) if maybe she really should look for a more soul-engaging job, at least part-time. She could fit the mindfulness sessions in around a part-time job, and it would give her something to talk about other than cleaning, or the mindfulness sessions that at least for now she wasn't letting herself mention.

"What is your goal?" Gordy said. His eyes were his teacher eyes.

Zoe felt abruptly irritated about him being in teacher mode, particularly because he knew what her goal was, or he should, anyway. Mindfulness center mindfulness center mindfulness center! "I'm still working that out," she said.

Gordy started, "Well, I just think it's a good time to—"

But Zoe jumped in. "Totally. For sure. I'm working on it. My trajectory is good. I can feel that."

"Okay," Gordy said. "Okay."

They were silent for a few moments.

"What did Janine say to you last night, really?" he said. He'd already asked that once, during breakfast, and she'd sort of shrugged and said, "Not much."

Now she said, "She just asked what my story was. I told her I was from Philadelphia."

"I wonder what she meant by asking that," he said, mainly to himself.

Zoe shrugged as casually as possible.

"She's just really not together in some important ways," he said. "Or, well, I guess what I mean is that she's not entirely kind-hearted."

"That's what you've said," Zoe said.

Gordy looked at her very ambiguously. Inside herself, she squirmed.

Zoe spent that afternoon wandering around about as aimlessly as it was possible to wander around. Somehow she didn't want to sit in the coffee shop—a little bit she didn't want to take any chance that she might see Brittany—and she couldn't think of anything else to do. She saw a bunch of restaurants and bars and houses and a couple clothes stores and little side streets. They all seemed interconnected in some way that she had yet to discover. She even passed a theological seminary at one point. People inside were presumably getting closer to God or the universe or all of it and then they were going to come out and help everyone else get there, too. *Maybe that's what I ought to do*, she thought.

She also picked up a copy of the *Phoenix*, and this time she opened to the apartment listings. She didn't make any calls that day, but she definitely started thinking about it.

Tuesday was better. On Tuesday was her first meeting with a woman named Mary. They had set it up over the phone; Mary had said, "I could use a break. I'm a stay-at-home Mom. So I could really use a break."

When she showed up, Mary looked pretty much the way Zoe expected: harried. Of course, most people looked harried, when you got down to it, but this woman was maybe a little extra. No makeup, her hair up and ponytailed but a lot of it not staying there, lots of brunette flyaway, eyes kind of sleep-deprived. She came in the door and looked all around jerkily for Zoe until she saw Zoe waving for her attention, and then she got to the table saying "Hi, hi, thanks, thank you," and as soon as she sat down—her bag hitting the floor heavily—her fingers started drumming.

Zoe felt harried herself at that moment—the previous night she'd kept waking up from weird dreams and found herself sort of checking on Gordy, like to see if he was really asleep or if he was just faking or something. She knew it was weird of her, or at least she realized it the next morning—of course he was just lying there, asleep—but you really can't help whether you wake up nervous or not, or at least it's not easy. So she had spent too much of the night hazily studying Gordy. When he was asleep, he made small sleep-sighs over and over, in a rhythm. Nothing else. Just sleep-sighs.

And then she'd seen Brittany again that morning for the first time since their semi-attempt at friendship. Brittany didn't act weird about it, but she didn't really act anything, in fact. Zoe ordered her beverage and Brittany made that beverage and handed it over in her signature deadpan style. She had even said, totally flat, "*Voila.*" Basically nothing had changed about the way they interacted. Well, between all of those things, the bottom line was that Zoe was a little sleep-deprived, first of all, and also distracted herself. It wasn't the right way to start a session. She decided to gather both her and Mary into the moment:

"What are you hoping to get from this experience?" she said.

Mary puffed out her cheeks and then blew all the air out. She said, "I just need to re-ground myself. I'm totally un-grounded."

Zoe nodded. "That's what we'll do, then." After a moment, she added. "Let's close our eyes, if that's okay with you."

And so they did.

It was a good session. Much smoother than her first try with Eleanor. They went, step by step, through a visualization and a bunch of steps of becoming aware of the body and then the sensations of the world. Mary just put herself right into it, quiet and intent on the experience. Things went so smoothly, in fact, that Zoe started getting a happy kind of jumpy and had to refocus herself several times, which she did manage to do. She added some things about becoming aware of oneself, one's inner essence, one's goals and needs and so on. At that, Mary, too, cried a little, but it was a really nice cry, a self-loving cry. Zoe held Mary's hands through it, brought them back to the body, the breath, of course the light.

When the meditation was over, the two women smiled at each other. "That was so great," Mary said. "I'm going to come back for sure."

"Great," Zoe said. "And also do you think you can find time to just do some stillness on your own every day, just a little bit, like we were doing here? Even if it's five minutes?"

Mary was nodding her head slowly. "Five minutes? I've got to be able to find five minutes. Right?"

Zoe nodded. "That would do a lot, I think. You could think of it as a little gift to you, which you deserve." Mary teared up at that again. "And also a gift to your children, too. I bet they'd be happiest with a grounded Mom."

Mary breathed in deeply and then breathed out again. "Yeah. You're probably right about that. Do you have kids?"

Zoe's mind flashed to Taylor instinctually, but of course that wasn't right. "No," she said. "Just me."

"Oh, well," Mary said.

Zoe nodded. She found that her hand was in her pocket, touching the bear.

It was such a good session that, all that afternoon, Zoe really wished she had someone to tell about it. Her knees bounced whenever she sat down.

She couldn't tell Gordy, obviously—though maybe he'd be more okay with the idea if he knew that she already had three clients, if you counted the one she'd be meeting with for the first time on Friday, and that things were going really well with one of them—but really she just couldn't tell him. Not yet, anyway. Not yet.

And although this was the kind of news you might normally tell your parents, and though her particular parents had left a couple messages on her voicemail over the last few days, Zoe knew she couldn't tell them. Her father would be wondering when she was going to get *real* work, and her mother would be too busy being worried in general to really take it in.

Dr. Charles? There was a while in her life when he was the main person she went to with her news, but now? No. He was for sure going to be against this whole new start to Zoe's life. And so was her brother, underneath his fakey I'm-on-your-side routine.

As for friends, well, there was Brenda, and also Grace. But Brenda was in the disapproving category, and how close was Zoe, really, with Grace? Grace was hard to pin down. And when did they last hang out?

The fact was—Zoe had to admit this when she thought about it—Zoe had not ever been able to hang onto friends long-term. Or, well, that put things in a negative way. Really the thing was that she was interested in growth, in moving forward, in developing as a person, and not everybody wanted to stay with you for that kind of journey. Consider the way Brenda had backed away after they had that disagreement about Zoe moving to Maine. They both had. And the people she'd actually spent most of her time with in recent months—the other staff in the Office of Parent, Family, Community Engagement & Faith-Based Partnerships of the School District of Philadelphia—well, they just weren't people she was able to get close to. Nisha, for example, told some funny stories sometimes, but the relationship never got deep. And Constance was as stern as they came. She was not going to call Constance, who had been so mad when Zoe gave only the minimum required notice before leaving her job, right toward the beginning of a new school year. That hadn't been pretty. But things never were with Constance. Right now she would be sitting stone-faced at her desk, enduring another day of life. Zoe didn't think it would be fun to call her just to say, *Hey, I've got this great mindfulness practice going!*

Then, too, she looked across the room—she was thinking about all this while she was still in the coffee shop—and Brittany was already gone.

Zoe let her mind jump around from person to person, along with little interruptions of *Table!* and *Mural!* and so on.

Wait—she knew who she could tell! She almost yelped with happiness. Jonathan Schiff: her teacher, the man who'd hoped that she'd leave Philly in peace and arrive in joy. She thought of his face—so calm, so unlined. You couldn't tell how old he was, really, even with the gray in his hair—there was just a kind of serenity that kept it all ageless. In a flash she was looking up the phone number for the Mt. Airy center, and then she was dialing it.

A woman answered. "Carpenter Lane Community Center," the

woman said. She probably said it a million times every day, but she still seemed like she meant it.

"Hi," Zoe said, semi-breathless. "I'm looking for Jonathan Schiff. The teacher."

"Okay," the woman said. "I'm pretty sure he's not here right now. Let me just—" a pause, some shuffling—"Yes—no—he's not here. He doesn't teach today."

Zoe felt that news deeply, felt gut-punched. She really wanted to tell someone, to tell *him*. She could feel it in her body. Maybe she could call back, but it would have to be a whole other day. "Do you have a home number for him?"

"Oh, I couldn't give that out. I don't know what we have, but I couldn't give it out."

"Right." Zoe thought fast. "Does he have some kind of voicemail where I can leave him a message?" she said.

"Well, I could *take* a message."

Zoe pictured that. The next day, this woman handing off a piece of paper that said something like *Zoe Tussler called. Arrived in joy. All best.* Zoe persisted. "There isn't any kind of voicemail?" she said.

"Hm," the woman said. "Well, you could call right back, and I could just not pick up, I guess. I could do that."

"Really?"

"Sure. Just call right back, so I know it's you."

"Great!" Zoe said, kind of loudly. "Thank you!" Still loud. She was excited.

As she redialed right away and let it ring, she pictured her old teacher. During meditation class you could almost feel him breathing from his place at the front of the room, even if you were in the back. It was like the room expanded when he breathed out and then it held them closer when he breathed in. She felt that—expanding and contracting, expanding and contracting—with each ring of the phone.

And then the voicemail prompt came, something about the center and hello and welcome and a few phone options, but Zoe hung on until it beeped for a message.

"Oh, this is a message for Jonathan Schiff, please," she said. "If you could just give this directly to him, that would be great. I mean, you know, this is for him. Anyway." She paused, like waiting for them to pass it along or something, and then got going again. "Jonathan, Teacher," she said, "It's Zoe Tussler. Do you remember me from your classes? I'm the one who worked for the crazy school district and had all those things going on and I recently moved to Portland? Maine? Well, you gave me such words of hope and possibility when I left, and so many people just didn't believe in me at all—which is still the case, and I just—but, no, you sent me off with, well, with all your wisdom and hope, and I just wanted to tell you how much that meant to me—I can't even tell you—and, well, I wanted to tell you how wonderfully things are going here now. Here's the thing: I'm a teacher, too! I've started a private mindfulness practice—did I tell you I was going to start a center? I can't remember. Anyway, it's different than I was thinking, but the point is I learned so much from you that's helping me as I do it. Like, remember that image of light pulsing like soft waves from the center of the heart? I've been using that, and in general just the peaceful way that you were always modeling for the rest of us. That's what I'm trying to do up here. I mean, it hasn't been easy. I have this one client, Eleanor—she's a real blast of wind, and the last time I was basically just trying to stay on my feet the whole time. I mean, wow. I think the thing with her is—well, I don't need to go into that. But then just now, well, like an hour ago, I was working with another woman named Mary, and she's this exhausted mother, really needing some support and some, some *tranquility*, some *serenity*. And she cried a little—they both cried, actually. It's just so powerful, what we do. I mean, what you do and what I'm starting to do. Well, I *am* doing it. That's what you'd probably tell me. I *am* doing it. And it feels great. And I just wanted to thank you. I think I really might be making a difference in the universe." She felt like she was expanding as she was talking, filling up with light herself. "Oh, Jonathan," she said. "Do you know what I mean? I just—I just feel so *good*, like if the universe was missing this one piece and maybe it was *me*, that piece, and I've been searching around for the spot where it was missing and maybe I've *found* it. And I've searched *everywhere*. Believe me. I don't think I ever told you about it, but believe me. Everywhere. But all of that was part of this. Like, it wasn't wasted. I had to do all that in order to get here. And now that I've found it, now that I've found it—"

Then a computer voice interrupted, a simulated woman's voice. *If you are satisfied with your message, press pound*, it said. *If you would like to replace this message with another one, press star.*

Zoe, her breath held in her throat, stabbed the pound key with her finger. In fact, she sat there for another minute, pressing that key, watching as the coffee shop, which had sort of vanished while she was talking, reformulated itself around her. Mural, tables, people. The sound of talking and the foam machine. Around her and her fast breath.

That afternoon, on the way home, Gordy said, "I talked to Janine today."

Zoe felt a throat-squeeze of panic, though for no reasonable reason. "You did?" she said.

Gordy chuckled, maybe bitterly. "Yeah."

Zoe looked out the windshield at the road, which was moving underneath them, past them. The tires were connected to the road. She didn't know what to say. Still she said, "Huh."

"You know what?" Gordy said. "I think she wants to be friends.

With *you*." Zoe turned to face him, and he gave her a wry look of his own. "She said I should tell you that she'd be happy to make you lunch one of these days."

"Really?" Zoe said, very aware of her accelerated heartbeat.

He fixed her with a brief stare. "What *did* you two talk about?"

"Nothing," Zoe said. "It was so brief."

Gordy frowned at the road, like an unconvinced person. Like a suspicious person. "I wonder," he said. *I don't want to hurt you*, he'd said.

"What should I do?" Zoe said. Gordy did like to give advice.

He nodded, shrugged. "She makes a good egg-salad sandwich."

"Huh," Zoe said.

He gave her another one of those looks. "You might just want to check it for poison before you take that first bite."

The next day she met with Eleanor again. And this time she was ready.

On the night before this Eleanor appointment, while Gordy slept, Zoe had thought it through. She said to herself, *Eleanor is going to be late.* And she thought, *Eleanor is going to be slippery and all over the place. She is going to be a challenge.* And she added, *But last time you did her a lot of good. You were a palm tree, and, okay, then there was that balloon part, but overall you got her to a powerful place for sure.* She remembered her realization that Eleanor was slippery precisely because she was afraid to be held still. Which meant the woman was wounded—who wasn't?—and that all the things that made her difficult were what made the mindfulness such an opportunity, so urgent. This was why the mindfulness teaching was a mission.

Zoe felt that the thing to do was to try to be the palm tree again, but maybe just a little stiffer. Like every session she could stiffen just a bit more, until she was holding Eleanor completely in place and showing her that it was safe after all. Zoe sighed in satisfaction. And checked on Gordy just once. He really did seem to be sleeping.

The next day, a rainy day, Eleanor blew into the coffee shop about ten minutes late, so it was like the last time, except that she wasn't quite as late—maybe a good sign?—and this time Zoe had her eyes open. Ready.

"I did it again," Eleanor said. "I'm terrible with time. I'd better just admit it here and now. You should know it about me."

"It's okay," Zoe said, making sure to be as calm as a Buddha. "You're here now."

"Oh, barely," Eleanor said, dropping her closed umbrella on the ground with a clunk.

And maybe she was about to continue along those lines, but Zoe stepped in first. "But you *are* here. That's what counts. Let's be here, one hundred percent. But, before we begin, would you like to get some tea for yourself, or anything else? We should clear away all the distractions first."

Zoe could see it in Eleanor's face—the extra firmness in the palm trunk was reaching her.

"Maybe I'd just use the bathroom?" Eleanor said. "And get some tea?"

Zoe nodded sagely.

And so Eleanor did those things, and the tasks took a little longer than maybe they would have if someone else was doing them, and when she got back to the table with her tea, and Zoe's, Eleanor started going off about food, and how snacking seemed to be the new American pastime and how the snacks you could get out in the world so often pretended to be healthy—ahem, yogurt parfaits—but actually they were full of sugar or fat or, really, salt, in a lot of cases—but meanwhile Zoe was running an approximate sort of clock in her head, giving Eleanor some time and space to reel on for a little while. Because that was how this woman got ready, and Zoe respected that. She just wasn't going to let it go on forever.

Eleanor was just on the verge of topic-leaping—Zoe could feel it—when Zoe leaned forward and said, "Well, I don't want us to cut into your session too much, so maybe we should get started."

Eleanor said, "Oh, absolutely. "Don't mind me at all. I just—"

"Definitely," Zoe said. "I'd like us to close our eyes." She was going slightly off-plan, being firmer than she'd originally intended, but you had to follow your instincts.

"Well—you're really raring to go, today, aren't you?" Eleanor said.

Zoe paused and then took her client's hands. She spoke with that intentional calm. "I have an idea."

Eleanor's eyes were a little wide. "Okay."

"Would you be willing to close your eyes?" Zoe said.

Eleanor's lids fluttered closed. "Okay," she said. Zoe kept her own open this time so that she could study Eleanor's face.

Zoe said, "Now, I think you were just about to go from one thought to another." Eleanor's face squinched up slightly, a *you caught me!* kind of face. Zoe continued. "But, just for the moment, keep that thought in your mind, only in your mind. What I want you to do is to picture your mind as a stream. It's right in front of you. You're looking at it. It's a stream that's running as fast as your thoughts run. Can you picture a stream like that?"

"Yes," Eleanor said, her face a little squinty. "Okay. I—"

Zoe gave her hands a gentle *hold on* squeeze. "And I want you to reach into that stream, to cup your hand and reach into that stream. Okay? Picture that. You're reaching for that thought that you were about to speak aloud, but instead of speaking it aloud you're going to dip your hand into the stream—feel the rush of it—and scoop that scoop of, you know, water-thought out of the stream. And I want you to keep your hand cupped very tightly, so that none of that water can drip out. Okay?"

Eleanor nodded. Zoe felt a buzz of excitement inside.

"And then you should look at that thought in your hand, really see it, see what you were going to say about it, see it completely. Can you see it?"

"Yes," Eleanor said. Her face was still tight.

"Okay," Zoe said. She paused for a long moment, making sure her knees didn't bounce under the table. She watched Eleanor's face, tense, concentrating. "And now open your hand up. Let that thought fall back into the stream."

Eleanor's face dropped open, including her eyes, her wet, sparkling eyes.

Zoe squeezed her hands again. "Try to keep your eyes closed," she said. "And watch the thought pass back into the stream, moving along, moving out of sight. Let it go."

Eleanor closed her eyes, which pushed loose a tear from her right one. *Signature Zoe*, Zoe thought, and then she rebuked herself for letting her ego jump in at a crucial moment like this. She shook her head slightly and said, Buddha-voice, "Keep looking at the stream. There are so many more thoughts in there. An endless supply. More than you could ever hold. But the thing is that you are not the stream. You are not the stream. You are watching the stream, but you are not the stream. You can see thoughts stream by, you can see them…see them eddy in place a moment, you can even dip them out. And you can let them go. They are not you, and you can let them go."

Another tear got loose, this time from Eleanor's left eye. Zoe couldn't help it—she was excited. This was really, really good. She was bringing important wisdom to a woman who needed to hear it. She said, "Let's just watch the stream for a few minutes. Okay?"

Eleanor said a watery "Okay."

They were silent for a little while, and then Zoe starting speaking again, getting into the imagery of a river, and the light playing off it, and just developing that awareness of the thoughts that went by all the time. This wasn't her creation, this conception of how the mind worked—it was something she had learned. Maybe from Jonathan? Maybe before him? It was the kind of thing you heard if you did enough meditation classes. But it had always held a special meaning for her, because certainly her own mind was like this more often than she wanted. While she talked to Eleanor, in fact, and especially once she'd opened up a period of silence for them to dwell in, she closed her eyes and kind of drifted into her own stream a bit, particularly in being proud of herself for having internalized this wisdom enough to share it with someone else, and just how well her still-brand-new practice was doing. All on her own! Maybe she could even tell Gordy about it. Wouldn't he end up being excited if he heard how well it was all going? Or not? She couldn't tell if she was worried about nothing or something. But in any case it was really happening, and who knew what it would lead to? Maybe even—

"What are you thinking about?"

Zoe almost jumped out of her chair. It was Eleanor who had spoken. Whose eyes were open. Who was looking with curiosity at her mindfulness coach. Zoe cast around for words but didn't find any.

"I can see it on your face," Eleanor said. "Must be something good."

Zoe opened her mouth but didn't know what to say. She was aware that there was a lot of irony going on at that particular moment.

"It's okay," Eleanor said. There was something a little weird on her face—a kind of satisfaction, it seemed like. "I guess we all do it, huh?"

Zoe was suddenly hearing again all the crash and bang of the coffee shop and its machines and conversations. Everything was hitting her senses.

She realized that she could just claim to have been in a very deep place that looked distracted from the outside—but she didn't do that.

"Well," she said instead, getting her voice back, "I'm really sorry. I think I did wander off. You're right that everybody does it, Eleanor. And what kind of news is that, for you?"

Eleanor's face got quizzical. "News?"

"What I'm suggesting is that maybe it's good news. You're not alone. You're not strange."

"Well, I never said I was strange," Eleanor said, drawing herself up with dignity.

Zoe's heart was going fast, but she took a chance. She said, very deliberately, "No, that's true. You never *said* it."

Surrounded by the sensations of the coffee shop, Eleanor and Zoe stared at each other. It was a moment that could have gone either way. And then, finally, Eleanor's face broke—not completely, not into sobs or anything, but just a hairline crack, sort of between her eyebrows and eyes. "Oh," she said, "Oh, Zoe."

Zoe took her hands, feeling like she'd somehow dodged a steel jaw trap. "Let's get back to the bank of the river, okay? Both of us."

Eleanor smiled a wobbly smile and they both closed their eyes again.

Zoe only allowed herself one final fugitive thought before she committed fully to the exercise. She thought: *I almost ruined that, almost ruined it because I let thoughts of Gordy get in the middle, in between me and the woman in my care.* Well, she thought that, and then she pictured a little ceramic bear, sitting there with her on the bank.

When Eleanor left the coffee shop that day, she did it without a word. She put the money on the table and then, almost without eye contact, she went. Was it because Eleanor was just so moved? Zoe sat there with the sixty dollars in her hand, which this morning she didn't feel like bronzing. Eleanor was going to come back the next week, wasn't she?

And now it was kind of big, the sense of distance she felt from Gordy. That night she had dinner with him and his parents and it was the usual silent thing, and Zoe felt like she was watching it from the other side of the room, or maybe from above. *Look at those people not saying anything. What is going* on *with them*? She even saw herself that way, found herself wondering what that woman was doing among that strange group. She was a woman who liked to talk, connect, and here she was in a group of people who spoke as though words cost a hundred dollars each, and double or triple if the words were about something deep and personal.

The room was full of a psychological syrup, everyone suspended in it. The same stuff that sometimes filled her up was now around her on all sides. Things were probably more upbeat at the correctional facility down the road.

At the same time, possibly to keep her mind from shutting down altogether, she re-studied the room they were in, the dining room with not all that much in it. Same old wood-paneling walls, same old sail-boat painting, same old light. She looked at the family photos on the banquette, from one to the next, all the standing around in place. But for some reason this time she noticed something she hadn't noticed before, maybe because of the way the photo of the Bouchers dancing had grabbed so much of her attention. "Who is that?" she said.

Everybody froze a little. It wasn't like she'd interrupted a conversation, but she'd definitely interrupted a non-conversation.

"What's that, dear?" Mrs. Boucher said.

"In the photo." Zoe pointed. It was a shot of the Bouchers, from clearly a while back, with teenager Gordy and everything, but there was also a girl there, a little younger than Gordy. She was wearing a blue shirt. "I never noticed before. Who's she?"

Gordy paused in his chewing. "That's my sister. Kathy."

"Your *sister*?" Zoe said. He had never ever mentioned a sister.

He nodded, unruffled. "Kathy," he said.

"But you never mentioned her. Ever."

Gordy and Mrs. Boucher both looked confused. Confused mixed with consternation, as in, *What's the big deal?* But Mr. Boucher was the one who responded, shrugging: "She lives in Massachusetts," he said. It sounded like, *She vanished into thin air one day—and we never really looked into it.*

Everybody Boucher went back to eating. Zoe continued to stare at the blue-shirted girl. She stared, but from her own distance, swimming steadily up through the syrup toward the surface.

Zoe was definitely awake a lot that night. Who has a sister and never mentions her? She and Gordy had talked about it a little when they'd gotten back to the trailer, and it was clear that nothing had gone really wrong between Kathy and anyone else—"We talk on the phone," Gordy had said shruggingly, not understanding what the issue was—but who *does* that? Who never thinks to mention that a whole sibling human being exists? And then who finds it weird that you find that weird?

At some point that night Zoe decided she was going to have to sit down with Janine and hash it all out. She looked at the nothing much of the bedroom ceiling and knew it was time.

One problem is that she somehow didn't know Janine's last name, so she couldn't look her up in a phone book, if anybody even had a phone book anymore, or online instead, or whatever. But there were, she realized, other ways.

After a very helpful yoga class at the studio the next morning, Zoe went out to the Longfellow statue and sat on the bench she liked, and she closed her eyes. Mindfulness, she knew, was its own reward, but it also led to lots of other great things, too. And now she used it to go back in time. Specifically, she went back to Sunday night, when they were in

Janine's driveway. She pictured the house, the brown and leaning house. She could spot that place if she was on that street, obviously—it was distinctive-looking—but she wanted more from her memory than that; very slowly and deliberately she cast around in her mind—there was the front door, the walk up to the front door, et cetera—until she saw the mailbox, which she'd noticed as they pulled back out of the driveway. She saw it again now. A white mailbox on a pole. And yes—there on the box was not only the number of the house but, and she really had to slow her mind down and go by the mailbox a few times to get this, not only the number, which was *73*, but also the name of the street. Janine lived on *Dunhull*. She could see it very clearly, even when her eyes snapped back open. 73 Dunhull Road.

She looked at the statue kind of rapturously. "Henry, I did it," she said.

It took a little more research to get it all totally nailed down, because what town was that address in, anyway, so Zoe had to poke around on her phone until she figured that out, and then there was the distance, which was not nothing. They had taken the truck to get there the first time, of course. But Zoe had been biking a lot, and she certainly had faith in herself.

The bottom line is that she went.

On the way, she had to stop sort of frequently, because she was using her phone as a GPS and didn't want to try to look at it while actually riding, and although it said directions out loud they were a little muffled from her pocket.

It was such a different thing, she noticed for nowhere near the first time, though it was still striking every time, seeing the world at the speed of a bike (especially with stops) instead of, for example, at the speed of a truck. Everything looked different, almost unrecognizably different. The unfolding was slower, obviously—you had time to see the

houses one by one, the trees, each leaf glowing in its own natural halo—
so things weren't blurry and general but dazzling, million-detailed.
Though that wasn't even quite it; traveling this way was more *connected*. The road wasn't invisible underneath you; it was right there at your
feet, with its speckles and cracks and sprouts of occasional grass close to
the edge, all a part of the road. She saw the tree roots levering up sidewalk, the squirrels dashing from one side of the street to the other, saw
the branches shake with animal movement. Her old meditation teacher
Jonathan had once said, "Mindfulness does not have to be reserved for
special occasions, for this hour we spend together. Mindfulness can be
for when you do the dishes or drive your car or speak to other people."
Something like that. And Zoe, on the bike, she was completely there,
right in the world.

The ride went smoothly. It took a while, but the phone told her
where to go. And the length of time—along with giving her the opportunity to actually see everything, Maine just at the cusp of fall, it also
made the journey seem more epic, which was a bonus. And it *was* epic,
she considered. In some sense her whole life was an epic journey, where
a determined person faced all kinds of obstacles and just kept going forward in triumph. It wasn't really her thing to picture herself with a sword
battling dragons or something, but metaphorically there was something
to that idea.

At one point Zoe stopped at a very residential intersection, sweaty
and her muscles saying *Time to stop for a minute*? She could have used
some water, and in fact she'd passed a convenience store a while back,
but it didn't look like Janine's house was much farther, according to the
phone, and Zoe could wait. Definitely she wasn't going back for sup-
plies at this point. For a minute, though, she paused in the intersection, which had houses on three of the corners—standard, white Maine
ones that you saw all over—and mini-woods on the fourth. She had this

quick thought that, what if she were just to move into one of these three houses? What would that be like? These houses were cute—not too big, not really loud about themselves. Little driveways, shutters. Zoe stared at one in particular—the one to the right of the woodsy corner—and thought about what it would be like to sit in that living room sunk into some very cozy chair, looking out at the trees. Tea in a mug in her hands.

Zoe let the fantasy play out for a while. There would be a garden in the back, lots of ceramic pots around the house to remind her about being grounded in the earth. It would be quiet. It would be like that time from her childhood.

After a few minutes, though, a face appeared in the window of that house—not in her fantasy but in real life. An elderly woman was there, staring out at her kind of concerned-looking. *Fair enough*, Zoe thought. When you were an elderly woman, you had to be careful about people who stared at your house. Zoe gave her a friendly wave before getting back on her pedals and resuming the epic journey, her muscles like old, weary warriors. Or something more peaceful than that, but tough and nonetheless definitely weary.

For sure she was feeling excited as she turned onto Dunhull Road, a right. She double-checked with her phone that it was a right, and then she went that way. The odd-numbered houses were on the left side, which matched Zoe's memory of the side Janine's house would be on, and they counted down by eights for some reason, starting at number 93. The breeze dried out her mouth even more as she grinned her way down the road. Soon there would be the reward of water.

She had just passed number 79 when the phone said something from her pocket. She recognized it as that self-satisfied tone of voice the GPS got when it had brought you all the way there. She loved that little bit of emotion in the machine. Like it was trying to be professional as it said, *You have reached your destination*, but couldn't quite suppress its pride at another job well done.

Zoe smiled as she slowed, as she got off the bike, even though—even though something inside her was already raising a question.

The house in front of her was numbered 71. And it wasn't brown or leaning. It was a yellow, upright kind of house.

Zoe looked back. House number 79—a somewhat dirty white—was one lot over. There was nothing in between them. And the street did look overall different from how she remembered it. Of course, everything looked different on a bike, was what she'd been rediscovering. But not this different. The house had to be brown and leaning, and this one wasn't.

The next few minutes she spent walking the bike down into the lower numbers, just in case they got bigger again at some point, but they didn't; the street ended in some more woods, the last house on the left being number 15. And the houses on the other side of the road stayed even instead of odd. And they were un-brown. Then she got back on the bike; maybe it was 173 or 273 or something, if a number had just fallen off the mailbox—she could picture the mailbox very clearly—and the bicycle would let her check things out more quickly.

But the block past the intersection was different from her memory, too, more space between the houses, and hillier, and after a while it got to 221 and then stopped altogether in a T with another road, a county highway or something, and there hadn't been any brown house.

Zoe stood at the T intersection, breathing a little hard for more than one reason. In her mind the image of the mailbox and the writing on it—it was all so clear. But it was wrong. But it was *so* clear. The light was glaring harshly off every wrong surface.

She tried closing her eyes again, but she was feeling both exhausted and also pretty jittery all of a sudden and it didn't seem like she was going to be able to get her mind into a state where she could dig out the real answer. Or maybe she wasn't capable of that even under the best of circumstances, apparently. But she had used this technique successfully before, hadn't she? To find her keys or her phone, right? Hadn't she? But maybe—maybe she was fooling herself. With her eyes closed, it felt like a car was going to abruptly blast up the road and wipe her out. And when she did open her eyes again, she saw that she was, in fact, straddling her bike alone right in the middle of Dunhull, like she was about to go into the intersection but just couldn't decide which way to go.

"Isn't that the way it is?" she said aloud. Because it was. Basically, she was always standing at some intersection, clueless about where she was supposed to go.

Very soon she was crying as she stood there. She was so tired, felt so old in her body and mind, that she couldn't get herself to go to the side of the road, but at least no cars came up Dunhull or along the other road, either. There was no sign of human activity anywhere. Maybe, she thought as she cried, she had been lured into some abandoned place where people used to be until they could no longer stand it. She turned back and looked at the last odd-numbered house on the block, partially obscured by a few trees, but a blue-gray and with a car on the lawn. This street wasn't *anything* like the one Janine had been on. It was completely wrong, and Zoe just didn't understand how it could be. Even the *phone* had thought there would be *something* at 73 Dunhull Road—it took her right there.

Zoe bent over and put her forehead on the stem of her handlebars. She wondered what the universe was trying to say to her. The crying went on and on.

The trip back to town was very long. And she did have to go back to town, because, as much as she still wanted to find Janine, she was short on time; Gordy would be taking her home in the truck that afternoon. The magic truck that somehow found ex-girlfriends' houses that didn't actually exist. She cried a little on the way back, but mainly she listened to her body protest the whole thing.

On the way, Zoe did stop at the convenience store for water. The man behind the counter looked South Asian and had a little bit of a South Asian accent. Or at least she thought so—he didn't say enough to be sure. Wherever he was from, he had picked up the whole taciturn Maine thing just fine. He barely said a word to her during the whole transaction. Zoe wondered what would happen if she ricocheted her water bottle off his counter and said something obscene. But of course she didn't, and instead she just got back on the bike and kept going back to town.

That night Gordy made a kale salad with miso sauce and edamame and they ate it in the trailer. The kale was right from the garden and it was good. Still, Zoe didn't have much to say as she sat at the little fold-down trailer table and put food into herself, packed it in around the heavy emotional thing that was lodged in her gut. Luckily, Gordy didn't notice for a while, or at least he acted like he didn't notice. Unlike when they were at his parents', he had a lot to say. Above all, he was chafing about the way Autumn and Melanie ran the studio. Well, really Melanie, who was the soft and sweet one.

"She's a lovely soul," he said, "but unfortunately I do think you have to make your peace with it being a business, too."

Zoe thought about how if he was unhappy with the way the women were running the place, maybe he should be thinking about that mindfulness center they'd talked about. But she didn't say it. She just ate more kale.

"I mean, Autumn," he said. "I think she understands that—you know, it's distasteful, obviously, but it's a reality. We have to strike that balance between the idea of the place and the nuts and bolts of the place.

I think Autumn is sympathetic to that."

There was something about hearing Autumn's name twice in close succession like that. Zoe found herself wondering why he was so fixated on Autumn. She pictured the woman, lean and ponytailed and firm. In her mind she felt a throb; in her gut the weighty thing got a little spiky.

"And the truth is that it's not exactly sincere," Gordy said. "Do you see what I'm saying? Melanie has this very mothering way—you know what she's like—but she's not interested in feedback. It's not really a family, even if she pretends it is. I think a yoga studio needs sincerity."

"Like Autumn," Zoe said, staring at him.

"Well, more so," he said. "I think so." There was a look in his eye that Zoe couldn't decipher. Maybe suspicion? Maybe guilt? What was hidden back there? After a moment, he continued. "The truth is that I don't understand their ownership model. I mean, they're not a couple, so it's just two friends who own a business together. I guess it's probably fifty-fifty." He shook his head, obviously wishing Autumn owned more, so that he could, well, somehow do something with that. Zoe speared a piece of kale a little hard. He looked up at the sound. "Is the salad okay?" he said.

Zoe noted that he was eager to change the subject. "It's good," she said, which it was.

"How was your day?" he said. Again the look was in his eye.

"You don't have to switch topics," Zoe said. "Maybe you have more to say about Autumn."

"What?"

"I'm just wondering what else you have to say about Autumn," she said.

He set his fork down. "Are you okay, Zoe?"

"I'm fine. Why wouldn't I be?"

"You don't seem all that fine," he said. He declared. He judged.

"What's that supposed to mean?" Zoe stared at him hard, her vision almost lightning.

His own eyes were sparking a little. "I mean exactly this. What's going on with you?"

"You know," she said, "I moved a long way to come here." Zoe gestured around at the close walls of the trailer, almost smacking her hand on the damn sink.

"I know you moved a long way. That doesn't tell me why you're acting like this."

Zoe stood up. "Like what, exactly?" Her voice was loud; it ricocheted.

"Like *this*," Gordy said. He stayed in his seat. "Yelling, getting agitated. And not only this, but you've been moody for days now."

"Moody? *Moody*?"

"Yes. Moody. That's exactly the word I want. One minute you're withdrawn and standing at this remove from everything, and the next you're, you're—"

As he groped around for a word, she thought, almost hungrily, *If he says "manic" I'm going to explode.*

"Listen," he said, giving up on the word search, running a hand through all his long hair. "You need something to *do*."

"Something to do?"

"Are you trying to get more work?"

Zoe, who had been pacing a tiny circuit, froze; a chill ran through her anger. She stared at him, at Gordy's watchful face. "What are you getting at?" she said, narrowing her eyes at him.

"What?" He threw his hands in the air. "What is going *on* with you? You're completely out of balance—I can see it from here."

Labels and diagnoses! She said, almost spitting it, "You can't see *anything* from there. You're not all-knowing, Gordy. You may be some kind of mister guru Gordon whatever who thinks he's got all the answers, but let me tell you—you're not all-knowing. There's *plenty* you don't know about me."

"I don't have any idea what to say to that." Gordy shook his head.

"And I know plenty myself," she said. "I see plenty."

"Zoe, what—"

She said, "I didn't move here for you, you know." Her heart pumped rage and fear in alternating beats.

He stared at her, his mouth open. And then, "*Fine*," he yelled, finally standing up himself, throwing his napkin onto his plate. "I was trying to help you. But if you don't want to be helped, that's in your hands, then. Because right now—right now, you're isolating yourself. You're—"

"Oh, just stop with all the enlightened language," she said, turning her back on him. "Maybe *Autumn* goes for that kind of thing, but I don't."

"What? What is going on in that mind of yours?"

Zoe gave out a little scream of frustration, and said, "I said stop with that!"

"Okay—then I'll tell you what," he said, loud. "You're being *crazy*. That's what. How about that?"

Zoe spun back around, incredulous. He wouldn't use that word. But he had. "You—" she started. Before she knew it, she was right in front of him, and she had given him a strong shove that sent him stumbling backward.

But just for a moment. Because then he was in her face. "If you want to let your crazy take over, just go ahead," he said, pushing roughly past her to the bedroom, knocking her into the wall. There was a pain in her shoulder. He had said he didn't want to hurt her, but. "I'll sleep over at the house tonight. And—" he stopped to point at her, his finger quivering with rage, his eyes, oh, his eyes *burning*—"you need to get your head screwed on straight again by morning. Because I'm not going to live with this." He grabbed some clothes from his dresser, and then a couple of things from the little bathroom.

Zoe finally found herself able to talk—or scream, as was the case. "Get *OUT!*" she yelled.

"I'm leaving," he said, shoving past her the other way now. He looked back at her with something like disgust. "But this is *my* place. And I'm not putting up with this again."

Zoe let out a wild scream as he left, as the door closed behind him.

The dinner dishes broke easily in the sink. The ones in the cabinet did, too.

Ten

Zoe slept in spurts that night, woken up repeatedly by all kinds of feelings. Regret was in there—part of her wondered what had just happened, what she had just done—but competing with that was an anger that wouldn't tamp down or quite name itself, and also there was fear. When she heard sounds outside, were they Gordy? He had been furious when he left, and he'd already been rough with her that night. Would he come back, unlock the door, come in to do more? Anything seemed possible somehow.

Be safe, Janine had said.

I don't want to hurt you, Gordy had said.

After a bunch of hours of off-and-on sleep, Zoe got out of bed. It was more than an hour earlier than she normally would have gotten up, if Gordy had been there. She windmilled her arm slowly to see if her shoulder still hurt, which it fortunately didn't, and then she got dressed in the quiet and the still-mostly-dark.

At the little window over the sink, which looked out at some trees that she couldn't see all that well in the early morning, she ate a cold piece of unbuttered bread. It was about all she could handle right then.

And then, without asking herself too closely what her plan was, she started throwing some of her clothes into her backpack. As much as would fit.

On the way into town—she had taken the bike—she could feel the ceramic bear in her pocket. She didn't know why she was still hanging onto it, exactly—it seemed like things had gone beyond Janine, beyond whatever inside scoop Janine had to offer on Gordy—but she was comforted to feel the bear there anyway.

The escape had been a close call; it had looked like the kitchen light was on in the Bouchers' house when Zoe came outside, and she definitely saw a light go on upstairs as she walked the bike down the driveway. But she hurried up and got onto the road as fast and as quietly as possible, and now she was zooming along. There was some soreness in her muscles, but she was free.

Not that Zoe knew what that meant. She was pointed generally toward town but didn't one hundred percent know where she was going. She also didn't know when she would see Gordy again. Or maybe the question was more like *if* she would see him again. For the time being, anyway, everything in her was saying *Get away, get away, get away*.

But to where?

She whipped past the trees and each one started to come to life in the rising sun. Each one was like a thought, an idea.

For sure she couldn't spend the day in her usual spots, because that was the neighborhood where Gordy would be. She could go back to the USM campus, or that park on the water at the end of the East End. That could be good. Or maybe there was someplace perfect that she didn't even know about yet, a place where she could think this all through. She could certainly start an apartment search for real. Of course, whatever she did, she couldn't go too far—she had the mindfulness appointment at that client's apartment later. Rose was her name. Zoe wasn't going to let that get derailed. Not because of Gordy stuff.

Which reminded her that she also needed to call Eleanor to just make sure that she would be coming back. Just to make sure.

In the end, because she couldn't decide what else to do, she defaulted to JoJo's. Not that she was going to stay there—she had to be long gone by the time Gordy came around—but it was a place to collect her thoughts, and she figured it would be open early, and that Brittany would be there.

Those things turned out to be true. With the bike leaning against a lamppost, Zoe went into the coffee shop, which was mostly empty, and spotted Brittany behind the counter. The barista was studying her hands. Her arms only had traces of the old temporary tattoos. Scraps and wisps of cute monsters. Zoe's heart leapt toward the young woman, and Zoe, in more measured steps, followed.

She got to the counter and made watery eye contact with Brittany, who looked nervous. "It's so good to see you," Zoe said. She felt one of her tears break the eyelash barrier and roll down a cheek.

Brittany now looked alarmed. "Yeah," she said. "Are you—" But she didn't finish the thought.

"I'm fine," Zoe said. "I think I'm fine. I may be on the verge of some big decisions. Or sort of big decisions. It's not like all of this was about Gordy, anyway."

Brittany spoke as though speaking to an escaped somebody. "Right," she said carefully.

"Don't look at me like that. I'm fine." Zoe felt some tension in her voice. "Just *relax.*"

"Okay."

Zoe stared at the mural for a second, trying to calm herself. It was such a crazy mural. All the weird bodies and heads. "I just—I just had a big fight with the guy I'm living with. That's all. And I know that's not such a big deal, but sometimes I *know* what's going to happen, what to do, and I think that could have been the end. It's really abrupt, but sometimes you know."

Brittany looked down at her hands, or her rings, or the scored wood of the counter, gathering herself. And then she looked up again, frowning with consternation. "Listen. Zoe?"

Zoe nodded. She already didn't like the tone of this.

"I'm just. Listen—you seem like a very earnest, soulful kind of person with a very big emotional life. But this just really isn't my thing. I can't do the whole—" She lifted her hands, shook them in front of her symbolically—"*intense* thing. The intense emotion thing. I can't. I really—I can't do that."

Zoe stood very still and heard what Brittany was saying.

"I'm sorry," Brittany said. "My friends and I just sort of sit around and listen to music and whatever. Binge on Netflix. And I—I can't get into a whole thing. It's—" She stopped abruptly and shook her head. "I don't know. I'm sorry."

Zoe nodded. She'd never heard Brittany say so many words in a row. There was something moving about it, if it weren't sad and disappointing.

"I—you know what I want, really? If I was going to be honest?" Brittany said.

Zoe raised her eyebrows as if to say, *Tell me.*

"What I would want is to get you a beverage. Some kind of beverage. And then we do the commerce thing." She paused. "That."

Zoe nodded for a few seconds, breathing in and breathing out. Maybe half a minute. And then she said, "I would like a large black coffee. In a travel mug."

Brittany's face was a flushed mix of apology and relief, but she nodded, too, and went to make the coffee. Zoe stared at the mural. It was a mural of people who had been twisted, who were not straight up and down. It was a wall of Zoes and possible Zoes. She felt her eyes go wet again, and said to herself, *Whatever.*

When Brittany gave her back her travel mug filled with coffee, Zoe paid for it, and she said, "Thank you." Then, having half-turned away, she turned back again. "Being honest is the right thing to be," she said. And then she went over to the door, and out.

On the sidewalk in front of the coffee shop, Zoe gathered herself, emotionally. It took a little time, and mostly it involved setting her emotions aside for the time being. She gathered them, and she set them aside. There was enough to deal with right now without adding the whole Brittany thing. Okay. Then, after a few more deep breaths, Zoe returned mentally to the sidewalk in front of the coffee shop and considered her options, awash in the smell of the dark roast rising from her cup. She was present enough to think that Gordy was insane for not keeping this stuff around. It even made the *air* better.

Basically, she needed to get out of the neighborhood, and probably pretty soon. But to go where? This street had become the heart of her Portland life. Not that she actually had a Portland life.

Still. She got on her bike, and pointed it sort of arbitrarily toward downtown. Because why not?

But she stopped again after just half a block—some light had caught her eye off a window, and it was the window of the cryptozoology museum she'd first spotted early in her time here. Bigfoot and the Loch Ness Monster. At the time it had been too much even for her, but on this morning she stopped. Feeling the shortness of time, she leaned the bike against another pole, and then just went up to the place. The front doors said they wouldn't be open until eleven, but she could look in the window.

There were a couple of mammothy elephant models in the window-seat display, and a skull of some kind, and a couple of *hooray for this particular museum* kinds of articles taped to the glass, but of course the big thing, literally and psychologically, was the Bigfoot manikin standing in the mostly-darkness. He wasn't facing the window, but you could see the side of his very hairy head and face. Seemed like a pleasant-enough face—fangs were not bared or anything. But of course how did anybody know anything about Bigfoot, if there actually was a Bigfoot? It's not as though this was an actual one, taxidermied up for this little display. Zoe was pretty sure that would have made the national news.

Suddenly she wished she could go in there, though she didn't exactly know why. Well, there was the fact that it was a museum for hidden animals, and she felt like a hidden animal herself in some ways. But it also seemed like another world, and she needed another world right then. And then, also, well, she just wanted to go in. Hang out with Bigfoot. Zoe even went so far as to try the front door, but, true to the posted hours, it was locked. Still, in a surge of anger, she rattled and yanked on the knob again, and then again, as though she could make the place be open by force of will, and then again, with all her strength, and she banged on the door with her other fist. Nothing. Of course, nothing. Obviously. She stopped herself and stepped back, kind of panting. Maybe it was good. Maybe she was only meant to see this from the outside. In any case, she took a steadying breath and, in a symbolic gesture, she pulled the ceramic bear out of her pocket—where it had itself been hidden—and pointed it at the Bigfoot to allow them a moment of mysterious connection.

From her bike, the landscape quickly turned to offices and busy people. She passed the art museum and a bunch of restaurants and some stores and the occasional historical-seeming place popped in among taller buildings which looked like real estate sellers or lawyers should be in them. She'd been down here before, of course. She'd fliered the area because it was so active, and gone through it up to the East End and that big waterfront park—it was called the Eastern Promenade, she remembered—and also, before any of that, the library was here, the one she went to when she made her ads and her fliers in the first place.

The memory of the library made her stop there. She was very much going on instinct right then, and she felt good about that. Now her instinct was talking library. But the library was closed, too, until ten. Hm. Straddling her bike in front of the glassy face of the building, she considered some more. Certainly she had started to become aware of her stomach. The coffee was good, but it had been a while since that piece of bread over the sink, and she was feeling hungry, too. For sure there were a lot of places to eat around there.

Her phone rang then, and Zoe saw that it was Gordy calling. She ignored it, put the phone back in her pocket with a shudder.

Zoe had another instinct. So far that morning she'd been flailing a bit, and eating was often just another kind of flailing. What she really needed was to figure things out. And she had time until her client meeting early that afternoon—not time to burn, but time as a gift, time she could inhabit in order to help her come to some conclusions. Zoe took another swig of coffee from her travel mug, and got back on her bike.

Back on the Eastern Promenade, Zoe found a grassy area away from the parking lot where she could sit. It was damp in the grass, with the sun still burning off the dew. It made her feel part of the great ocean in front of her. Or bay—she remembered Gordy correcting her about that. And she remembered his face, the way it could get irritable or even angry. Who *was* he? *Be safe*, Janine had said. Of course, who was Janine, anyway? Who were any of them? Especially after the bomb Brittany had dropped that morning—those emotions wouldn't stay set aside forever—Zoe realized that she'd dropped herself into a world of strangers. Or that maybe she was always in a world of strangers.

But before those thoughts took over completely, Zoe closed her eyes and then brought herself back to the light. When she was there, she took off her shoes and stood up in the grass, stood up tall into a sequence of sun salutation yoga poses. She reached her arms up, and then bent down and went into a lunge, a plank, into upward and downward dog. All the while she thought about it not abstractly but with the consciousness of the actual sun, with the intention of actually producing a heartfelt salutation.

From there she went into other poses, feeling the sun on her face, the damp grass under her feet and between her toes and on the palms of her hands, the air off the water. She felt her stomach ask a question or two about breakfast, and she answered back about the power of fasting.

Zoe had not grown up in a religious household, but a handful of times her family had gone to the annual High Holy Day Services in the synagogue's giant opened-up space that they made by opening partitions between one hall and the next. They were especially likely to go when she and Noah were still in Hebrew School. Zoe had particular memories of Yom Kippur, when all the dressed-up adults—there were so many of them—seemed wobbly on their feet. Her father would shake hands when he knew the people, and would say, "Easy fast," each time. He once told her, after greeting some people, "They're fasting—they're not eating," and he'd said it with a kind of bemused and condescending wonder, the way some people might say, *It's a museum about Bigfoot.* It was a funny thing, being a child and holding her father's enormous, dry hand and thinking he was a kind of all-knowing, all-powerful being, while at the same time just beginning to think something like, *I'm not sure I think the same thing about fasting that he does. I'm not sure it's so dumb.* And feeling a chill go through her, learning that it was possible to differ.

She felt that chill now. Her whole life had in some sense been about learning what it meant to differ. And honoring the difference. And trying to find the right way to support herself in it, trying to find the world that would help her support it.

Wait, she thought. *That's it.*

Zoe opened her eyes. She looked at the green space that led up to the water.

When the library opened, Zoe was there. She wasn't the only one, in fact; a little crowd formed outside the doors in the minutes before they opened. These were Zoe's fellow searchers and journeyers. Who knew what they were looking for? You could make guesses. The young man with the enormous backpack was clear enough—he was reading a novel already, and Zoe was pretty sure he was up for more of the same. He was going to read his way to adventure. The young mother standing off separately was clear, too, because she was saying to her child that she didn't know if his favorite books were going to be there or not, and that they would be able to see in just a couple of minutes if he would just be patient, and so on. And then there was a man who appeared to be homeless, though you couldn't be sure. Well, you could be pretty sure. And he was probably looking for a bathroom and a sink to wash himself in. His not-so-clean hands shook a little as he waited. Different people had different-shaped and different-sized quests. Zoe knew that instinctively. She studied an older woman who was nearby and who had a very grandmotherly vibe, with her comfortable pants and button-up sweater. Zoe wondered if she was going in for crosswords or a few books for her grandkids or, who knew, maybe a guidebook to hiking through Norway.

Zoe, meanwhile, jumped up and down on her feet, barely able to contain herself, her hand in her pocket touching the bear. The light was glary all around. When the doors opened, everybody got in each other's way in their rush, and then on the other side of the door they went off in various directions, Zoe zapping off toward the computers, almost colliding with a couple people on the way. Having gotten herself set up at a station, she paused to look at the open screen, the little icon for the web browser, which could take you anyplace. Not spiritually, of course—that depended on you—but otherwise.

She set the bear on the desk next to her. And then she began to search.

Zoe didn't have much to go on—it had been decades since her parents had taken her there, and she couldn't ask them for more information, or even her brother, because then they would know what she was looking for and they would assume the worst and try to get in her way, and she just didn't want them to know. It wasn't like she was planning to *go* to the little town where she'd had that revelatory childhood vacation; she only wanted to know where it was. Look at some pictures, maybe.

So first she pulled up an online map and worked her way up the coast town by town. But she couldn't be sure the map was catching all of them—sometimes it would ignore littler towns if you weren't too close, but then if you got too close you got more information than you could really handle, especially because she was feeling a little jacked up, to be sure. Her knees were bouncing all over the place under the desk.

Okay. She switched away from maps and just did a search for "Maine beach town" and looked at pages and pages and pages of pictures in the hopes that she would recognize something. There were shots of beaches, of course, endless shots blurring together, and even in her excitement she was very aware that she wasn't going to get anywhere with those. She found some A-frames, but they all blended together, too. And seafood restaurants, and streets without stoplights. All of it looked exactly familiar and like she maybe hadn't ever seen it before.

Zoe sat back in her chair, trying to remember. Was there anything particular that would narrow it down?

She searched for "quietest Maine towns" and "quietest Maine beach towns" and "quietest Maine beaches," all the time getting more worked up about the stillness she had experienced there. Even in the library there were sounds—two people talking louder than you would expect at one of the tables nearby, a librarian thunking books down onto a cart, incongruous beeps and bloops from somewhere. It was a very coffee-shop kind of library, busy and buzzing. But she knew there was a place out there where you got rid of those last little noises. Of course, everywhere had gotten louder—the world was getting louder—but this was Maine. And the one thing about Maine was that it said *No* to things. Good things, sometimes, but also bad and unwelcome things. She wanted the Maine that had said *No* to loud.

Unfortunately, that wasn't easy to find. There were plenty of maybes and possiblies, but nothing that determined any damn thing. Nothing. Abruptly she slammed her hands palms-down on the keyboard, making a very loud sound indeed. To the extent that a few people turned in her direction and Zoe saw in a panicky way how she herself was tangled up in noise.

Then she had a flash of inspiration. Jumping up out of her seat so fast that she almost knocked it over, she grabbed up her stuff, including the bear in particular, and started to roam the library. She was looking for a librarian—a librarian with some years on her or him.

After a while—there were stairs to climb and descend, stacks to maze through—she spotted a woman at the Information desk who looked promising. She had white hair but a lively spirit, palpable as she dug among her desk things searching for something or other, and she was wearing a very funky necklace with orange stones in it.

Zoe went right up to her. "Hi," she said. "I do need information."

The woman paused mid-search and smiled, though she also looked a tiny bit startled. "Yes, dear," she said.

"Can I pull up a chair?" Zoe pointed back at one of the nearby semi-occupied tables. "I really want to get into it."

"Well, okay," the woman said.

And so Zoe did. She pulled a chair up to the Information desk, and she said, "I'm looking for a town. A particular small Maine beach town that's very quiet at night. And I tried looking on the internet, but, well, *bupkis.*" The woman didn't look like she knew what *bupkis* meant, but

Zoe pressed on. "So I didn't get anywhere that way. And that's when it occurred to me: computers are great and everything, but they're not *people*. Computers are so literal and they don't have intuition. They don't have real insight. Do you know what I mean?"

"I think so," the woman said, folding her hands in between them. With her folded hands and her glasses and her white hair she very much looked her part. "Would you like my help finding this town?"

Zoe made a sound somewhere between a choke and a sob. And then, "Yes," she said.

"And I take it you don't have a name for the town."

Zoe shook her head.

"Well. What *can* you tell me about it?"

Zoe was breathing fast. She leaned forward and put her own hands on the desk. "Well, okay. Like I say, it was a very quiet town when I was there. Especially at night. But even during the day there wasn't much going on there. Maybe one or two restaurants."

"How long ago was this?" The librarian was actually looking at her over the top of her glasses, which was classic and somehow very reassuring.

"Well, about twenty-five years, I guess."

"So we know that the town might have changed." When Zoe's face fell, the woman added, "Still—this *is* Maine. What else can you tell me?"

"Okay. So, one or two restaurants. It was the kind of town where there isn't much of a downtown. Maybe a grocery store. The beach, for sure. But no lighthouse. I'm pretty sure there was no lighthouse." Zoe thought. "We went to museums, but they were out of the town, I'm almost positive."

"Hm. How far up or down the coast was it?"

Zoe opened her mouth to answer but didn't actually have an answer. She shrugged instead. "I was a kid," she said. "Wait—there was a state fair. Or a county fair."

"Okay," the woman said. "Right in town?"

"No. No, we had to drive for a little while to get there. There was this one ride that whipped you around in a circle. The bottom dropped out. I didn't go on it."

The woman looked at her, still over the glasses. She was waiting for more information.

"We stayed in an A-frame house," Zoe said, a little desperate.

The woman almost said something, but Zoe kept going to forestall what was coming. "There were pictures of cats on the walls," she said. "The porch had four chairs on it, but mainly I was the one who sat there. The beach sand was pebbly. We made—we made omelets. My mother made omelets."

The librarian's face was pinched with concern. She looked like she was coming to conclusions about Zoe.

"Do you—do you have any ideas?" Zoe said.

"You can imagine that there are a lot of towns in Maine like the one you describe," the librarian said, in a measured way.

Zoe knew it. Still, "There's only one like this one," she said miserably. And then she put her head down on the desk, just for a moment, and lifted it back up again.

"I'm sure," the woman said, glancing around the room elsewhere. What, was she looking for a security guard?

"Only one," Zoe said. "I'm sorry," she said, a whimper, before getting up and getting out of there so that nobody would have to throw her out.

Zoe tried to rally. It wasn't like she was going to actually go to the town, anyway. She had only wanted to know where it was, to have some kind of contact with it. Again she thought about calling at least her brother, and in fact she dialed his number as she stood on the sidewalk in front of the library and let it ring once before hanging up again. Noah would only try to shut her down somehow. She wasn't going to be able to count on her family. In fact, she couldn't think of anyone that she was going to be able to count on. Just herself. And maybe that was better, anyway. She was down to the one person who definitely understood her.

Zoe developed no further plans as she waited for her next appointment time to roll around. She thought about it, certainly, sitting up on the Eastern Prom again, still fasting, but nothing happened. She didn't even get herself a newspaper to check apartment ads, though that was perhaps kind of urgent at this point. She just did nothing, experienced nothing—except for a call-back from Noah, that is, which Zoe ignored. She also ignored a second call from Gordy. The thing was that it didn't really matter what either of them had to say. This just wasn't about them. She had made it about them in the past, but this wasn't the past, and things were finally going to be about her.

She did call Eleanor at one point, got voicemail. "Hi," she said. "Just wanted to make sure we're still on for next Wednesday. That'll be great. Thanks. Okay."

Eventually it became time to find her way to the client's house and meet with her for an hour. Or almost time. Maybe it'd be good to get there a little early, and in any case Zoe just couldn't wait any longer. She had gotten the address in a text, had discovered that it was in town and where exactly it was. And now she just had to get there. She climbed back on her bike. Maybe it had been a sign, not being able to find the beach town, and having the appointment instead; maybe the universe was reminding her that her life was in Portland now. It wasn't clear what that life would be like, but it had to be in Portland, didn't it?

Rose's apartment was in the West End, or at least the phone said so. Only like a half-hour early, Zoe drifted to a stop in front of a house with a porch, painted white but grayed with dust and so on from the street, and parked her bike against a pole. She hadn't been down this street before, though she had fliered a convenience store nearby. This block was quiet and humble—down-to-earth, lived-in houses plus a few trees.

The porch steps all creaked like wooden porch steps should, and so did the porch floorboards. At the side of the door she saw the several buzzers; the bottom one, #4, labeled *R. Knapp*, was the one she wanted. She felt relief when she saw it; the phone hadn't steered her wrong this time.

Should she wait? She *was* a half-hour early. It wasn't the *most* professional to be there so early. But she couldn't wait. The buzzer even made a nice, humming sound when she pressed it.

Zoe stood there touching the bear in her pocket, tapping one foot and then the other. She wasn't a hundred percent clear on why they were meeting here instead of at the coffee shop. She had suggested the coffee shop as an option in one of the texts they exchanged, but the woman wanted to do it at her apartment, which was an option that Zoe had offered in her ads. It had been an edgy offer, she recognized—she knew it wasn't necessarily the safest thing to be going to strangers' houses—but you had to take a few chances in order to get something going, didn't you? And you had to be receptive to the universe being abundant and kind. Anyway, Zoe said yes; Rose's apartment would be fine. And maybe the woman was going to reveal herself to be in a wheelchair or something else that made her not so mobile—though the porch did have steps to climb, so maybe it was something else.

In any case, after a minute the door opened, and a young woman was there in the opening, a very small kind of young woman, almost kind of elfin except the white-woman dreadlocks and the dirty sweats.

"Rose?" Zoe said, a little loud.

"Totally," the woman said. The woman was totally Rose. Zoe suddenly felt unexpected relief; she didn't know until that moment that she had been worried, but she clearly had. Since everything had been done by text and because so many things had been going wrong lately, Zoe's subconscious had apparently been sort of wondering if Rose had been a fake name from some serial murderer guy who just lured freelance people to their deaths. But no—here was a Rose, blinking at her vaguely.

"I'm here kind of early," Zoe said.

Rose said, "Oh, wait—are you Zoe? Did I say that right?" She kind of giggled.

Zoe laughed, too, a little. "Yes—Zoe. I'm a little early. If that's not okay—"

"No problem," Rose said, and then took her arm—stronger than she looked—and more or less dragged Zoe into the house. "My apartment's straight back," she said, as they went along the dim hall and some more loud floorboards into the open door of the apartment. Zoe was not loving the grip Rose had on her arm.

But then she let go. They were in a living room, lit by the windows on the far wall, the kind of living room that had beanbag chairs in it. And down on one of the beanbag chairs *was* a guy, kind of lumberjack-looking with his beard and shaggy hair and flannel shirt and the general sizable size of him.

"Oh," Zoe said. She wasn't expecting anyone else to be there, of course.

"Hi," he said, a big smile on his face.

"This is Andreas," Rose said. "Is that okay?"

"Um," Zoe said. "Is what okay?"

"You know," Rose said. "Andreas. Being here."

"You want to do the session, too?" Zoe said.

The two of them looked at each other. His bushy eyebrows were way up. And then Rose said, still looking at him. "I don't think—probably not. Right?"

He squinched his face a little.

Rose turned sharply back to Zoe, her dreads flying. "No. He just wants to watch."

"Uh, sure," Zoe said. "If it's okay with you. If you think you can concentrate."

"I told you," Andreas said to Rose, grinning, his eyes bright bright bright.

"Great," Rose said, and then she dropped down onto him, so that she was sitting on Andreas who was sitting on the beanbag chair, all in a stack.

For her part, Zoe wasn't sure whether she should try a beanbag chair or just go right for the floor. After a moment of uncertainty, she chose floor.

"Wait," Rose said, her eyes wide, her hand stretched out toward Zoe. "Do you want anything? Tea or anything?"

"I'm okay," Zoe said. In her mind, she was orienting herself toward the situation. It wasn't like anything too strange was happening, exactly, but she was feeling edgy all the same. She had the feeling that she was going to need to be very palm tree for this one.

"Great," Rose said. "Because we really want to get started."

"Great," Zoe echoed. *We*? And they were in a hurry even though she was early? "So what are you hoping to get out of this session?" She directed the question toward Rose, though she was aware of Andreas' bright eyes taking it all in. She wanted to say, *Are you going to sit on him the whole time?* but she didn't, for the moment.

"Well," Rose said, "what kind of things do you do, anyway?"

Zoe was ready for this. "Mindfulness," she said. "My practice is to help people find their center, to get grounded, to get in touch with themselves, with the moment." It wasn't a canned line, exactly, though it was pretty good, she thought.

"Get in touch with themselves," she said.

"I told you," Andreas said quietly.

"I know some people don't like that language," Zoe said. "New age and so on."

"Oh, no," Rose said, smiling knowingly. "We're cool with that."

"Okay." Zoe laughed a slightly nervous laugh.

For a minute they all just sat there. Then Andreas leaned forward, which leaned Rose forward with him, and he said, "Listen—speaking of touching?"

"Speaking of touching?" Zoe said.

"Yeah." He grinned. "So, you do massage, right?"

"Do I do massage?"

He nodded, a strange smile on his face. Rose's eyes were fuzzy. As for Zoe, the room suddenly felt a little closer all around her. It was like the light dimmed.

"I don't do massage," she said. She remembered—re-felt—that unsettled feeling that had driven her out of massage training in her late twenties. And she also was remembering some other things, looking at this couple that was looking at her like this. She was remembering Samuel and Phebe from that commune that she really, *really* didn't want to be thinking about.

"But *would* you?" he asked. "Do massage?"

"I," Zoe started, before faltering. *Extremely no,* is what she was thinking, but things were going back in the other direction, getting kind of glarey again. Was the sun changing in the windows?

"It's cool," he said. "Don't flutter. We're, you know, aware that people who put those ads out sometimes offer a little more than the ad says.

181

Especially in the *Therapeutic* section. And we're not cops or anything."

"Uh-huh." That was not a thing she had been wondering about.

"So you don't have to worry," he said.

Rose nodded, her eyes closed now. And then, while Zoe sat there almost hypnotized, Andreas gently took hold of the hem of Rose's sweatshirt and lifted it up over her head.

Which left Rose in a state of complete upper-body nudity.

Zoe was on her feet in a flash—so abruptly that Rose's eyes snapped open in surprise.

"Are you okay?" Rose said.

"No," Zoe said. The light in the room was undulating, going from bright to dim to bright to dim. And her one thought was, *No, no, NO, NO—not* this, *too!* "I have to go."

"No, you don't," Andreas said gently. "You don't have to go." And he got up, lifting still-half-naked Rose up with him. The two of them stepped forward. Their faces were strange, confused.

"What's happening?" Rose said.

"Oh, you little bird," Andreas said. He reached out and took hold of Zoe's wrist. "Don't flutter."

Zoe pulled back, but couldn't get her hand free. "I need you to let go of me *right* now," she said.

"But we want you to stay," Rose said dreamily.

Abruptly Zoe was flailing, wrenching on her left arm and swinging her right one, hitting at Andreas and yanking away from him at the same time. There was a sharp pain near her elbow, the one she'd broken back one of the times when things got really, got really—and then she was free, falling to the ground. She hit it hard. Andreas and Rose stared at her like she was the crazy one. But Zoe was up on her feet fast again, and back to the door, finding the doorknob and throwing herself backward through the door.

Andreas reached out, and Zoe slammed the door shut. Or almost—

the door bounced off Andreas' wrist, which was there in the space between the door and the jamb, and he howled.

Zoe only stood for a second by the mostly-closed door, while her body went into extreme shaking. Inside there was howling and swearing, and then the door started to open again. But Zoe didn't see who was opening it.

Because then she ran.

Zoe was several blocks gone on her bike before she stopped again, and then only to look her destination up on her phone. There was one close by. Off on her bike again, racing. Like her legs were trying to keep up with her heart.

On the way, right before she got there, she passed the Miss Portland Diner—the sight of it hit her at first like a neon Picasso mess, in her mental state, though actually it was just sitting there silently and smugly like usual in the middle of nowhere nowhere nowhere. Zoe sped up, shaking her head violently as she put the place behind her, and then, a block later, pulled into the parking lot that she wanted, among all the shiny vehicles, basically threw the bike against a post where it collapsed to the ground, and then went in through the glass door, feeling like she was breaking into many pieces.

The man, a doughy twenty-something kid of a man, looked up as she came in. His face asked, *Can I help you?* from behind the counter.

"I need to rent a car," she said.

Eleven

Life was two pockets. That was one of the things Zoe remembered from her time in that mystical Judaism cult that she did a few years ago. It was one of the things she hung on to. Lior had told her that it was an idea from one of the old rabbis, that everybody should carry two pieces of paper with them, one in the left pocket, and the other in the right. On one paper would be written, *I am nothing but dust and ashes.* On the other would be written, *The world was created for me alone.* She didn't remember which one went in which pocket, but in any case, the bigger idea was that both statements were true at the same time, though most people usually only looked in one pocket at a time. And the two pockets thing was a pretty amazing idea just by itself, for Zoe, but Lior explained that there was more to it. He said it was about creation and destruction, about the fact that life, the universe—these things were at all times a mixture of creation and destruction, and that you couldn't have one without the other. In order to make something—good or bad—you had to break what was already in place; whenever you ended something, you began something else.

So Zoe reminded Lior about that stuff when she told him she was leaving the group, because he got angry with her about it; she said she was ending one thing but beginning another. He told her she didn't have a real understanding of the idea. He told her that some things, in fact, were pure destruction.

Zoe had been twenty when she fell for the first time fully into the pocket of ashes. There wasn't any particular starting point; she was in college, doing the same things everybody else was doing, basically: going to classes, pulling all-nighters. Except that increasingly that year, junior year, she was really staying up all night a lot—not just for tests and papers but also talking with friends about all kinds of ideas for how the world worked and how it ought to be, and sometimes, more and more often, on her own. It seemed urgent, somehow, that she not waste her time on sleep, on *unconsciousness*. What an idea that was, spending so much of your life *not conscious*. Wow. Once she recognized that, it was hard to justify going along just because other people were sleeping a lot.

College had not been an easy transition. Or, more exactly, it had been as hard as all the other transitions. She'd thought that leaving home would get her out from under the umbrella of her family's dysfunction and so fix everything, and basically it did the first part, but then she discovered that she didn't feel any different about life than she had in high school. It was still the frenetic, harrowing thing that had harassed her from the beginning. Her classes were interesting—she was trying everything, slow to settle on any one major—and the people were cool enough, but they were like everybody else, really. Like everybody else, most of them seemed to be able to live in the world just fine, and to not even notice that things weren't totally fine, in fact.

Her college friends had nicknames for her. They called her Gonzo, and Zoomy, and one guy who was kind of into her even called her Protozoe for a while. Even Becky, who was more like Zoe than the others, used the nicknames sometimes. And all of it was theoretically affectionate, but she knew what they were all saying. She was the wacky friend in their unwacky lives. Which was a fun role to play sometimes. But not forever. And it hid the truth that Zoe had started to discover—that yes, there was a difference between her and them, but that her friends were actually seeing it the wrong way around.

Late at night, Zoe would keep the main lights off in her room so that her roommate, who was a generally exasperated woman from Missouri somewhere, could sleep, and Zoe would turn on a little clip-on book light and huddle over one of her books from this religion class she was taking, or over her spiral-bound journal, writing so intensely that the force of the ball-point pen grooved many pages underneath the one she was writing on, like her ideas were already creating ripples in the universe. She'd always been a big journaller and had often had stretches of insomnia, but that year both really piled on, to the point where she was building a stack of filled notebooks beside her bed. There in the dim, close dorm room at night, her little book light glowing, she felt that she was alone, singular, in the pupil of a vast eye. She wrote about knowing God, about talking with God, about being part of God. In her most transported moments, she wrote about being God altogether—an audacious idea, but one that was hard to deny once you'd thought of it. Sometimes the lined notebook paper ripped under the force of her pen, which she took to be significant.

Her friends expressed concern—Zoe also wasn't eating very much, and they suggested she was becoming a little extra unpredictable, missing classes and arranging her desk in patterns upon patterns (stacks and side by side and overlapping rectangles and the pens spiraling out and so on) and showing up at their rooms in the middle of the night with breakthrough ideas that they didn't seem to be moved by or even really get. They expressed concern. Zoe heard them, but distantly—they were not having the revelatory experiences she was having, and so they couldn't understand what was happening to her. Maybe their unconsciousness—that was the difference, really—kept them from those experiences. And what she was doing wasn't even so weird, she thought. There was all kinds of precedent in Judaism, for example, for fasting, for studying all night, times on the calendar when you were traditionally *required* to do those things.

Not that it was just some kind of rededication to Judaism; it was so much bigger than that. In her class she read about the Hindu ascetics and Christian martyrs, the Buddhists who set themselves on fire during the Vietnam war; she recognized herself to be in those lineages, too.

One recurring specifically Judeo-Christian image she did have was Jacob's ladder; she saw herself climbing up with the angels on rungs that were hotter and hotter to the touch as she climbed. Or, not hot, exactly, but so bright with light that they felt hot, like they were blinding her hands. And with each night spent pouring her thoughts onto the page, she got higher on the ladder. A skipped meal, too, was a bunch of rungs. But each time she dozed off accidentally, she fell; each time she gave in and ate she fell; when she talked to other people she felt them yanking on her from below. And so increasingly she worked to keep herself focused, laser-like, on the ladder. She did what it took.

The world took on many colors.

One day Zoe went to the dining hall as a kind of mortification. It would mean more to be around the food and not eat it than to avoid the food by staying in her room. She walked very slowly through the door and across the wide, boxy room to the food, saying to herself, *God, God, I am God. God, God, I am God.* Each step—she was awfully tired and things were hazy and her steps felt unsteady, like she was stepping onto a see-saw—each step was a syllable, the syllable *God*. Around her there were people, like blurs of people, so that she felt surrounded and pressed in upon. Like they were reaching their hands for her. They were mortifications, too. She started saying the syllable out loud, and louder, and as loud as she could. And when she reached one of the food lines, she was suddenly aware that everything being served there was dead—not just the animals but the vegetables, too. Later, when she was in the mystical Judaism group, she heard the story of the Israelites in the desert, eating the quails that God sent down when they complained, not knowing that the quails were a punishment, a plague. Those people all ended up dead. But back in college, before she ever heard that, she understood what was happening, and the role she was being given. It was so clear: the world was created for her—*by* her—alone.

Nobody was injured. Somehow nobody was injured, or at least not seriously, when she grabbed plates from the stack of white, shatterable plates and started throwing them. She threw them at the sneeze guards over the food, at the people serving the food, at the people coming for the food, the people swarming around all the dead things. From her place on the ladder, she threw the plates and raged in order to ward people away, including the security guard, and then the other security guard. Eventually there was a third. She was surrounded by blue.

It was blue, but nothing at all like sky.

She felt her hands—she tried so hard to hold on, but she couldn't—she felt her hands come off the rungs. And she felt herself falling.

That night. That night, in the hospital, alone. Her family was flying in, even including her brother. But that night, in the hospital, she was alone, and both pockets were open. The slips of paper were blowing wildly in front of her face. She was God; she was ashes. She was dust; she was at the center of the universe. She was at the top of the ladder; all her bones were broken on the hard ground at the bottom.

In fact, her left elbow *was* broken, from when she'd been wrestled finally to the tile floor of the dining hall. The pain of that, even given the painkillers and the sedation and the temporary brace they'd put on, was like a magnet, pulling her to the bed. The white-gray ceiling was like a force pressing down on her. She was pinned there, even now that the restraints were off. And in the bed, with no journal, no book-light, the IV running food into her arm, and all the awful human sounds from out in the hallway outside her room, in the bed all the binaries slowly resolved themselves. One of the slips of paper blew further away, and then it was gone. The world was not created for her alone. It was not created for her at all.

Gradually, that night, her body collapsed only into ash.

Her parents referred to that whole thing, forever after, as the "episode." As in, "That was right before the episode" (when they were trying
to figure out what had happened to cause it), or "You're not having another episode, are you?" (when they were worried about her) or, above
all, "Now, be careful—you don't want to have another episode, do you?"
She and her brother had even occasionally joked about it over the years,
when she could handle joking about it. If her parents were worried
about her, he'd say in the voice of a TV announcer, "And now, get ready
for another very special episode of *Zoe!*" But mostly she couldn't handle
him doing that, even including some of the times when she pretended
to handle it.

The other word they liked to use was "cycle," as in, "This is just part
of your cycle, Zoe," whenever she had an idea to get her moving forward.
They said, "Now you're in the up part of the cycle, but, before you know
it, you're going to be down," and they said, "You've been here before." Dr.
Charles said it, too. More gently, but he said it.

They pointed to the different therapies she tried, and especially the
non-traditional and non-Western ones, as well as the several kinds of
corrective body work, and certainly the mysticism. They brought it up
when, that one month, she consumed only liquids, and during the period when she was fruitarian, and the raw foods experiment and the mac-
robiotic diet and the Ayurvedic diet. They were especially bothered by
her more spontaneous leaps, her wildly unplanned things, like the vivid
repainting of her apartment walls, or her burning of her journals, or the
broken bathroom mirror. Really, they were especially bothered by *her*.

And that didn't change. When, about thirteen years after that time
in college and about a year before she made the move to Portland, she
woke up one morning full of *go go go* and so she jumped in the car without planning and just drove straight west, tearing out of Philadelphia and
into the whole rest of the world, she knew her family would have said

episode and they would have said *cycle*. But she also knew that she had to go; it was something she'd known, known, right when her eyes had opened that morning. The *why* of it was less clear, but you couldn't always wait for *why*. So she drove, and the route took her straight through central Pennsylvania, right past a town that you couldn't even see from Route 70—just some silos and a numbered exit—but which, to her mind, was almost a place on fire in the middle of the landscape, a place she'd been avoiding for years, and she felt that passing it was part of why she was making that trip. She passed it and nothing stopped her. She kept going.

Zoe was all energy the whole time. She fueled herself on small amounts of tolerable roadside food and also on what little promising images she could see in towns along the way, but more on her own inner surge of power. She had gotten past that Pennsylvania town.

In the end, it wasn't her that gave up; it was the car. The car started vibrating really hard and making a thunking noise just as she got past the Ohio border into Indiana, so she got off at the first exit she saw. Alongside the off-ramp was a giant cross and, maybe separately, maybe not, a huge billboard promising guns. And suddenly, amidst the vibrations and guns and thunking and Jesus, Zoe was nervous. Where *was* she?

The people she met in this Indiana town seemed as wary of her as she was of the town. The guys at the car place were definitely put off by the way she talked—she had led with "I come in peace"—and they said guarded things in their unexpectedly southern accents—"Well, *somethin'* needs fixed, anyhow"—but ultimately they were able to pinpoint what was wrong and they were able to repair it, not at all inexpensively. In the meantime, she spent a couple nights in a grim hotel that was part of a strip mall that seemed to go on forever—maybe it was the town itself—and she ate her meals there, too, people all around her eating themselves unconscious and smoking at the same time. It was not a place that made you feel like everything was definitely going to be okay.

When she first got the estimate on the car, she actually made the mistake of calling her father; she wanted to be sure she wasn't getting ripped off, and he knew something about cars. But it was for sure a mistake.

"You're *where*?" he said.

"It's for a conference," she said, looking out her hotel window at a very large parking lot.

"A conference? What conference?"

"You know," she said. "You know, a kind of—an educational. Like a—you know, fine. There's no conference." She was not the best liar. "I was just driving."

"To *Indiana*?"

Zoe could hear her mother in the background, getting agitated herself. "Listen—can you please just tell me if this estimate is reasonable?"

"*Now* she wants to be reasonable," he muttered.

The parking lot blurred in front of her.

When the car was fixed, Zoe packed it in and went home. The energy that had driven her west—that was all drained away by then.

"Thank God," her father said when she told him she was returning.

Although the trip back was just thorough grayness, and though she felt like an automaton driving, she had enough initiative to do one thing: she took Route 80 through Pennsylvania, the way-out-of-her-way Northern route so that she didn't have to see that little emotionally burning town in the middle of the state again. Not when she was coming home in defeat.

It had come up in her repressed memories therapy, back when she was doing that in her late twenties. A lot of things did, but the commune in central PA showed up more than once. In the end, it was probably the only thing that came up that was even real. So much of the rest of it wound up insubstantial, smokelike. The therapist, Cathy, kept trying to get her to *discover* things about her childhood—intense, traumatic things—and for a while she went along. There was even a period of time where she cut off all contact with her parents because she'd accepted the possibility that they'd somehow *done* something to her. Physically. But after a while she had trouble maintaining that possibility. Outside the therapy room, it just didn't make that much sense, didn't seem quite right, and inside the room she sometimes felt like she was guessing, trying to figure out what exactly the therapist was going for. Was it abuse, Cathy? Was it neglect? Am I getting warmer? All of which eventually became kind of silly, even for Zoe, who was constitutionally committed to being open to all the possibilities.

So eventually she quit that—she never called Cathy to tell her, just stopped coming—and put it behind her. Everything but the one memory that was definitely real.

The commune in central Pennsylvania had happened not long after college ended. In fact, it was her college friend Becky—the one who was the least critical of Zoe's sanity—who drew her into it. The idea was a group of maybe a dozen people farming and making their own clothes and so on and trying to be off the grid as much as possible.

"Why me?" Zoe said when Becky called her.

"Are you serious?" Becky said.

"Yeah. Why me? I don't know anything about farming. Or building things."

"You'll learn," Becky said. "There's this one couple who's going to be here, and they know everything. And besides, you're a total visionary. That's why you. You're the only one I thought of."

Zoe looked around herself. She was living at home again, staring at a room that had last been updated toward the end of high school. On the wall, there were motivational posters with—it's true—cute animals on them. Maybe some kind of an unconscious nod to the past, to the cat pictures from the vacation house in Maine? Regardless. She'd redecorated frequently when she was still in high school—from dark paint and closed curtains to bright paint and no curtains or from bare to full of natural things like pinecones and leaves and so on to batik sheets as wall hangings—but the last iteration had been a little wince-worthy. *Hang in there*, said a cat dangling from a tree branch. It was almost like a stranger's room, and she was living in it. "I'm a visionary," she said.

Her parents were so predictably freaked out by the idea that she didn't even tell them where she was going, exactly. She just said at the last minute that she was joining a working farm, and left without more detail, and—once she was settled in—only kept in touch via sporadic emails sent on the rare occasions that she could get to the nearby town's public library, emails where she was careful to never give them any clues. She talked about things that could be happening in any rural place anywhere, said she was learning how to sew, working hard in the soil, that she collected eggs.

All of which was true. After a small amount of training she was working hard all day out in their modest field or huge garden or whatever it exactly was, and more and more saw her hands as the powerful tools they were. She loved the fact that it was impossible to get the dirt out from under her nails completely. In some ways it was so idyllic. At night, after dinner, she'd sit outside on the unpainted porch with some of the people, practicing her stitching, and there'd be guitar music and drumming and some of the women had really beautiful voices. Becky, who was from New York City, could sing "Angel From Montgomery" so sweetly it made you want to cry.

Though other things were true, too. There were almost two dozen people at Home Farm instead of one, which meant that people were packed in. It wasn't a calm place, really—it was a full place. And that would have been okay, except that it wasn't. It felt like someone was always watching you. Especially Samuel and Phebe, that couple that Becky had mentioned on the phone. They had been raised on farms, or at least that's what they said, so they directed all the work that was to be done. They were also the founders of Home Farm and so they set the rules and framed the ideology everybody was working under; Sundays they liked to bring everybody together in the parlor of the big house to explain their growing, spreading vision for the commune. They would sit in these two old armchairs—mostly it was the floor for other people, but Samuel and Phebe liked their chairs—and they would take turns leaning forward and talking, her soft brown eyes focused past everyone and his bright blue ones scanning the group sharply, person by person. He could fix you, arrest you, with a look. But that wouldn't have been so bad, either, but, well, after a while it was clear that they saw themselves as more than just farmers, as something bigger and more prophetic. One time Samuel said, "Home Farm is going to be the center of the world someday. The beginning. And Home Farm began here," reaching out for Phebe's waiting hand and grasping it. He held up their clasped hands. "You need to understand that this is the center of Home Farm." That was during one of their disciplinary meetings.

Because there were definitely rules. Rules about how the work was to be done, of course, and about chores around the house, and about what was okay to wear, but also about possessions—after a certain point, nothing was supposed to belong to individuals, but instead to everybody—and about when and if it was okay to communicate with the outside world, which Phebe called "the failed world," shaking her head, and about sleep and toilet schedules and how people were supposed to talk and show respect and so on. The possessions rule, anyway, shouldn't have bothered Zoe much—frankly, she was pretty sure that people weren't supposed to own things individually anyway—but she discovered that she didn't like the repeated feeling of having things taken from her, especially as the things piled up in the bedroom of Samuel and Phebe, which the two of them occupied all by themselves. At least most nights.

Because that was the other thing about the possessions rule: apparently it applied to bodies, too. As in, certainly nobody owned anybody else, and monogamy wasn't okay—that was what made Becky finally take off, one night while everyone was sleeping—but also meaning that your own body, and Zoe really, really hated to think about this part, wasn't your own to control either. She remembered, on those occasions when she couldn't shut it out, the roughness of the sheets in Samuel and Phebe's bed. She remembered Samuel's eyes, that never stopped looking at her, and Phebe's, which never started. The sharp blue and the yielding brown. She remembered the next-morning view through their window, the upper branches of a tree, like fingers, the hand open for more. That— that was what made Zoe run.

Vigilance had been high since Becky bolted, so that you always found yourself around either Samuel or Phebe or one of the other people they trusted most, but after a while it settled down again, at least enough to let Zoe slip off on a town run one day while Phebe was in the bathroom of a gas station, in a bathroom for the umpteenth time. Zoe was convinced that Phebe was pregnant, actually, which seemed like an inherently tragic thing under the circumstances. But Zoe only thought about that distantly as she ran around a couple of corners, found a phone, made the call, and then hid out behind an unoccupied house in town to wait for her parents to get there.

Though it wasn't her parents who got there first. Apparently they contacted the police before they got in their car, and Home Farm was raided that day. She learned that from the police themselves. When they found her, she thought they were there to arrest her for trespassing, but the officer, a pretty big and round man, held her by her shaking shoulders and said, "It's okay. It's okay, darling. We've got you." And the way he said it, it was a good thing to be got. She hugged him like a father.

It didn't end like Waco or anything, she eventually found out—no violence, nobody died—though there were arrests, and Home Farm was shut down that day. When the police were done talking with Zoe, her parents were there, and the looks on their faces—she had never seen her parents, not in all their anxious years, ever look quite like that. They didn't say anything. They just held her and then took her to the car.

All the way home, Zoe sat low in the backseat, her eyes level with the bottom of the window. Her parents said *episode*. They said *cycle*. They said those words again and again, all the way home.

For months after that, Zoe lived at home again filled with a thick, thick syrup. She did the traditional therapy that her parents demanded she do, and otherwise she stayed in her room, almost immobile. Her therapist—a man who always had a cold, it seemed like—had his own things to say. All kinds of things. And then she went home again, each time, and sank into her mattress. In a way it was even worse than the time she'd been in the hospital. Certainly it was longer. When she counted her blinks, she got to numbers that mathematicians had yet to even name.

Remembering any of that time was like cutting a window in herself. Cutting it with a serrated knife.

For her part, Zoe knew that the word "episode" was wrong. It wasn't something episodic—and it wasn't cyclical, either. She knew that things had gone wrong when she was twenty, that she'd basically fallen apart, but she thought of it as part of something more continuous. In fact, she saw it as the culmination of two decades of having her dials turned wrong for this world, and nobody noticing, or at least nobody *helping*. And she knew that other things had gone wrong, too—plenty of things. But that was part of the continuousness too. The problem was that people just didn't see things in enough dimensions. Because, think about it: if you look at something and it looks like a circle, you might just be seeing it in two dimensions, and if you were to step to the side, to get an angle on it, you'd see that the person isn't circling but moving along on a path that's more like a spiral, or the thread on a screw, or a coiled spring. These things because, each time she came around again, she wasn't where she started. She was further forward. And maybe the spring was partly submerged, so that she repeatedly ended up back down in the syrup, but she also repeatedly came out of it, and when she did she had made forward progress.

She first glimpsed that truth when she was in her bed, in her old room, in her parents' house, a few months after Home Farm. She was heavy with the syrup, deep in the mattress, but there was a moment when she saw in her mind a huge spring, but so vividly that it was as though the spring were suspended in the air above her. At first she didn't understand—it was just a vision without an explanation. But after a few days of studying it, the shine of it, she saw that a spring was in fact a line. It was not a straight line, but it was a line. It didn't matter how many things went wrong on the way—it still got you somewhere. All you had to do was stay on it and believe.

At some point Zoe finally sat up in bed. In front of her was the encouraging cat poster, and that poster was not, in fact, wrong.

Twelve

The Maine countryside rolled along, mainly very green. Things had gotten quiet on the road after Zoe had put Portland some distance behind her and then turned off 95 onto a state road that seemed to keep her closer to the water. Highway lanes were empty, the sky vast above the trees on all sides. It was almost as though the world was opening the way for her.

Zoe tried to meet that world halfway by getting her own mind under control. Fundamentally, she just tried to get some calm back. She focused on the action of her heart, slowing it down, reassuring it to just do its normal job. There was no need for fight-or-flight; the fighting was over, and this wasn't flight so much as directed movement. *Slow down, heart*, she said, one hand warm on her chest.

She also had to talk to her stomach a little, since it was starting to really assert itself about needing some food. And Zoe wasn't even sure she was fasting anymore—wasn't that a lifetime ago?—but she was also pretty sure there wasn't anything along this highway that was going to work for her, eating-wise. And so, *Hang in there, stomach*, she said, her hand down on her tummy now.

As for her mind, she worked hard to stay away from thoughts of that Andreas man. His grip on her wrist. His eyes. *Her* eyes. Zoe had stopped at a gas station a while back, thought about calling 911 to make an anonymous report, but what was the point? She didn't want to file a report, because it would just get her wrapped back up in everything. So there wasn't any point in dwelling on him and his face, his hands. She certainly had to try to let him go. Instead she focused her attention on the bear, which was on the dashboard behind the steering wheel.

A car went around her to pass—a massive pick-up truck, actually, with very large wheels. Not Gordy's, obviously, though she'd had a moment of fast-heart all over again when she first spotted the thing. And then it roared off, on its own urgent mission.

"Good luck to you," Zoe said aloud, her hand up in a gentle fare-thee-well. Though inside herself she was not having gentle feelings.

Zoe didn't have an exact plan. More like a two-part intention, one part of which—getting out of Portland—she'd already accomplished. The second part was the harder one, but she was still putting it out there, to try to do it. She was going to find that town from her childhood. She was going to find it, and she was going to root herself down there.

And if she couldn't find it? That was another thing she couldn't think about. Can the syrup actually drown you? Can you let go into it and never come up again? Would that, in fact, be better than a world that never gets right?

Zoe knew, though she had always been careful not to articulate it to herself, that it was optional: going on, keeping going. Being alive. She knew you didn't have to do it.

She shook this out of her head, vigorously. She had to find the town.

The problem was that she obviously still didn't know where it was or what its name was. And she still didn't think she could call her family about it, no matter how important the task was. It would be like drawing them a map for how to find her. Zoe very definitely wanted to be un-found.

And so what she figured—what she needed—was that openness was going to have to get it done. Zoe was going to drive and drive until she spotted something that just plain felt right.

Miles went by, and time. She kept her eye on the road signs but didn't recognize any of the names of any of the towns there. She did get a few calls along the way. Gordy, Noah, her parents. Of course she let it go to voicemail every time, and eventually even turned the phone off altogether. Whatever those people had to say to her no longer mattered at all.

It was mid-afternoon when Zoe finally saw something promising. Not a name, not even really something concrete—but she had come over a modest rise in the road, and in front of her was a vista that seemed somehow familiar. Not that it was even very different from anything else she'd seen on the road—dense trees to the left, dense trees to the right— but the slope of the land, the distribution of green from left to right, the slightly curving line of the road—it just rang a bell somehow. It was like looking at your own bed, the way you'd rumpled your own sheets, and knowing, because you knew your body, that it was you who had rumpled it. The landscape was like a familiar bed. And she could hear the little girl in her say, very quietly, and without a lot of intensity, but still saying it, *Oh—this place.* A contented little girl voice. Zoe drew in an awfully deep breath. This was not any kind of time to be turning her back on her own intuition; she looked for the next opportunity to jump on a south-heading road, and she grabbed it.

On the new road, Zoe pulled over at the very first gas station she found. The attendant was a bone-skinny young guy with a Patriots baseball cap on.

"Are there any beach towns around here?" she said.

His eyebrows went up a little. "Beach towns?"

Zoe nodded very seriously.

"Well," he said, revving up slowly, like it was the first question he'd been asked all day. "If you stay on this," he said, pointing over at the road that ran right alongside the gas station, the one she'd just been on, the only one around, "you know, this road he-ah?" She'd thought the Bouchers had Maine accents—but this was a whole lot more.

"Sure," Zoe said, looking over at the road.

He scratched at his chin, which had some scattered stubble on it. "Well, if you take that a ways down, you'll run into Casper, sure." *Caspah*, he'd said. *Shoo-ah*.

Casper. Zoe let that bounce around in her mind. *Casper.* "That's the name of a town, right?" she said. "It's not a person, right?"

The kid's face fell open, and he threw his head back to laugh. When he finished, he shook his head with pleasure. "A person—no. Not a person. It's a town. A beachfront town."

Casper. That could be familiar. Couldn't it? "Is it a very little town, like with not much going on there?"

"Not much at all," he said, sounding wise beyond his years. "You could keep going on to Bar Harbor"—*Bah Hahbah*, he said, of course— "if you wanted more to do. People do seem to like that one."

"No," Zoe said. "That's okay. I like it quiet."

He nodded his head at her, bemused.

"And do you ever have county fairs around here?"

"Oh, not this time of ye-ah," he said, taking off his cap to wipe his forehead with the back of his hand. "That would be back in August."

Zoe's heart leapt up and down like a child. "Thank you," she said.

"Did that help?" he said, surprised.

"I don't know for sure," Zoe said, "but I think so."

The state road wound its way down toward Casper, the landscape closely woodsy for most of the way but slowly turning over to something rockier and more open. And then there was water on her right—she could see the other side, so it was just a bay, but it was a good sign. An extremely good sign. Zoe tried to keep her expectations under control. She tried a little. But then there was water to the right *and* left, and there wasn't any way she was going to be able to relax about this. By the time she got to the bridge that was going to take her into Casper—there had been a bridge in her childhood, hadn't there been? Hadn't there?—she was cloud nine-ing it all the way.

"WooHOOOOOOOO!" she howled.

The town itself was just the kind of sleepy place Zoe was thinking of. She couldn't be a hundred percent sure that it was the exact sleepy place she was looking for—did it feel familiar because it was the *kind* of place she'd been, or because it was *the* place she'd been?—but certainly it was definitely possible. *Casper,* she said to herself. *Casper.*

Downtown Casper, all two blocks of it, had a very small grocery store in it, a church, a bank, a hardware store, a family-style restaurant, a handful of scattered houses, a post office, and a couple of antiques stores that seemed to be shuttered for the off-season, all of it peppered along Main Street. Everything was white or a relative of white, and pointing up in the way of New England buildings. Zoe discovered it all on foot, having parked the car to step out into the salt air. Oh, and it was salty. It went beyond smell to something you could *taste.*

There were a few people out on the sidewalk. Well, a few in the sense of there being exactly three people that she saw—one older husband-wife-looking pair and a man in overalls that had been made unclean through some kind of hands-on work. And they definitely saw Zoe, too; each one looked at her the way you would look at a brand new lamp that suddenly showed up in your living room with no warning or explanation. Despite her profound excitement, Zoe remembered that this was Maine and she managed to not hug the people, and not even to wave or say hello. There was some nodding back and forth, though.

In any case, her mind was busy. It was pretty all-consuming, trying to decide whether this was the place from her childhood. Did the hardware store, there on the corner, strike a familiar chord? Not that her family would have had any reason to go in there, but a hardware store on a corner—wasn't that a memory? Or the ice cream case right on the inside of the window of the little grocery store? She was sure there had been ice cream, and she thought it might have been from a case like that. A case right up against the window. Wasn't it? Her intuition was deliberating quite a bit over the evidence at hand.

After the sort of mostly commercial part of Main Street there were two more blocks of houses, and then—she could see it coming as she walked—there was the ocean. She came down to the bottom of Main Street as it opened up into a perpendicular line of dark wooden docks, mostly empty of boats just then, and stood at the edge of those docks, her feet on the weathered planks. And there it was.

But really—the ocean. It had to be, this time. There was no land anywhere in sight ahead of her. And this water, this great, wide, vast water, had a calm and certainty that suggested ancient power. Power and intelligence. Zoe watched as little white patches—foam—happened and disappeared here and there on the surface, like neurons firing. Like the fluid, unconcerned thought of the earth on display in front of her.

Swaying in the breeze, Zoe actually swooned a little. It was all so— it was so amazing, and then, too, maybe she was at the end of a long, long journey, so incredibly long, and here in front of the ocean and everything, so a little swooning went with it. Though it was probably also partly about her being pretty hungry, when you got down to it. That realization came to her. And although she wanted to stay longer, right then she saw on one of the docks a crate of fish that a solitary man was working with—he was the only one around—and she thought about how the fish were dead, and then for some reason she thought about Rose's guy Andreas, even though he was obviously alive, unless something unrelated and bad had happened to him since she left. But the thought was enough to shake her.

"Listen—" she said to the ocean before she turned away, "I'm going to see you again soon."

Whitecaps sparked something like a goodbye. Something like an *I'll be here.*

As she'd anticipated, the family-style restaurant wasn't open—it wasn't quite four o'clock yet—but the grocery store was, so Zoe tried that instead. Inside, the woman behind the counter, a stout and grandmotherly type, took a good look at the brand new lamp in the living room and gave one of the town's signature hello-nods, which Zoe returned before grabbing a plastic basket and tucking herself into the aisles. There were only three aisles, all of them empty of people, the whole thing almost as small as a convenience store would have been in Philly. But there was produce—Zoe picked up a pair of bananas and three peaches. Wandering, she also got some bread—they only had the very heavily-processed kind, full of chemicals, but at least it wasn't expensive—and some peanut butter for protein. She got bottled water. It was a start. To what, she didn't know—but a clear start.

The woman behind the counter rang up the items silently. Zoe realized that she hadn't heard anyone in the town speak yet—and wouldn't it be interesting if the thing was actually that the whole town had taken a vow of silence for religious reasons, and maybe that this was a place of ultimate peace? Zoe hardly dared open her own mouth. But then the woman finally finished the ringing-up, and said out loud the number for how much it all cost. "Twelve twenty-one," she said. It was almost like a code.

Zoe took out her money and paid. And then, the spell broken, she herself said, "Thanks. And hey—that's the ocean out there, right?" She pointed off toward the docks. "It's not a bay, is it?"

The woman gave her a look. "No, de-ah. That's the ocean." More of the hardcore accent here. Though Zoe was nearly too excited to notice it.

She pressed on. "I don't know if you would, but do you happen to know if there are any A-frame houses in town? Like, pretty much right on the beach?"

"A-frames?" the woman said thoughtfully, bagging the food.

"Maybe a rental?"

"Oh, well," the woman said. "All those ah shut down since the summah."

Zoe clasped her hands together to keep them from shaking. "Wait—do you mean there *are* A-frame rental places?"

The woman made a *well, sure* face. "Up to Haven Point Road you'd find a couple."

Zoe actually literally took a step back. "Did you say?" she said. "Did you say *Haven* Point Road?" It wasn't that she remembered the name, but that it was such a *perfect* name.

The woman didn't even respond—she just looked uncomfortably at Zoe.

"Sorry," Zoe said, buttoning up the best she could, even though it was like buttoning an extra-small sweater over an extra-large happiness. "Thank you very much."

The woman nodded warily, her vow of silence back in full effect. Part of Zoe wanted to toss the woman a peach just to get her to lighten up. *Do you know how wonderful this universe is?* she wanted to say. But instead she just collected her plastic bag of nourishment and, with one more solemn nod, let herself out of the store.

Hungry or not, first things first, is how Zoe saw it. So she walked fast toward her car, meanwhile getting her phone to pull up a map of where she was at that moment, and then she spotted it—Haven Point Road. It ran along the coast up the island a while, apparently—she wasn't sure of the scale—and not much branched off from it after the first couple of blocks. It was just itself, reaching out and up toward—well, Zoe meant to find out exactly what it was reaching toward, and she meant to find out immediately.

The road, lined with quiet houses and unpopulated beaches, was only a mile and a half long, it turned out, but it also turned out that that was long enough—she checked the whole thing, eating a banana and a peach along the way, until it ended in sand and big rocks—long enough to contain exactly two A-frame houses, both of them dark brown triangles planted on the right side of the road—the beach side. They were basically identical, a little more than a tenth of a mile apart and with a more tan and square house halfway between them. Zoe parked the car fairly erratically in the driveway of the one further from town and got herself out to look closer.

For sure the place looked uninhabited—no cars in the driveway, and nobody and nothing on the front porch, and off past it she couldn't see anyone at all on the part of the beach that was visible, couldn't hear a thing aside from the general soft sound of waves in the near distance, and in general the house just gave a closed-up vibe, a vibe of stillness. In contrast with herself, which was a trembly, heart-pounding chaos. The house was smaller than the one in her mind, but she knew that was a common thing with childhood memories, because childhood things took place when the rememberer herself was smaller and when everything else seemed bigger. So it didn't prove anything. She told herself it didn't.

Getting out of the car, she self-consciously climbed the two porch steps and went up to one of the front windows, and, screw it, she looked in through that window, her shaking hands shading her face to keep the glare out. She could feel her pulse in her temples, where her hands were. Inside was also completely still and, well, inside it was very A-framey.

The walls were slanted like the triangle shape demanded and there wasn't a ton of room—Zoe remembered that she and her brother slept upstairs in a sort of cramped attic kind of space that they got to by climbing a built-in ladder, and that their parents slept down in the living room on a couch that folded out. Was this that couch, the shadowy one she was looking at? Well, first of all, there was no reason that she should have expected it to be, after more than two decades, and second, it was pretty dark in there, and third, she just didn't know regardless. It didn't look like a very new couch—none of it looked anywhere near new, the chairs or the kitchen table or the cabinets or anything—but as to whether it was *the* couch, whether any of it was *the* stuff, well, she just didn't really remember what it had been like.

And so Zoe took her face off the window and tried something else. Climbing back down off the porch, she went around the side of the house to see what was behind it. There was no way that she was going to be confused about this part. Her feet crunched through gravelly sand— this home was right at the edge of the dunes—and her heart thundered, as though she was sneaking up on a rogue elephant or something. At one point—and it was only a very short walk!—she had to put her hand on the house and lean there, panting, duney weeds swaying by her side. But then she kept going. The whole thing must have taken twenty seconds, but twenty seconds spent sneaking up on an elephant are not twenty regular seconds. In any case, she got there, to the back.

And everything in her slumped. There was no porch here, facing the water. There were only some steps that came out of a back door right down to the pebbly sand. And it wasn't like there could have been a porch that had since been replaced by steps because, first of all, why would you even ever *do* something that stupid—Zoe actually felt herself getting angry—and also the steps looked as old and weathered as the rest of the house. They looked like they'd always been there.

Zoe felt tears on her face. She was aware of the part of her that could easily collapse. The part of her that would lose any sense of a path forward. Everything shook, threatened.

But no—no. This wasn't the only house. There was one other one.

This time, having relocated her car, askew again, to the driveway of the other place, Zoe started with the crucial part, going around back first, this time in apparent pursuit of a herd of elephants, if her heart was any indication.

But this time, when she got there, it wasn't like the other place. Oh, it wasn't. It wasn't, because in back of this house there weren't just steps. No—here there was a structure, a structure that was, by anybody's definition, a porch. A porch that was jutting rectangular out over the sand just the way the one in her memory had. A porch big enough for four chairs, and made out of wood that was dark just the way she remembered it—and it had two steps that led from it down to the sand, exactly like the picture in her head.

Zoe took her shoes off, very intently, and then she climbed up onto the porch, all of her nerves on fire. Her footsteps—bare feet on rough, cracked wood—felt like they were making ripples in the universe.

There were no chairs to sit on—they were probably packed up inside for the off-season—but she sat down on the porch itself, very gingerly, as though something might break. Because something always might break. That was a thing that Zoe knew for sure. Gingerly, she planted herself down on the boards of the porch, settled herself into a lotus, though with her fingers touching the rough planks. And then she dared herself to do it—to look at the ocean.

On that vacation, so long ago, Zoe had spent night after night on the back porch of the house, looking out over the water. If there was one thing she definitely remembered, it was that—the look of the water from that porch. It was the whole horizon, of course, and then where it met the sand and pebbles it did so at a kind of an angle—or maybe the house was at an angle?—and there was a little slope to the beach, too. Very slightly uphill in the direction of town. She knew it wasn't uphill the whole way, or even as far as the next house, but it was on this particular stretch of the beach. Above all, the main impression was of everything wide open, not a thing between the house and the immensity of this endless ocean.

Whereas between *this* house and the water things were totally different from that.

Between this house and the water there was a substantial pair of dunes—you could see over them to most of the empty beach, but they were definitely a presence, with a path running between them to the water. It was not—there was no way around it—was not what she had encountered as a kid. And the water, too—she looked at it with eyes that were tearing up—it was nearer, and it didn't meet the sand at any kind of noticeable angle.

It didn't matter how important this was, no matter how much Zoe wanted it, no matter how much she needed it—this was definitely *not* what she had seen as a kid. Not even close.

She was panting again, but now more on the path to hyperventilation. And she felt dizzy, not only from hunger and the blood pulsing in her head but because this just wasn't right. She had come all this way—not just from Portland to Casper but all the way along the long, long twisting spring of her life for decade after decade after decade—and this wasn't right. It was wrong. It was wrong wrong wrong wrong wrong.

Zoe fell from lotus onto her side on the porch, the tears just coming and coming now, her lungs still straining wildly, desperately, her hand clawing at the wood, trying to find a grip. She tried to scream but couldn't get the breath. She didn't see the dunes or the ocean anymore; she saw the faces of Gordy and his parents and Brittany looking scared of her. And she saw the faces of her parents and Noah. And then, too, Lior from the mysticism group and also her friend Brenda who didn't think Maine was a good idea, and her old college friends, and even, she even saw Samuel and Phebe, their faces, in front of her. Phebe's eyes that wouldn't let anything out or in, and Samuel's eyes that wouldn't let you go. She even saw Rose and Andreas stacked on each other, watching her. She saw these people as she lay on the rough planks and gasped and sobbed, every one of the faces filled with pity, with contempt. On every pair of lips the word *cycle*. On every pair, *episode*.

Why was she even there on that porch?

Why was she still trying?

Why was she there?

Why was she anywhere at all?

Suddenly she was on her feet, full of terror and fury, and kicking at the wall of the house again and again, and then, with her horrible reflection caught in one of the back windows, she pulled her arm back and punched.

She punched right through that window.

The sound of glass shattering.

There was a shocked silence, which, after several seconds had passed—she didn't know how many—pain entered. Zoe held her hand up and saw that there was blood. Blood on her hand, blood starting two lines down her arm.

Zoe looked around sort of wildly, as though there was going to be somebody nearby with a big Band-Aid. Nobody there, of course. It seemed, from what she could see, like the square tan house was empty, too. And so she turned to the house whose porch she was uselessly on, and stepped toward the back door.

Zoe paused for just a second, just long enough to say, to maybe no body or nothing, "Come on." She said, her right arm up in the air, "Just give me this one."

Then, when she tried the doorknob with her left hand, it actually opened. A new tear or two found their way out. "Thank you," she whispered. Things were very low at this particular moment of her life, and she was probably not done with how low it was getting, but at least the universe had been able to cough up this one tiny kindness for her.

She stepped inside, where it was as dark as the other A-frame had been. Too dark to really figure out where the first aid stuff might be. Zoe felt around on the walls, found the switch by the back door, and flipped it on, filling the space with a yellow light—dim but enough to see by. Enough, for example, to see the walls. Walls with pictures that were not the pictures of cats that she remembered from her childhood. And she saw the furniture that also didn't look familiar. Not that she had expected any of it to match. And enough to see the window glass on the floor inside. Oh, God.

She found the bathroom, and there was a sink where she could wash out the cuts on her knuckles and the back of her hand, and there were bandages. She forced herself to focus on the task. She wrapped her hand, and the pain dulled a little. The blood didn't seem to be coming too fast—the bandages stayed bandage-colored. That was something.

In a sort of haze Zoe looked around the unfamiliar living room. She picked up the pieces of glass and, feeling helpless, she put them back down on the floor under the window. Then, slowly, without intention, she looked through the rest of the house, which, even slowly, took very little time to do. There wasn't much to the place. Up the ladder, the little second floor wasn't decorated at all, just beds and a couple plain wood built-in bookshelves, and the kitchen was fairly non-descript, too. It could have been anyplace. It might as well have been anyplace. Certainly it wasn't hers.

Exhausted, like a person filled with liquid exhaustion, Zoe fit herself into the couch. She knew she didn't belong there, was even trespassing, had broken and entered, but she let herself lie there anyway. She let herself fall asleep.

Zoe woke up to a sharp sound.

It was so sudden that she woke up not heavy with grief but instead immediately and totally disoriented, thrown out of a nap of some unknown length into confusion. The objects around her swayed dangerously as she sat up. Sat up and got up, almost in one dizzy motion; Zoe was on her feet, not steady but standing, before she had really thought things through, and then she weaved to the front door. Because the sharp sound had been knocking. Only as she opened the door did it begin to occur to her that she was opening the door to a house that she didn't own and wasn't renting and had no official business even being in, and opening it to she didn't know who.

Who turned out to be a police officer.

Thirteen

"Good evening, ma'am," the man said.

Zoe didn't even say anything at first; she was too busy taking the situation in. On one side of the door: her, trespasser in the house that was not the house that she'd been searching for for practically her whole life, but there she was anyway. On the other side of the door: a square-shouldered, clean-shaven, pink-faced kind of maybe-in-his-fifties man wearing an all-blue police officer uniform, and more importantly looking at her very expectantly with clear, blue eyes. Behind him it was not, in fact, quite evening, but they were getting there.

"You don't have a Maine accent," she said. She was not a hundred percent in control of what she was saying.

The man laughed a single, surprised laugh. "No," he said. "No, I don't." And then his face returned to its expectant look.

Zoe shook her head. She was starting to really catch up with what was happening. It was not a pleasant experience. "Can I help you, sir?"

"Are you renting this cottage, ma'am?" he said, friendly enough in a *Let's see where this goes* police voice.

Thinking for a while about how to answer that question was probably not the wisest thing to do, but it's what Zoe found herself doing. What would happen if she told the truth? Was this a jail kind of situation, technically? With the broken window, probably. Oh, God. But what if she lied? Could he just find out the truth anyway, and then it would be a case of lying to a police officer, and was that an even more jail kind of situation?

"Why do you ask?" she finally said.

The man sighed. She had the impression that he wasn't wanting things to go the way they were going. "Well, ma'am," he said. "Can I ask your name?"

"Zoe," she said. "Zoe Tussler."

"Officer Allan McClung," he said. He extended his hand, which she shook without thinking, and she winced as he lightly squeezed her injured hand. "Looks like you had a mishap there," he said, looking down at her bandages. The bandages had definitely become spotted with red since she put them on.

"I did," she said.

His stare, now back at her eyes, became pointed. After a moment, he said, "Well, Ms. Tussler, as you may have gathered, Casper is a very small town."

"I haven't seen much of it," Zoe said. "Yet." She was becoming aware of how awkward it was, both of them standing on either side of an open door. She thought it might be good to lean casually on the door jamb, but didn't trust herself to stay upright if she did lean.

"Well, it's a very small town. And so people notice things. One of the residents noticed your car in the driveway and word got out about that, and people generally had the impression that the owners of this particular house—they don't live in town—weren't renting to anyone right now."

"A ha," Zoe said, as though the two of them were trying to solve this mystery together. She had put her right hand behind her back.

He rubbed at his ruddy chin, like a man who had had a beard until recently.

"Okay," he said. "And then Mrs. Collins—she's the owner of the store in town—said that she talked to a woman who was asking about A-frame houses."

"I see," Zoe said, kind of looking around to scope out the casual leaning opportunities to her right side. They didn't seem promising; the jamb was a little in front of her, and she didn't want to step forward.

He said, "A woman matching your description."

"Huh," she said.

He paused for a moment, maybe hoping that Zoe would jump in with a confession at this point, but she was sticking with simple expressions of mild interest until they stopped working or until she came up with something better. Then he continued. "So we called the owners," he said.

Zoe could feel her face flush. "Ah," she said.

"So, you see where I'm going with this," he said.

Zoe just kept her mouth shut this time. She had a feeling that this was going to be the last time she was going to be able to get away with pretended innocence. Meanwhile, her nervous system was starting to buzz pretty actively.

"You're not renting this house," he said.

Zoe breathed in and out three times. "Technically," she said, "no."

Officer Allan McClung nodded. It was almost a sympathetic nod.

"Do you want to come in?" Zoe said, stepping back.

"I think I'd better," he said.

Then the two of them were inside, standing side by side, looking at the space.

"Can I ask you to sit down?" he said.

Zoe went over to the couch—there was a knitted blanket all bunched up on it, which she must have been sleeping under, a couple minutes earlier—and she sat.

"I'm just going to look around a little."

"Okay," she said.

It didn't take him long to find the broken window. In fact, he saw it as soon as she finished saying the word *Okay*. "Ma'am," he said, pointing at the glass. "Is this how you hurt your hand?"

Zoe felt tears coming. "I wasn't trying to break in," she said. "I really wasn't. I was on the porch out there—" she pointed— "and I was so upset that I lashed out, which is something I never do, something I really almost never do, and I punched—I punched the window." She pointed at that, too, even though she didn't need to. "And then the door was unlocked and I came in just to see if there were bandages." She held her hand up. "Which there were. Which I'm so grateful for."

He sighed a sigh full of disappointment, watching her hold her hand up and cry quietly. "Okay," he said. "Am I going to find any additional disturbance if I look around this place?"

"No. No. Definitely not. I think I even washed the blood out of the sink all the way."

He shook his head, and then he nodded, and off he went to poke his head into the bathroom, and then he went high enough on the ladder to scope out the second floor a bit. Zoe had a brief, wild thought about making a dash for it while he was several steps up, but she was immediately pretty clear on just how terrible an idea that would be. So instead she sat there, waiting and buzzing and working on her breathing in order to try to get her tears to stop, which she eventually was more or less able to do.

When he was satisfied that nothing else had been disturbed, Officer Allan McClung sat down on the green-brown armchair across from Zoe. On the wall behind him were a number of pictures that were not of cats. He leaned forward, folded his hands with his forearms on his thighs. It was the most expectant he had looked yet, though maybe also a little sad.

"So, what's going on here, Ms. Tussler?" he said.

Her name. She thought to herself that there was really no way out of this one, since she had been unguarded enough to give her actual name to him. She could feel some flapping start up in her chest. "Do you really want to know?" she said.

"I do," he said. "This is not a good situation. I'd like to know what's happening before I decide what to do next."

And that was certainly a frightening thing for him to say. Zoe looked around the room, trying to gather herself, like trying to gather heavy stones while in a mild panic. And then she began, speaking probably too quickly. "For pretty much my whole life, you have to understand, I've felt like all my dials were set wrong. Set wrong right at the beginning. You know?" She looked at him, and his face conveyed very little. "Like I just didn't fit. Like I was carrying around the wrong stuff."

"I'm going to need you to get to the current situation," he said.

Zoe took a deep breath. "Okay. Definitely. That's exactly where I'm going. It's just the kind of story where you have to know the whole thing for it to make sense. Is that okay?"

After a hesitation, he gave one small nod.

"Thank you. Okay. So I've been looking for a way to get things right." She shook her head. "I mean, for *years*. I've tried everything. Everything!" She could feel the edge of tears again as she said that, but she got a hold of herself. The adrenaline of the situation was helping her from sinking under. "But then I met this guy. There's probably always a guy, right?"

Officer McClung's face was noncommittal on that one.

"And he lives in Portland, and he seemed really healthy and amazing, and I didn't move up here *because* of him or anything, but it was like a doorway opening. Because all the while I was remembering this vacation I took when I was ten years old. I grew up in Philadelphia—"

His eyebrows went up.

"Why?" she said. "Where did *you* grow up?"

"New Jersey," he said tersely. "Cherry Hill."

"How about that?" she said, feeling the tiniest bit of surprise and interest in the midst of everything else. "That's why no accent, huh?"

"Well, no *Maine* accent," he said, which was a kind of nice response, though he delivered it in a flat voice.

She shook her head again. "Here we are," she said. "Two transplants from the Delaware Valley. Both here. Normally maybe this would make me think that definitely God is real, or anyway a force in the universe or something. Normally."

His eyes squinted a little, which she gathered meant, *Let's get back to the story*.

"Okay," she said. "So there was this vacation. And I was coming from Philly, which as you know is kind of a very crazy place."

He tilted his head. He knew what she was talking about.

"Right. So we came up to Maine, and it was *so* peaceful, so amazing, so calm, so wonderful. It was like nothing else in my life, before or since." She looked down at her hands, one bandaged and one not, saw that she was leaning forward, too, sitting just like him. "So, I came back up here and there was the guy in Portland, and when things didn't work out with him—I guess they never work out, right? With a guy?"

Noncommittal again. His face really was pink. Like a sunburn, but Zoe didn't think it was a sunburn.

"Well, when it didn't work out," she said, "I decided that I had to find the place from that vacation. I know, right? Crazy. Crazy!"

That word. Saying that word. She had tried to never say that word about herself. Meanwhile he was looking concerned.

"You know, that's what everybody thinks of me. That I'm crazy. That's what everybody's always telling me. And the thing is, maybe I am. Maybe I am." And now, adrenaline or not, she could feel the danger of sinking under again. Inside her rose more panic, the panic of a person who can't swim and who's out on the water, on a small, unstable raft. "I mean," she said, talking even faster over the loudness of his increasingly concerned expression, "I came here with nothing to go on. I didn't remember the name of the town or anything. I tried to get some clues at the library in Portland, but nothing. Nothing. All I knew was that it was up here somewhere. So I got in the car, I rented a car and got in the car, and I started driving. All I had was my intuition, whatever *good* that turns out to be. I saw this one view and got the idea I had to turn off the road I was on, so I turned. I came down here. And I wasn't sure at first, but the town seemed maybe familiar, and then I checked the two A-frames." She was practically panting.

"Ma'am?" he said.

"But they're not right. Neither one is the right one. They're totally wrong!"

"Ma'am?" he said again, a hand up as a caution. "I'm going to need you to stay calm. The situation is already bad enough."

There was force in his cautionary hand. And she sort of did get calm, in the sense that her momentum collapsed inside her and she didn't say anything else. She just hung her head and stared into her lap, lost. The word *crazy* was in her head now. Was the biggest word in there. "*Ms. Tussler,*" he said firmly. He dipped his head down to try to catch her eye.

"Yes," she said, not allowing her eye to be caught. "I'm sorry. I'm just." She suddenly felt very serious. "I know I shouldn't be here," she said. "I…I get kind of big ideas sometimes."

He nodded, still trying to secure eye contact.

"And those ideas haven't changed anything," she said. "They haven't changed a thing," she said, and really she was telling herself.

Zoe looked up, finally. Looked him in the eyes.

They stared at each other a good long time. For his part, it seemed like he was reading her very closely. Looking for something important inside her. She didn't know what it was, though, and didn't know if she had it.

After a minute, his face softened a little bit. It was like he'd found whatever he'd been looking for.

Like he'd seen something not bad.

Her question came out abruptly. "Do you think you can perfect yourself? Perfect your life?" she said. "Like, a life where everything is totally *right*?"

The man sat back in surprise. "What?"

"I just—you seem very steady," she said, because he did. "I wonder if you think a person can get their life just right."

Officer Allan McClung rubbed at his face, clearly trying to decide what to do with Zoe and the situation she was presenting him. And then he sighed and said, "A perfect life?"

Zoe nodded earnestly.

The man, blessings upon him, he put his hands on the arms of the chair and actually seemed to consider what she was asking. He thought for a little while, looking up at the ceiling, and then back at Zoe. He said, "No. No, I don't think so."

She pressed him a little. "But you moved all the way here from New Jersey. You must have been trying to perfect things. Weren't you?"

"Well, I *liked* it here," he said. "I first came here on a vacation, too."

Zoe's eyebrows went up a little.

"As an adult," he clarified. "With my wife. But we did like it a lot, and we always thought it would be nice to live here. We made the move about, well, about eight years ago now, when the kids were all in college. But we weren't trying to make things *perfect*, exactly."

"Okay," Zoe said. She was still leaning forward, forearms on her thighs.

"Ms. Tussler," he said, "I doubt if there's anything that's perfect out there. And listen—"

Zoe nodded, her throat tight. "I think I thought," she said. "I think I thought *I* could be. Perfect. Perfected."

He shook his head. "Ma'am, listen—we're a long way from where we should be in this conversation." But she saw it in his eyes—that same sympathy from before.

"I know I'm in trouble," she said. "I know I'm in a lot of trouble here. But I just—can we just talk for a couple more minutes before you do anything?"

After a deep breath, he said, "About what? Perfection?"

"Exactly."

"I don't know," he said. "I just think that's impossible."

"Perfection? Or talking a couple more minutes?"

At this he gave another surprised laugh. "The first thing," he said. "It's impossible."

"So, if that's not even possible, how do you do it, then?" she asked. "How do you get through it all okay?" This felt like maybe the most important question she'd ever ask.

The officer shook his head as he thought about that. "You—well. Huh." He rubbed his chin again. And then, after a minute, "How am I supposed to answer that question?"

"Like," she persisted, "do you have any problems? Do you have anything that's set wrong in you?"

"Well, I've been pretty fortunate," he said. "I'm grateful for what I have."

Zoe nodded, feeling abruptly alone in the room even with him right there.

He saw that. She saw him see that. He decided something else and added, "Maybe you mean something like, well, there's my health, I guess."

Zoe felt a mix of things. Part of her was almost grateful that he might have something wrong in his life, too; part of her went into immediate mourning for the both of them. "What is it?" she said.

He shrugged, looked away. "Garden-variety diabetes is the one thing."

"Diabetes," she said.

"Yep."

"They don't have a cure for that, do they?"

He shook his head. "But it's not so bad." Officer McClung looked back at her, having worked off whatever embarrassment he'd been feeling. "I take my insulin shots, and I'm okay. The doctor says I'm doing all right. I feel all right. I live my life."

"Huh," she said.

There was a pause, and then he looked at her expectantly again. He really did want them to get back on track.

"Do you think I'm crazy?" she said.

"I can't answer that one, either, ma'am. That's not a thing I know how to answer."

"Okay," she said. "Sure."

"But *you* keep saying the word 'crazy,' is the thing," he said. "I have to know. The question for me, getting practical, is how worried I ought to be."

Zoe shook her head. "If I'm crazy, I'm not the kind who's dangerous to others or property or anything." She looked at her bandaged hand. "Not anymore, anyway."

That wasn't what he had meant. "What about dangerous to yourself?" he said quietly.

She sat back and thought about that. She looked inside. Finally, when she had checked in thoroughly, she told the truth of what she saw. "I'm not going to hurt myself right now or anything," she said. "It's just that in the long term I'm going to be totally miserable."

Officer McClung said, "Now, come on."

Zoe said, a little loud, her hands in the hair, "But I've tried *everything*! And I'm always the same!"

222

"The same?"

"Yes—I'm the same miserable person. The same *crazy* person."

He looked like he was having trouble understanding what he was hearing. "What do you expect?" he said abruptly, throwing his hands up in the air.

"What do I expect?"

"Yeah. What do you expect? *You go to bed, you wake up, you're the same person*. Like the rest of us. You get out of bed, you're the same person. You have breakfast. You go to work. Lunch, dinner, bed. Right? All the same person. Who are you supposed to be, anyway?"

Zoe was a little taken aback herself. It was a big speech, by Officer McClung standards. "Well, don't you want to be different? Be the guy without diabetes?" she said.

"But I'm not going to be," he said, flustered. "I just deal with it."

Somehow that hit Zoe kind of hard. She came up short and didn't have anything to say.

"Hey," he said. "We're miles off the road, here. Miles. The main thing is that you're not supposed to be in the house."

"Okay," Zoe said, but still a couple seconds behind, thinking about what he had said about dealing with it. When she caught up, she said, "You're right. I'm not supposed to be here."

The man took another deep breath. He seemed very glad to be back on track. "Right. And I think what we're going to have to do is—" he was coming to some decisions right in front of her, and it occurred to her that she was about to be arrested—"we're going to have to get you to write a check or something for this window."

"A check?" she said. "I have a checkbook in the car."

"Okay," he said. "So that's good."

"Okay," she said. And even through the relief—he didn't even seem to be thinking about arresting her—she felt another couple of tears form.

"I don't know," she said. "I just wanted that quiet. The sunset, the ocean, the quiet."

"Listen," he said. "Let's go outside."

Zoe nodded again, and she set about straightening the blanket on the couch as he watched. Then the officer locked the back door to the porch and he pressed the button on the inside knob of the front door, and then he held the door open for her before closing it behind both of them again. Which left it locked. They were all the way outside.

From the porch she saw their cars. His was blocking hers into the driveway; good thing, anyway, that she hadn't tried to make a break for it.

"Could you go ahead and write a check? You can make it out to Sam Cooper. He's in town here. Fifty dollars and he'll fix that window up."

"Really?" she said. And after he nodded she went and got her checkbook—it was from a Philly bank, an account she had left open when she moved—and wrote one out, and the officer folded it exactly in half and put it in his shirt pocket.

After that, he put his hands on the railing, looking not at her but off across the road at another house. It was starting to get cool out. "So, of course, you can't go back into the house here," he said.

"I know," Zoe said, heavily. "I promise I won't even try."

"Let me ask you something."

"Okay," she said. "Of course."

Is it *like* the place where you went as a kid?" he said.

"Kind of," she said. "It's the kind of place that would remind me of it. Why?"

He didn't answer that. Instead, he said, "Do you have anyone you can call, to check in with someone, tell them what's going on?"

Zoe thought about that, her mind slow. There was Gordy, but no. For the moment she couldn't even be sure who he was or who he was to her. There were her parents, which no. There was Noah. "I could call my brother," she said, shrugging.

Officer McClung nodded. "Good. I think it'd be good to check in with someone. Just check in."

"Okay," Zoe said. Maybe she could call Noah.

"And I'll talk to with the Meginnises, see if they can rent you a room for tonight at the inn."

"Really?" Zoe said.

"Sure. And tomorrow you can see Dr. Evans about the hand, if you want." He nodded at it.

"Wow. Okay," she said.

"Anyway, it might take a little while to get things set up at the inn. They don't get a lot of business this time of year. You might have to wait a little while."

"Sure," Zoe said. "Of course."

He looked at her, sighed. "I guess I don't think it would be hurting anybody," he said, "if, while you wait," pausing, and then, "if you just sat on the back porch here this one evening." He pointed over his shoulder at the house they'd just left.

"What?" Zoe said.

"You know, for the sunset."

"What?" Zoe said.

"You can come into town after that."

It took her a minute to understand what he was saying, and then, when she did, Zoe put her bandaged hand to her mouth. She said *Really?* with her eyes.

He nodded. She could tell that he wasn't a hundred percent sure, but he was going to give it a shot. "I know it's not the right spot," he said. "The right house. But we get a pretty good sunset here."

Zoe shook her head in a slow, astonished, quiet gratitude.

"We can give you one sunset," he said, almost to himself. Deciding once and for all.

"You're one of the nicest people," she said.

He smiled a small smile and shrugged that off. "I doubt if it's a competition," he said.

Zoe watched him drive off, feeling all the thankfulness. And then she got a sweatshirt and her food from the car, made a peanut butter and banana sandwich using mostly her fingers for utensils, and sat on the back porch to eat.

Well, eat and call Noah. He'd left several voicemail messages on her phone, along with her parents and Gordy and even Eleanor, who did, it turned out, want to meet the following Wednesday. Noah's most recent message was just him saying, *Zoe, please. Please just call me.* Please.

She dialed, one number at a time, telling herself she could stop putting the numbers in at any point if she wanted to stop, but then she put in the last one and made the call, and the ringing started. In front of her were the dunes that weren't supposed to be there, though it's true that beyond that was the ocean. There was a salt breeze on her face, cool but very soft.

The ringing stopped. "Hey," he said. Maybe a little anxiously.

"Herro," she said, her mouth gummed up with peanut butter.

"Zoe?" he said.

She swallowed. "I'm just eating a peanut-butter sandwich," she said, a little annoyed at the tone in his voice. Like always assuming something was wrong with her. Though this time she had to admit that maybe there was reason to worry. The word *crazy* was still with her. In her.

"Oh," he said. "What are you up to?"

She set the sandwich down in her lap. "I'm at the beach."

"Huh," he said in a soft voice. "You're at the beach a lot up there. I guess it's a good place for beaches."

"Yeah," Zoe said. "But this time it's the actual ocean, not just a bay."

"Nice," he said. They were both speaking cautiously, delicately, distantly. It struck Zoe that having that distance with her brother was a very painful thing.

"I'm sorry," she said.

There was a pause, and then, "For what?"

"For all this," she said, waving her free hand around, which was the bandaged one. She meant, *For the craziness*.

At that moment, Noah took her seriously, too. He didn't deny what she was saying. "It's okay," he said. And then, "I just want to know that you're okay."

She could have said a lot of things. In the many times the two of them had talked about her, she had said many things. But this time, she said, "I'm not sure I am." It seemed like a very big thing to come out of her mouth.

"Oh, Zoe."

Before he could add anything, she said, "Do you remember how we used to be kids?"

It took him a second, but then, "Yeah?" he said.

"Like, little kids?"

"Sure, Zoe."

"I didn't know it would turn out like this," she said, a little whimper coming out with the words.

"Zoe," he said with a quaver, "I'm worried."

"I know," she said. "Does it help if I might be worried, too?"

"I don't know." He thought about it. "Maybe."

"Yeah," she said. "You know, I just met a guy who says that you always stay the same. That you don't change. And he says you just deal with it. Do you think that's true?"

"You just deal with it?"

"Yeah," she said.

"Huh. I have to think about it, I guess," he said. "But maybe, yeah. Maybe so."

"Maybe so," Zoe said, looking out at the dunes. They weren't going anywhere. She looked at them. "Maybe so."

Neither of them said anything for a minute. Zoe realized that she could actually ask him the name of the beach town from their childhood, but she didn't. She just didn't. Instead Zoe asked, "Hey—what are you even doing right now?"

"Now?" Noah said. "I'm sitting in the car. I'm in the parking lot next to the grocery store."

"Huh," Zoe said. She could picture him, sitting back against the seat, one hand maybe in his curly hair while the other one held the phone. The seatbelt still on. "Like, what are you going to buy?"

Noah sighed. "Everything, basically. I ran out of everything."

"What's everything?" Zoe said. "Tell me."

"Really?" Noah said. "Well, milk, I guess. Fruits and vegetables. I want an avocado or two. Beans. You know."

"Yeah," Zoe said. "Tell me more things."

"You really want me to tell you what's on my grocery list?"

Zoe nodded, mainly for herself. "I want to hear something ordinary."

Noah laughed a little. And then he started. "I need eggs. And pasta," he said. "And tomato sauce. Olive oil."

"Keep going," Zoe said. "Tell me more."

And he did.

After they were done talking—Zoe promised she'd call him again soon, and she meant it—she finished her sandwich and cried and thought about everything and looked out at the landscape in front of her. At those unchanging wrong dunes, the wrong slope of things. She thought about what the officer had said, and about Noah, and about a lot of other things. She was thinking slowly, rolling it all around. *You go to bed, you wake up, you're the same person.* And *You just deal with it.* And *Maybe so.* She rolled it around. Not like something magical was going to spring out of there, but more like she was getting familiar with the thoughts. Getting to know them.

Eventually, though, something caught her attention. Or, not caught, but slowly, slowly drew it in. Because what she noticed consciously, a while after she had noticed it subconsciously, was that actually things were very quiet all around her. *So* quiet. So calm. The ocean just breathed over the land. The salt air kind of thick and steadying. The sun doing its silent last work of the day. This wasn't the same house, the same spot, no. But the stillness—there was recognition in her—this was a kind of stillness she had not experienced in a long time. It was like the stillness she'd been looking for, actually. Maybe it was in more than one place.

It was so simple, in a way. Just that air and her and the sun and the dunes—the grasses swayed almost in slow-motion—and the little bits of driftwood and small piles of seaweed that she could see past the dunes out on the sand and pebbles of the beach and, of course, above all, the ocean, which rolled itself onto the sand in a rhythm that only the water understood fully. Zoe felt, sitting there, that she understood some of it, though. She watched the water and knew that the moon was out there contributing its part and that the land must be, too, and all the fish, and that—well, that maybe even she, Zoe, was playing a tiny, tiny role in what was happening. Maybe? Maybe so. She sat and sat and let it all flow into her, or out of her, or between everything and everything else. She drank water to keep herself hydrated—the tears weren't stopping, though it was not all sadness that was behind them. Not a hundred percent. After a while she ate one of the peaches.

And then, eventually—she waited and waited for it, somehow anxious for it to come and also, at the same time, willing to wait—the sun started to go down. It was almost as though it was the first sunset she'd seen in the last twenty-four years. The porch must have been facing south-ish, because the end-of-day glory happened off to her right, off in the direction of town, which was how she remembered it happening at the other house, actually. And so there was this experience of looking back and forth, slowly, first at the cloudy fire of the day's last minutes and next at the ever-ongoing roll of the ocean, and back again, and back again, and back again. While she faced the ocean the sun warmed the side of her face, and while she faced the sunset the ocean spoke to her ready ear.

Everything got even quieter, even more still. The sun down, the world in front of Zoe became indistinct in the growing blue-gray. Visually indistinct, anyway. Certainly the ocean never stopped talking. In fact, it got clearer as the sun made its way. So, as everything went over to dark, Zoe listened very closely—more closely than she had ever listened to anything else ever before. And the ocean told her old, old secrets. One of which was that there were no old secrets, and for sure no new ones. The ocean told her a long story, a story about what it meant to be, to just be the ocean. It said, *There's nothing to be done.* It said, *There's nothing to be done.* It said, *All there is, is being.* Although everything was so calm and steady, in a way the story shook her. She couldn't say in what way, but she felt it. Meanwhile, up above, the stars made their one-by-one appearance, even more than had been above Gordy's trailer. And of course the stars had even older stories, though their stories were pretty much the same as the ocean's. They talked to each other, too, the stars and the sea. They said, *Some of us are meant to burn.* They said, *Some of us are meant to roll in and to roll out again.*

David Ebenbach

Zoe didn't know what she was going to do with her life. She didn't know what she was going to do the next day. Home, whatever that was? Meds? A few days more in Casper? All she knew is that, for those moments, she was listening very closely.

Some of us are fire, and some are water, is what she heard.

She heard, *There's nothing to be done, but be.*

Meanwhile the ocean rolled itself onto the beach; the ocean rolled away. And the night, carrying all those stars—the night just walked its steady course.

Acknowledgments

This book is a book because of help. I'm pretty sure that every book that's a book is a book because it had help, and certainly that's true for this one. First of all, I'm incredibly grateful to my close writing friends who gave me feedback on drafts of *Miss Portland*: the writers West Moss (author of the excellent story collection *The Subway Stops at Bryant Park*), Margaret Luongo (author of the excellent story collections *History of Art and If the Heart Is Lean*), and Emily Mitchell (author of the excellent story collection *Viral* and the excellent novel *The Last Summer of the World*). These great readers/writers (I mention their books because you should go read them—believe me) enabled me to take this project from something with very wobbly legs to something that can, I hope, stand on its own.

Then you've got the wonderful people at Orison Books, who have made this whole process unfailingly smooth, collaborative, a pleasure. Thanks, specifically, to editor Luke Hankins for his stewardship and Karen Tucker for her insight and sharp eye.

Of course, the foundation on which everything stands is my family. I'm grateful to my parents and my sister and my parents-in-law for all their support, and in particular I want to single out my mother and my sister-in-law, two women who taught me things about courage. Finally, and above all, there's my wife Rachel and my son Reuben. I don't know how it could get any better than the life I have with these two wonderful human beings.

About the Author

David Ebenbach is the author of three short story collections: *The Guy We Didn't Invite to the Orgy and other stories* (winner of the Juniper Prize, University of Massachusetts Press), *Between Camelots* (winner of the Drue Heinz Literature Prize, University of Pittsburgh Press), and *Into the Wilderness* (Winner of the Washington Writers Publishing House Fiction Prize, WWPH). He is also the author of a full-length collection of poetry, *We Were the People Who Moved* (Winner of the Patricia Bibby Prize, Tebot Bach), a chapbook of poetry, *Autogeography* (Finishing Line Press), and a guide to the creative process called *The Artist's Torah* (Cascade Books). Ebenbach holds a PhD in Psychology from the University of Wisconsin-Madison and an MFA in Writing from Vermont College. He teaches creative writing at Georgetown University.

About Orison Books

Orison Books is a 501(c)3 non-profit literary press focused on the life of the spirit from a broad and inclusive range of perspectives. We seek to publish books of exceptional poetry, fiction, and non-fiction from perspectives spanning the spectrum of spiritual and religious thought, ethnicity, gender identity, and sexual orientation.

As a non-profit literary press, Orison Books depends on the support of donors. To find out more about our mission and our books, or to make a donation, please visit www.orisonbooks.com.

12/16/21
14